STAR TREK
THE NEXT GENERATION

D1470816

STAR TREK:
THE NEXT GENERATION NOVELS

STAR TREK:
THE NEXT GENERATION GIANT NOVELS

STAR TREK

THE NEXT GENERATION

EXILES

HOWARD WEINSTEIN

TITAN BOOKS

LONDON

STAR TREK **THE NEXT GENERATION 14:**
EXILES
ISBN 1 85286 320 X

Published by
Titan Books Ltd
19 Valentine Place
London SE1 8QH

First Titan Edition November 1990
10 9 8 7 6 5 4

British edition by arrangement with Pocket Books, a division of Simon and Schuster, Inc., Under Exclusive Licence from Paramount Pictures Corporation, The Trademark Owner.

Printed and bound in Great Britain by Cox and Wyman Ltd, Reading, Berkshire.

For
Susan

Just because . . .

Author's Notes

Hello again. Welcome to my fourth *STAR TREK* novel, my second visit to the expanding universe of Gene Roddenberry's highly successful *STAR TREK: THE NEXT GENERATION*. It's been fun watching this television series and its characters grow and improve with age—which makes writing these novels more fun, as well.

As you settle down to read this one, I'd like to remind you of a sobering fact. Unless we humans change our ways, scientists estimate that we'll be causing the extinction of something like *one hundred* animal and plant species *every day* for the next thirty years.

What's that—? You say you didn't even know we *had* that many different varieties of animals and plants? Well, look fast—pretty soon, we *won't*. Think about it, okay?

Thanks and appreciation go to Dave Stern and Kevin Ryan at Pocket Books; Bob Greenberger, DC Comics' *STAR TREK* editor; Dave McDonnell and *Starlog* magazine; John Davis and the Colorado crew in charge of *STAR TREK: The Official Fan Club;* Marc Okrand, linguist extraordinaire and author of *The Klingon Dictionary;* Peter David; my family for bemused support of many kinds; my new wife, Susan, for extreme patience; and, as always, Mail Order Annie.

Chapter One

ZEILA WAS THEIR LEADER. But they would not let her speak.

With her usual brash stride, the Curister of the planet Alaj ascended the five steps to the platform and sized up the scene, watching as at least a hundred thousand people overflowed the Great Plaza of Swatarra City. Grim-faced, they waved their protest signs, pumping them high in the air, up toward a sky tarnished by a polluted haze. Zeila knew they were not here to listen.

It was she who would have to listen.

And she did. First, to a discordant rumble ragged with anger. Then the clatter of random shouts aimed at her like wobbly arrows, insults and accusations hurled at both her and her government. *Her* government, not theirs.

Perhaps there'd been a moment when she could have broken through the resistance and reached out to them. Perhaps not. In any case, it was gone in the space of a breath, overtaken by a collective chant that demanded the replacement of Curister Zeila and her regime.

From somewhere to the right of the podium, the chant changed. One small group along the plaza's edge began to sing. It took Zeila a moment to recognize it as the Alajian anthem. They sang it not with the stirring pomp of the march, but with the muffled cadence of a dirge. They sang with more than their voices. They sang with their souls.

The song spread until the city square trembled with the thunder of one hundred thousand voices, echoing off the dingy buildings bordering the perimeter.

Zeila stood transfixed, gripping the podium, the seven bracelets on each arm now bunched together at her elbows. Her bodyguards moved closer, but stayed out of sight behind the platform. All of them were well over the average seven-foot height of Alajian men, and all were conspicuously well-muscled compared to the slender norm. But no escort wedge, however large, had ever made her feel especially protected. She'd always believed that her own senses and abilities were her best source of security, and this situation was no exception.

On a world of physically imposing people, Zeila was shorter and more slight than most, yet she carried herself with regal pride. She had the pronounced facial structure common to her race, the prominent cheekbones and brow, the short muzzle formed by a delicate nose blending into the outward curve of the upper lip. Beyond that, her appearance was striking, with features like finely chiseled sculpture and a complexion ruddy and youthful despite her middle age. Her hair was clipped into a spiked style, shining black with flaming auburn highlights, matching the onyx and ruby stones studding her suede headband. Yet the feature she was best known for was a scar incised along the point of her chin, most visible when she smiled.

She was not smiling now.

As if by silent signal, the crowd moved forward, not with a mob's panic but with the inevitability of a tide. Barricades marking a buffer zone around the speakers' stand crushed under their feet. Uniformed troops ringing the plaza closed ranks and linked into a determined chain.

And that was the last Zeila saw as her own security squad hustled her down the back steps, through the building behind, into her idling flyer, and out of Swatarra.

The flight back to the capital compound in Port Arabok took an hour. Zeila's aides left her alone in her private compartment, and she used the time to review the near-disaster back in Swatarra. She was most frustrated by the fact that she'd not had the chance to say a single word. Even an argument in the street would have been welcome, compared to a hasty retreat and a silent departure.

Arriving at the Capital Forum, Zeila was met by her chief of intelligence and security. Lef was a big pale man, his broad shoulders stooped by a fatigue that seemed bone-deep. In contrast to Zeila's electric presence, he seemed cast in cool soft clay, his face lined deeply beyond his years. His hair was cropped close, mostly gray with some leftover streaks of its former cinnamon color. The jeweled headband and brightly colored clothing typical of Alajians of both genders looked distinctly out of place on him, but custom was custom.

He greeted his leader with just two words. "It's dead."

Her lips thinned as she recalled an undeniable truth uttered by someone wiser than she: *The most perilous moment for a bad government comes when it tries to mend its ways.*

A bad day had just grown worse. *Much* worse . . .

"You're sure it's dead," said Retthew, Prefex of the Council of State on the planet Etolos. With short, quick movements, he nervously nibbled brown seeds picked one after another from a plain ceramic dish on his desk.

His security adviser, Ozemmik, replied without hesitation. "Absolutely."

"When did this report come in?"

"Just now," said Ozemmik. "It happened two days ago. And we also know that Zeila's government on Alaj is covering up the news. They're afraid of even more widespread violence if their people find out."

Retthew pushed away from his rough-hewn desk and crossed the room to the bay window, his soft-soled moccasins whispering against the wood-plank floor. Even in private, he moved stiffly, like a man uncomfortable inside his own body. With uncharacteristic grace and tenderness, his fingers brushed along the half-dozen plants arranged in the window alcove, their leaves bowing toward the grow-lamps shining on them. Outside, it was twilight, and the plants knew instinctively where to turn.

Retthew wished his own instincts were as sure. As executive of the ruling Council of State, he knew he was privy to the most comprehensive information Ozemmik could gather, and he doubted he could ever find a security adviser as dedicated to the job. Yet the information Retthew received could not make his decisions for him and he'd often envied Ozemmik's decisiveness.

They'd known each other since their middle-school days, and even as youngsters Retthew had admired his friend's ability to focus his formidable intelligence with uncommon discipline. Retthew was just as bright, but known as the class scatterbrain—as Mik would often remind him.

Mik. Ozemmik had always loathed that diminutive. Some of their school chums had tried using the nickname just to provoke Ozemmik, but his response gave them no satisfaction. With icy composure, he'd simply remind them of his full name, and thereafter ignore anyone who failed to use it. Retthew never tested his friend's resolution on that or any other matter. From the day they'd met as children, both knew who was stronger.

But now, as adults, it was Retthew who was the leader and Ozemmik the servant. In name, at least.

"The plants are doing pretty well, don't you think?" Retthew said, trying to lose himself in the soothing music he always had playing in the background. "Considering they haven't seen natural sunlight stronger than that," he nodded out toward the dusky sky, "in four months. Don't you think?"

Ozemmik made no comment, refusing to indulge his leader's penchant for avoiding the issue at hand.

Retthew sighed. "Your sources—"

"The best."

"So." Retthew shoved his hands into the deep pockets of his pants, and shambled back to his desk. "It's hard to imagine there's not a single nefittifi left on Alaj, that the handful here on Etolos are the last ones anywhere."

"The Alajians are destroying their whole planet. What do they care if a sacred symbol goes extinct?"

"I think they care, Ozemmik. They just don't know how to change."

"They knew how to banish our people," said the security adviser, a pious edge spiking his voice. "If we'd been there for the past three hundred years, we could have saved the nefittifi. Could've saved a lot of life forms."

"Maybe. But we weren't, and we didn't. And here we are, trying to save our own world." Retthew got up again, drawn back to the window. He'd spent too much of his time lately considering the ironies of fate. How odd that two peoples, sharing the same origins yet estranged for centuries, now faced crises of such magnitude that both populations could be doomed.

Though there'd been no direct contact, Etolos had pieced together a rather effective intelligence network over time. Retthew and his predecessors in the prefex's office were kept well-informed about life on their ancestral homeworld. More than likely, the same was true for Alajian rulers.

If a group of Alajians suddenly found themselves wandering about the Council Center outside Retthew's office, they'd probably find little of great surprise. Even before the Great Exodus from Alaj, the forebears of today's Etolosans had developed some distinct differences in style and custom to distance themselves from the Alajian mainstream, differences that had naturally widened through the centuries.

In contrast to smooth-faced Alajian males, for instance, Etolosan men generally still grew full beards, although Ozemmik was an exception, carrying his flair for individualism to the extreme of also shaving his scalp. And unlike their Alajian cousins, Etolosans shunned extravagant clothing and ornamentation, preferring garments of simple cut and subtle color. In place of ubiquitous Alajian jewelry, Etolosan men and women both wore woven headbands with small cylindrical pouches stitched over the right ear and religious symbols embroidered all around.

But these were just the outer trappings. *What about*

inside? Retthew wondered. *Maybe we've come together without even knowing it. Maybe the Alajians eventually learned the same lessons we learned while we still lived there. What if that were true and we died without knowing it? Tragedy on top of tragedy . . .*

Ozemmik joined him at the window. "It's not our fault, what's happening out there."

"No. Volcanic eruptions are not our fault. And yet, there they were waiting to bury us in dust and darkness while we strolled along our self-styled path of righteousness," Retthew said with some bitterness.

"Cosmic injustice? Nobody ever said the right path included rewards, Rett. But we couldn't walk any other path even if we wanted to."

"Why not?" Retthew searched his friend's face for unknowable answers.

But Ozemmik always had an answer, one he believed in, no matter what the question. "Because we're afraid of what we'd become if we ignored the righteousness of what we've done, what we've built here."

"And what *would* we become?"

"Just like the Alajians, just like the people we hate the most."

"I don't hate them. Not after three centuries."

"I do," said Ozemmik simply. "And my polls tell me the Etolosan people will *never* forgive what was done to our ancestors, Spirit rest their souls."

"Polls. Sometimes I wish you wouldn't tell me what they say."

"You need to know."

Retthew returned to his chair, biting more of the brown seeds between his teeth. "Are you really afraid of becoming like them?"

"I'm not afraid of anything. But if I were, that would be my fear."

Retthew motioned to his adviser. "Sit down, my

friend. Do you remember that motto you had posted over your dormitory bed?"

"Of course. 'Once called, always committed.' You know it's still on my wall."

"Yes. In your office. You've never stopped believing in that, have you?"

Ozemmik's brow made a fractional arch, as if the answer was self-evident. And to anyone who knew him as well as Retthew did, it was just that.

"I've always envied that about you," said Retthew, "the way you can choose a direction and never look back. I can't tell you how many times I've wished I could be like that."

"You shouldn't bother, Rett," Ozemmik said, wagging his chin. "I go through life trying my damndest to get the universe to agree with me. It's a burden I don't think you'd enjoy."

"Well . . . some of us get that calling later than others."

"Hmm? What do you mean?"

"I've been thinking about . . . about taking an extreme step."

Ozemmik snorted a laugh. "You? Without opinion polls?"

"Don't be so sarcastic with your prefex," Retthew admonished, only half kidding.

"Forgive me, Excellency," Ozemmik said with a friendly smirk. "And tell me what you're talking about. What calling?"

"I've always been an administrator. The job does not encourage great leaps of courage."

"And that's always suited you," Ozemmik said, not unkindly.

"True. But the times are different. And they're demanding something greater from me."

"I'm not sure I like hearing you talk this way."

"Then I doubt you'll like what I'm considering." Retthew took a deep breath to steady his nerves. "This may be the time to open up a dialogue with Alaj."

Ozemmik's face pinched in startlement. *"What?"*

"No one else on the Council knows about the last Alajian nefittifi's death, do they?"

"No. I came directly to you, as always."

"I'll inform them at today's meeting," said Retthew, avoiding his friend's probing stare by chewing another seed from the dish.

Ozemmik rose from his chair, leaning halfway across the desk. "Alaj is our sworn enemy—"

"An enemy who has something we need," Retthew replied in a soft-spoken voice. But now he forced himself to lock eyes with Ozemmik. If he couldn't stand up to opposition here, he'd never be able to do it in the full Council meeting.

"What do we need from them?" said Ozemmik dismissively.

"A place to live, to continue our work. The fourth planet in the Alajian system. They've never settled it."

Ozemmik blinked, not quite believing what he'd heard. "Move our *whole society?* And even if we could, do you expect them to just *give* it to us?"

"There may be room for negotiation." Retthew tried to sound forceful, but knew he had failed. "We have things to offer Alaj."

Ozemmik stepped back, as if distancing himself from madness, his expression dark as a thundercloud. "There are powerful people who would oppose any dealings with Alaj. Perhaps with violence."

"Are you one of them?"

"I'm your security adviser. I serve you. Warning

9

you when I think you're about to do something very foolish is part of my job. The Council will never agree to this."

"Our survival is at stake. I think Alaj's may be, as well." Retthew's voice wavered. Then he stiffened both his back and his resolve. "If I have to, I can invoke the emergency powers of this office and act on my own."

Ozemmik shook his head. "The Council will revoke your election."

"The hearings will take months," Retthew said evenly. "By then, the process I've already started will have gone too far to stop."

"Already started—?"

"A message to the United Federation of Planets, an official request for mediation. A Starfleet Starship is on its way . . ." He squinted as he tried to recall the ship's name. "The *Enterprise.*"

Chapter Two

ARMS STRETCHED TO THE LIMIT, fingers straining, Lieutenant Worf reached high and snared his prey as it hurtled past. He clutched it to his chest. Even stark naked, a Klingon could still strike fear into any foe. Clad in protective armor, as he was now, Worf believed himself to be an ambulatory fortress. Unconquerable.

Like any good warrior, he'd prepared by briefing himself on his opponents' likely strategies, which seemed almost childish in their direct simplicity. He had no doubts he could stand his ground, and he knew there would be fewer than a dozen of them. He'd faced greater odds in past skirmishes.

But they came at him too quickly to be counted, their faces hidden inside helmets. Their feet pounded the sod as they charged at a dead run. With a Klingon battle snarl, he braced for the onslaught of the enemy phalanx. He was ready to make the ultimate sacrifice.

Few adversaries could make that claim. This would always be the Klingon advantage.

They slammed into him with stunning force, his

eyes wide with surprise. He recovered quickly, summoning all his strength and instinct with no time for thought. His warrior's blood boiled as he lashed out. But they overwhelmed him, too many against one. He fell back on the field, the battle over . . . the lone warrior vanquished in a matter of moments.

"Worf! Worf! Are you okay?" It was Geordi La Forge shouting, his voice racing closer from somewhere outside the pile of bodies pinning Worf to the ground. One body at a time, the weight lifted and Worf saw Geordi's concerned face peering through an opening in the heap.

"Of course," the Klingon rumbled. Another foe lying across his chest got up and Worf peeled himself off the turf. Commander Will Riker offered him a hand. The *Enterprise* security chief waved it off with disdain and rose to his feet, still clutching the oblong prize in the crook of his arm. "An invigorating experience."

Geordi and Riker, both wearing colorful helmets and padded uniforms similar to Worf's, stood there shaking their heads.

"Nice catch," Geordi said, "but you're supposed to run."

Worf's eyes narrowed in suspicion. "Why?"

"So you don't end up at the bottom of a pile," said Riker helpfully, stifling a smirk. He'd learned from assorted experiences that it was best not to smirk at a Klingon, especially a frustrated one.

"To avoid the defense," Geordi added.

Worf looked from one to the other, trying to grasp another of what seemed to be an endless supply of inexplicable human quirks. "If I avoid the enemy, where is the challenge?"

Riker and La Forge traded a quick glance of exasperation. Geordi took the football from Worf and began to reiterate the idea behind the ancient sport, but Worf stopped him with a sullen glare. "I believed I would better understand humans and their approach to combat if I experienced their more violent pastimes, but there are too many arcane rules and limits in this activity."

"Maybe you're right," Riker concluded. "Computer, cancel program." The computer obliged, and the football stadium and opposing players promptly vanished, leaving only the bare holodeck and its familiar yellow-on-black grid.

"You've got something in mind, Commander?" asked Geordi.

"I do," Riker said with a sly twinkle. "Worf, I think you need something more gladiatorial, more primitive, more like organized mayhem."

The Klingon's eyes gleamed with anticipation. "I was not aware there were any human games with those characteristics."

"Oh, there's one. I used to play it myself," said Riker. He looked at Geordi, who had caught the first officer's drift.

"What is it called?" asked Worf.

Riker and La Forge both answered at once: "Rugby!"

Before they could explain, the voice of Captain Picard filled the cavernous chamber. "Number One, Mr. Worf, and Mr. La Forge—to the bridge, please."

"Riker here, sir. We're on the holodeck. Permission to clean up first?"

"Granted," Picard replied. "Then report to the conference room. We've just received a message from Starfleet Command. The *Enterprise* must make an emergency diversion."

"I *thought* it felt like we changed course," Geordi muttered.

"How could you possibly tell?" said Worf.

Geordi shrugged. "Engineer's intuition."

"Where are we headed, sir?" Riker asked.

"The Etolosan system."

"Etolos?" Riker frowned, but the name didn't register. "Never heard of it."

"Neither had I, Number One."

"But I'll bet Data has," Riker said with a grin, "and I'll bet he's dying to tell us about it. We're on our way."

Captain's Log, Stardate 44429.1:

The *Enterprise* is en route to the planet Etolos. Although Etolos is not a member of the Federation, the planetary government has requested Federation assistance in ending long-standing hostilities with a neighboring planet, Alaj. It seems that the people of Etolos are descended from members of a dissident movement banished from Alaj some three hundred years ago.

"Long-standing hostilities," said Riker dryly, "would seem to be something of an understatement."

Jean-Luc Picard nodded in agreement, then addressed the group gathered around the long briefing table—Riker, Worf, Dr. Beverly Crusher, Engineer La Forge, Ship's Counselor Deanna Troi and Lieutenant Commander Data. "There are some odd elements involved in this mission. Not the least of which is the fact that Etolos is not a Federation member though Alaj is. Yet the request for mediation came from Etolos."

"Captain," Beverly said, "how do the Alajians feel about a third party getting involved?"

"After hearing from Etolos, the Federation contacted the Alajians. Apparently, Alaj expressed wary interest in the idea."

"I don't get it," Geordi mused, swallowing a sip of coffee. "These people haven't said 'boo' to each other in three hundred years and now, coincidentally, they both think it's a hot idea to sit down and chat about old times?"

"The circumstances are somewhat incongruous," Picard agreed. "It usually takes some compelling motivations to prompt such a rapprochement. Investigating those motivations will be part of our assignment. Mr. Data, the pertinent background, if you please."

The android officer's yellow eyes glittered with enthusiasm. Though Picard had experienced some initial misgivings about having an android on his senior bridge staff, he'd long since come to appreciate the manner in which Data tackled all tasks, however mundane: with nothing less than exhaustive (and, to those listening, occasionally exhausting) thoroughness.

"Sector Sigma-485," Data began, "contains sixty-six percent fewer habitable planets than average. As a result, worlds with sentient life and developed societies take on extra strategic significance."

Riker scratched his beard thoughtfully. "How many developed societies are out there?"

"Twenty that we know of. Only three are Federation members. The rest are nonaligned, and there has been considerable jockeying for power and prestige between them. Over the past fifty years, several small wars have broken out between assorted planets in the region. At least a half-dozen alliances have formed and shattered."

"Sounds incredibly unstable," said Riker.

"Instability," Worf said, "invites trouble."

"Precisely," Picard agreed. "The Federation is concerned about what may happen if one world manages to forcibly consolidate power over the others."

Riker grasped the implications immediately. "Possibly the birth of the next Romulan Empire or Ferengi Alliance."

"Big trouble," said Geordi.

Picard clasped his hands and rested them on the table. "By encouraging peaceful contacts and cooperation, the Federation is attempting to offer those planets some more fruitful alternatives to endless rounds of warfare."

"What about the Prime Directive?" Riker asked. "There's a fine line to be walked."

The captain nodded. "Indeed there is. Whatever the Federation does in Sigma-485 must be done by example and invitation. Which makes our diplomatic foray of critical importance. If we can mediate a durable detente between such old adversaries as Etolos and Alaj, it would clearly enhance the Federation's standing among the other societies of the Sigma-485 region."

"How long has Alaj been a Federation member?" Deanna Troi wondered.

"Ten years," said Data. "In fact, Alaj was the first planet in the area to join. The other two current members, Vorgon and Ta'Trosha 4, joined eight and five years ago, respectively."

"Although," said Picard, "the Alajians have kept largely to themselves during that time."

"Quite true," Data said. "In fact, the Alajians recalled their Federation ambassador three years ago, and the Federation liaison office on Alaj has not been staffed for the past two years."

"Isn't that unusual?" asked Dr. Crusher.

Picard shrugged. "But not unheard of. The Alajians were having serious internal problems and had an abrupt change of government. The new government never bothered to send a representative back to Earth. And the Federation's Interplanetary Liaison Office is always complaining that they don't have enough diplomats to go around. They evidently decided Alaj could do without diplomatic attention . . . until now."

"Captain," Troi said, "why would the Federation accept as a member a world which uses banishment as a way of dealing with those who disagree with government policies?" Her large dark eyes reflected deep concern.

"It's been quite a few years since Alaj last banished dissidents—"

"One hundred and eight, sir," Data volunteered.

"By signing onto the Federation Charter, they accepted that it upholds certain basic human rights," Picard said.

Riker leaned forward. "Just out of curiosity, Data, is there any record of how many times the Alajians banished groups they didn't like?"

"Twelve, sir, for various political and religious differences. They have had spaceflight capability for five hundred years. Their standard procedure entailed stocking a vessel with provisions and sending it off into space."

"Lovely," said Riker. "And that's how the Etolosans began?"

Data nodded. "Affirmative. In three hundred years, they have established a viable alternative society."

Beverly shook her head in sympathy. "No wonder they wanted nothing to do with the planet that threw them out into cold dark space."

17

"Captain," Riker said, "do we know why the Etolosans were banished from Alaj?"

At a gesture from Picard, Data fielded the question. "Our records do not include a great deal of detail on that, sir. There was a political movement known as Totality, which objected to Alajian government policies on land use and environmental standards."

Beverly Crusher's eyes flashed in disbelief. "And that got thousands of people thrown off their homeworld forever?"

Data looked over at the doctor. "Their protests grew to include violence."

"Maybe with good reason," Beverly countered.

"Doctor," Picard said with gentle firmness, "the origins and merits of the dispute are not ours to judge."

Grudgingly, Beverly accepted the point. "Understood, Captain."

"And their situation has now changed," Picard reminded them. "After the *Enterprise* arrives at Etolos, per Federation instructions, we will send a shuttlecraft with a small Etolosan delegation to Alaj. Number One, you shall be in command of the away team and supervise this preliminary round of negotiations."

"You'll also be making an unobtrusive survey of conditions on Alaj. It needs to be done quickly and as completely as possible, so I'd suggest you have Lieutenant Commander Data accompany you. The Federation needs to know what has transpired there since this new government has been in power, and what might be prompting them to make peace with mortal enemies. We'll be awaiting your progress report. If you find the Alajians amenable to further talks, the

Enterprise will be there within twenty-four hours with a full Etolosan negotiating team."

Dr. Crusher raised a skeptical eyebrow. "And what if the Alajians *aren't* amenable?"

"Then this three-hundred-year cold war will not end."

Will Riker rose from his seat. "It will if I have anything to say about it," he said smoothly. With easy confidence in his stride, he left the conference room. The other officers followed him out, except for Troi who remained with Picard.

"Counselor?"

"Captain, request permission to accompany the away team."

At times like these, Picard found himself wishing he had more than one empathic Betazoid, or that Deanna Troi could accomplish the magical feat of being in two places at once. Her ability to sense truth behind the most elaborately disguised deceptions made her an indispensable adviser whenever the *Enterprise* plied the treacherous currents of diplomacy. True, he was sending his first officer into dicey waters, with passions and suspicions likely to be running high on both sides. But William Riker had proven he could keep his wits about him. On top of that, his skill as a poker player had quickly become *Enterprise* legend, and Picard harbored not a shred of doubt in Riker's ability to handle this assignment.

"Etolos is an unknown quantity, Counselor. My two most senior officers will be off the ship. If I allowed you to accompany them, to whom would I turn for advice in delicate matters of interplanetary relations? Mr. Worf?"

At that image, Deanna's lips curled into a smile. "I see your dilemma, Captain."

"Thank you, Counselor." As she turned to leave, he spoke just before she reached the door. "One more thing—"

She looked back over her shoulder. "Sir?"

"Don't tell Worf I said that."

"Never, sir."

Chapter Three

THE *ENTERPRISE* SWUNG INTO ORBIT around Etolos and Deanna Troi was the first to notice the giant lake. It was an angry crimson, like a bloody wound.

"I've never seen anything like that," she said from her seat at Captain Picard's left.

With a deft touch, Data's fingers danced over his console and summoned a sensor display. "The waters are extremely high in concentrated sodium hydroxide, carbonate, bicarbonate and oxide. The only life forms able to survive in such an alkaline environment are red-pigmented bacteria. Thus, the color."

As the *Enterprise* circled the planet, the red lake was one of the few surface features clearly visible through a dark shroud of heavy dust and clouds. Picard rose from the command chair and took up a position closer to the viewscreen, his hand on Data's backrest.

"I've never seen cloud formations like that," the captain commented. "Never this pervasive—at least not where life thrives. Analysis?"

"The density of atmospheric dust is unusual, sir," Data confirmed. "I estimate it is blocking eighty-five-point-four-eight percent of normal sunlight over ninety-one percent of the planet surface."

"Perpetual twilight," Picard murmured. "Cause?"

Before the android could reply, they saw the cause. As the starship advanced in its orbit, the viewscreen revealed a line of fire girding half the globe from northwest to southeast.

"Magnify and enhance," said Picard.

Data complied. In three increments, the image grew until it was distinguishable as a continuous string of volcanic peaks stretching across three continental landmasses and a long archipelago. At this higher resolution, they could see that some of the craters spewed forth spasmodic pulses of molten lava, feeding the river of flame coursing down mountainsides and through valleys. But other sections of the explosive chain belched out towering spirals of ash and vapors.

Data projected a progressive series of images to provide a comprehensive overview. Awed by the totality of what they were witnessing, the bridge crew watched in silence. In that hush, Picard's mind sought to make some sense of what they'd been told about Etolos and what they now observed firsthand. He knew that life could *not* thrive in those conditions down on that dark and fiery planet. Was this why the Etolosans suddenly desired talks with Alaj? What did it all mean? What did they hope to gain? For the moment, Picard and his crew could be certain of only one thing: this mission had just taken a quantum leap in complexity.

The *Enterprise* continued its majestic arc around Etolos, and the wall of flame receded from view. Here and there, other volcanoes made their violent presence known, but much of the rest of Etolos was concealed behind its veil of volcanic steam and ash.

"Mr. Data," said Picard, "what do your sensors find under that curtain?"

Data swiveled a half-turn. "Readings indicate that Etolos is a geologically young and active planet, with greater than normal heat generation at its core. It also has a relatively thin crust—only twenty miles thick, compared with Earth's thirty-mile crust, for example. Those factors would enhance the likelihood of excessive volcanic activity." The android tapped a command into his console and the main viewer displayed a computer-generated rotational map of the planet, showing the surface which could not be glimpsed visually through the atmospheric soup below.

"This is how Etolos would appear on a cloudless day," Data explained. "My observations are necessarily incomplete, based as they are on only one orbital scan. Shall I proceed?"

"I have faith, Mr. Data," Picard said. "Continue."

"Sensors reveal unusually tall mountain ranges all over the planet. Twenty-thousand-meter altitudes are common—"

Riker's brows arched in awe. "That's more than twice as high as Everest on Earth."

"Etolos also has a high incidence of rift valleys and fissures," Data added.

Rarely had Picard seen such a rugged planet, certainly not one with abundant life. Data's computer map showed a world at savage war with itself, its surface riven by elemental forces great enough to create planets—or destroy them. And Picard knew, when it came to planets, creation and destruction were two ends of the same continuum. Worlds were not monuments from which some creator would stand back and proclaim them *done.* They were works in progress. Some survived the turbulence of conception, to receive foreign life or spawn their own, to evolve toward its own endings. But others died aborning. And for insignificant and short-lived creatures like humankind, stumbling upon a creation in chaos like Etolos, it was difficult to know where in its life span such a world might be.

Commander Riker absorbed Data's recitation and came to a succinct conclusion: "Etolos might make a great real-life geology lab, but it sure as hell isn't a great place to live."

"But people do live there," said Troi. "And they need our help."

Picard returned to his seat. "Let's find out what sort of help. Lieutenant Worf, open a channel to the prefex."

"They are hailing us, sir," the Klingon said.

"Very well. On viewer, Lieutenant."

Data's map of Etolos vanished from the main screen, replaced by a bland and fatigued face. *"Enterprise, I am Retthew, Prefex of the Council of State."*

"I am Captain Jean-Luc Picard, Prefex. On behalf of the United Federation of Planets, I extend good wishes to you and your world. However, at risk of breaching protocol, I think we should dispense with time-consuming formalities."

Retthew managed a wan smile. "Ah, you've scanned Etolos and you know what's happening here."

"Yes."

"Then you can appreciate the desperate nature of our summons."

"Indeed we can."

"Then, as you suggest, Captain, let's get right to it. We believe we have a special world here, with much to offer. We're doing important work of great potential benefit to the Federation and the entire galaxy."

Picard stood. "In order for us to best decide how we can help, it would be useful for us to visit Etolos."

"Then I invite you, Captain."

"Excellent. We shall beam down immediately. Picard out."

"*We,* Captain?" said Riker, a skeptical furrow creasing his brow. "Is there some reason why Counselor Troi and I can't handle this visit? We don't really know the situation down there, sir."

Picard let out a vaguely irritated breath and rubbed the back of his neck. "I do appreciate your preoccupation with preserving the captain's life and limb, Number One. However, you will soon be departing for Alaj and *I* shall be dealing with the Etolosans. Therefore, the value of this face-to-face meeting outweighs other factors."

Riker's expression made his displeasure clear, but he knew when his captain's mind was made up. "I suppose captain's discretion overrules first officer's objections?"

"Occasionally," Picard said with a wry twinkle. "Mr. Data, you have the conn. Number One, Counselor, let's not keep the Etolosans waiting." With that, the captain led the way to the turbolift.

"Never," Lef moaned. "We'll *never* survive this, Curister." The Alajian intelligence chief paced Zeila's opulent office from end to end, footfalls absorbed by the lush carpet.

"One dead nefittifi and you go all to pieces."

The quip halted Lef in appalled mid-stride, directly under the chandelier glittering in crystal glory. Zeila loved the stop-action effect it produced and she couldn't quite contain her amusement. She knew it was cruel to mock Lef's jittery nature, but sometimes she couldn't resist. Each time, she hoped he might react by cracking a self-deprecating smile. Instead, as usual, he simply glared at her as she sat curled in her chair. She leaned back into the deep cushions, one elegant leather boot braced against her desk and her arms crossed behind her head.

"With all due respect, Curister, we're going to be hauled from office, tried—*if* we're lucky—and summarily executed."

"Sit down, Lef. You're going to wear a ditch in that lovely rug."

"A ditch is where they'll throw our corpses," he muttered in total despair. But he did as he was told, folding one long leg up onto the other knee. The foot now suspended in mid-air twitched as if still pacing. "You don't seem to grasp the situation, Curister."

She pursed her lips playfully. "Explain it to me."

"We can't buy any more reprieves with promises of progress, barrages of statistics or speeches filled with grand plans. They don't want to hear the speeches any more."

"I noticed," Zeila said, recalling the crowd in Swatarra City.

"The people *were* willing to give us time to correct hundreds of years of abuses. They knew it couldn't be done overnight. But they're not seeing results, ma'am. There could be a revolution any day now." He rubbed his eyes. "If I had any honor at all, I'd quit."

"I don't want you to quit."

"Maybe they'll accept me as a sacrificial offering and give you another chance."

"Nobody will be sacrificed," she said as if soothing a frightened child. "And my job is safe."

Lef's jaw dropped. "How can you say that? The riots, the food shortages, the cities burning—"

"My job is safe," Zeila said lightly, "because nobody in his right mind would want it."

26

"So what does that make us? Lunatics?"

Zeila truly wished she could calm Lef's fears. She was touched by his loyalty, and valued his contributions to her regime. She believed she'd chosen wisely when she promoted him to deputy over other operatives with greater experience simply because she liked his integrity. Not once had he let her down, though sometimes she felt like she'd let him down. And sometimes it was impossible to make him understand her sweeping vision of possible futures for their world. But Lef gamely went along even when he wasn't sure of her plan, and that trust made Zeila feel a little more secure even when circumstances dictated otherwise. Now, for instance.

From Lef's point of view, the wave of popular adulation which she'd ridden to leadership had long since crested. Now they were drowning in the vortex left behind. Zeila could understand his dread of what might come tomorrow; to him, it appeared she'd run out of miracles. Or maybe old Lef had finally concluded there'd never been any miracles, just sleight of hand.

"Twenty-two days," he said. "The Feast of the Awakening is in twenty-two days." He was gripping the polished marble desktop so tightly she feared the edge would cut right through his palms.

"The most sacred day of the calendar . . ."

He nodded mournfully. ". . . when all Alajian leaders since before recorded time have presided from the overlook on Spirit Square with a nefittifi by their sides."

"And now," said Zeila, "the last nefittifi on our world is dead."

Lef spun out of the chair and resumed his pacing. "If you appear without the sacred symbol . . ." He waved his hands in small futile circles. "When they find out that the last nefittifi died while you were curister, they'll take it as the final outrage. They'll explode with anger like nothing—"

"Who says the people have to find out?" she asked in perfect serenity.

Beads of perspiration mottled Lef's brow. "How can we prevent it? What are you going to do, stuff the dead nefittifi and make it into a puppet?"

"Lef," said Zeila with an impish expression, "are you developing a sense of humor?"

"No—I'm just trying to understand the absurdity of what you're saying. There are no more of these animals—"

"On Alaj."

Once more, she'd stopped Lef short in verbal mid-stride. He recovered enough to look horrified as he realized what she seemed to be saying. "You can't be serious."

"Why not?"

"There's only one other planet with nefittifi— Etolos has a handful at most, and they're as sacred to the Etolosans as they are to us."

"So?" Zeila asked innocently.

"Alaj and Etolos haven't had direct contact in three hundred years. They hate us! For Spirit's sake, our ancestors *banished* those people. Why would they do us the favor of giving us a sacred nefittifi to save us from self-destruction?"

"They wouldn't. Unless *they* needed something from *us.*"

"They would have to be incredibly desperate."

"They are."

"Not desperate enough to forget three centuries of hatred," Lef said with a vigorous shake of his head.

"Don't be so certain. Don't you read the reports you give me?" she teased.

"Of course I do," Lef shot back. "Sometimes I just wonder if you understand the language."

"I understand forty-nine languages."

The burly security deputy resumed his pacing. "I should quit. I should."

"Lef."

"Curister, I just don't understand."

"That's because you see the Universe as something you can force into some semblance of order, if only you had enough information to put you one step ahead."

"And how do you see it?" he snorted.

"When I was a kid, my family moved from burned-out farmland in the Bahkk River Valley to Swatarra City. Not a nice place for a little girl to grow up, even then," Zeila said. As she spoke, she slid open a desk drawer and came up with a hefty pocketknife. The handle was gouged and weathered. But when she flipped the blade out, it gleamed like new. She used it to point to the scar on her chin. "I learned to use this when I was seven. I also learned there are no rules in a knife fight. You do what works. Little kids in alleys do. So do planets." Her smile was still there, but it had turned as cold and steely as the gleaming blade.

Chapter Four

PICARD, RIKER, AND TROI materialized in a courtyard just outside the Etolosan Council Center. The air was thick with ashy dust, falling like powdery snow, coating everything in sight. Trees in the courtyard were bare, and shrubs huddled in lifeless groups. The captain knew it was mid-afternoon, local time. He glanced up and saw a ghostly sun hanging in the leaden sky, a pale distant disk so dim it couldn't even cast a shadow. Lights glowed, as if it were night, in the windows of the low white-stone buildings comprising the government center. And it was damned cold, too. The dust made the starship officers cough, and their breath condensed in the chilly twilight.

A glass door opened and a lanky official moved toward them, extending a harried but friendly hand. "Captain Picard?" he said, looming even over Riker.

"Yes. This is my first officer, Commander Riker, and Deanna Troi, ship's counselor."

"Welcome to Etolos. I'm Sedge, the prefex's attaché. Please come with me."

They followed Sedge back through the same door. The building was as plain and utilitarian inside as out, without the impressive frills so often a part of government complexes. The walls were off-white, the floors simple tile; the only decoration was a heroic bronze statue in the atrium lobby, set in a reflecting pool with a small fountain. The *Enterprise* trio slowed to look as they passed by.

It was a bust of an animal. Standing nearly ten meters high and four across, its size alone made it imposing. But the sculpture portrayed a creature of blunt power, with a short curved beak, sturdy brow and grave, deep-set eyes, fearsome yet compassionate. To Picard, it was reminiscent of human-animal hybrids rendered as religious totems by artisans of several ancient Earth cultures.

Sedge noticed their interest and paused by the fountain. "That is a nefittifi."

"Nefittifi," Troi repeated, letting the word roll off her tongue.

"Not life-size, I hope," said Riker.

Sedge smiled briefly. "No. The nefittifi is our most sacred symbol. According to our lore, the Spirit gave us wisdom by speaking to us through the nefittifi."

"So it was native to Alaj," Troi said.

Sedge's face darkened as if by reflex at the mention of Alaj. Troi's expression flickered for an instant as she felt Sedge's emotions.

"Yes," came the stiff reply. It didn't take Betazoid empathic sensitivity to tell that Sedge would rather not pursue the topic. The Etolosan attaché edged away and they followed.

"Are there many left?" Troi asked gently.

The warmth in her voice melted a bit of Sedge's resistance. "No. We're not sure how many are left on Alaj. All we really know is that the numbers have been dwindling rapidly since our people left to come here."

"Are there any nefittifi here on Etolos?" Picard asked.

"Our ancestors brought a few on the Great Exodus. They live to be quite old, two and three hundred years sometimes. But they're very difficult to breed. So we only have a handful."

As they walked through a hallway off the lobby, they noticed other artworks depicting the nefittifi. There were some smaller busts resting on pedestals, and some framed paintings of the creatures' heads, done in styles ranging from primitive to realistic to abstract. But all were easily recognizable as the same animal.

Sedge led them around a corner into an open reception area with some simple wood-frame chairs and couches. He bowed slightly. "If you'll make yourselves comfortable, I'll tell the prefex you're here. I'm sure he'll be with you in a moment." The attaché left through a door and it closed behind him.

One curved wall of the reception area was all glass, and Picard drifted over to the windows. In the dusky outdoor light, all he could make out were some woods extending off into distant hills. Troi and Riker joined him and they sat on a pair of facing couches.

"Observations, Counselor?"

"Just the obvious one which I believe you both sensed as clearly as I did."

"Sedge is not fond of Alaj," said Riker.

Troi nodded. "Which is not surprising in view of the history here. But it is much more than a simple dislike or even a good honest dose of hatred. It is an abhorrence so deeply ingrained as to be virtually indistinguishable from the usual basic emotions."

"You mean something like instinct?" Picard said.

"Yes," said Troi emphatically. "Comparable to the automatic love and nurturing a mother feels for a child, or the fear almost all creatures feel when startled by an overwhelming threat."

"That *is* basic," said Riker.

Troi nodded. "If all Etolosans feel this as deeply, it could pose formidable obstacles in any negotiations between Etolos and Alaj."

Picard didn't like the sound of that. "Hmm. And if the Alajians feel the same way . . ." His voice trailed off as Sedge returned and ushered them into a large conference chamber.

Again, the decor was simple, just an elegantly austere oblong table surrounded by two dozen high-backed chairs made of wood, with tufted cushions on each seat. Small bowls of Retthew's favored snack seeds had been put within easy reach. Picard was not surprised to find another bust of the nefittifi glowering from a perch near a large observation window.

Sedge pulled out three chairs for the visitors, then circled to join his prefex and a matronly Etolosan woman already seated across the table. Retthew and the woman stood and half-bowed in greeting. Picard, Riker, and Troi returned the gesture and all took their seats as the captain introduced his officers.

"And this is Ambassador Navirra," said Retthew. "She will be representing us in the exploratory talks with Alaj."

Navirra's face showed her advanced age, and she exuded weighty dignity in both manner and dress. Her eyes moved in stately review, measuring these Federation emissaries.

"If this meets with your approval," Picard said, addressing his hosts, "my first officer will command a shuttlecraft which will take Ambassador Navirra and her party to Alaj."

"I *am* the party," Navirra intoned with deliberate diction.

Picard's eyebrows rose in surprise. "Oh?"

"Navirra is our most skilled representative, Captain," said Retthew.

"And I prefer to work alone," she said, "especially if the first task is to size up the prospects for success."

"As you wish. The *Enterprise* will remain here, enabling us to explore the possibilities of a closer relationship between the Federation and Etolos."

"Good," Retthew said. "I was afraid you and your ship would be leaving too quickly for us to show you around."

"Prefex," said Picard, "our records are somewhat incomplete on the history of your dispute with Alaj. Could you fill us in?"

At the mention of Alaj, Sedge again visibly stiffened. Retthew, who'd been holding a handful of the brown seeds, reacted by popping some in his mouth and cracking them nervously. Only Navirra showed no overt reaction, maintaining a perfect poker face.

"All we really know," Riker said, "is that your ancestors belonged to a movement called Totality, and they were banished for protesting against Alajian environmental policies."

"What else would you need to know?" asked Retthew tightly.

"If we are to mediate," Riker prodded politely, "additional detail would be helpful."

"Totality was formed by a prophet named Etol," Retthew began. "Our world is named for him. The government of Alaj sanctioned wanton abuse of the natural world. Etol and his followers tried to change those policies. But nothing deterred the government from overbuilding, overpolluting, and overpopulating —not even a series of great disasters."

"Did Totality turn to violence?" Riker asked.

Retthew closed his eyes in a moment of painful

memory. "Some did. Out of frustration. Etol never approved, but he was blamed. The government arrested thousands and convicted them—"

"Without fair hearing," Sedge huffed angrily. "All who wouldn't recant their beliefs were banished. As if we could shed beliefs like clothing. The Alajians never understood the sanctity of life and they *still* don't."

"We don't know that, Sedge," Retthew said. "Banishment may have been the best thing for our ancestors, Captain. We came here and found a pristine world. And we've kept it that way."

"You have a very small population," Riker said. "About two hundred thousand people—?"

"And it will never exceed that," said Retthew firmly. "Etolos was established to be everything Alaj was not: people balanced in perfect harmony with the natural world. The people of Etolos have settled just one small continent."

Picard cocked his head curiously. "Why is that?"

"Because the rest of Etolos has been kept wild, reserved for our work," Retthew said. For the first time, his eyes lit with passion. "We believe we are the galaxy's foremost experts at preserving, protecting, and renewing endangered life. We can take the last specimen, living or dead, of any species, and from that one sample recreate entire genetically diverse, self-sustaining populations.

"We can revitalize former native habitats and reintroduce extinct species to places they once dominated. Or we can build perfectly simulated replacement habitats right here on Etolos which will maintain renewed individual species, partial ecosystems, or whole planetary life systems for posterity."

Riker seemed unimpressed. "The technology to do all those things isn't exclusively yours."

"True," Retthew admitted. "But other worlds have

other priorities: trade, exploration, colonization, conquest. In just the known galaxy, a million plant and animal species become extinct every day. We believe that no life form is expendable. Natural death is one thing. But extinction brought about by the carelessness and stupidity of beings who should know better —*that* is a crime, pure and simple. Your own Starfleet credo is 'To seek out new life . . .' What if some more advanced species had caused *your* extinction millennia ago?"

"This is our sole purpose, our single-minded quest," Sedge added. "We have made long-term consulting arrangements with planets all over this part of the galaxy. We know there are many worlds that don't have the knowledge or resources—or the wisdom—to protect precious life while they've got the chance."

"Worlds like Alaj once was, Captain," said Retthew. "Worlds that could go either way, where perspective is in danger of falling victim to greed and uncontrolled growth. If we can get to those worlds before they pitch over the precipice, we can save them. Elsewhere, we can help civilizations find the harmony they've lost before they become unredeemable sewers like Alaj is now."

Sedge and Retthew took deep breaths, trying to recoup the energy expended in their speeches. That left Navirra. Her mouth took on a sardonic twist, the first break in her sublime neutrality. "We're the best, Captain Picard. We are a light of the galaxy, Commander Riker. Counselor Troi, we are wisdom personified. If you doubt any of this, we can demonstrate the truth of our words. There is just one catch . . ." She paused for emphasis. "Etolos is dying a cold, dusty death. We need a new world. Alaj may be able to provide such a world. And we need you to move us."

The enormity of Navirra's declaration caught Picard and his officers off-guard. After a moment of flummoxed silence, the captain was the first to find his voice. "Move your *entire civilization?* Two hundred thousand people—?"

"And six hundred thousand animals of various sizes," said Navirra. "As quickly as possible. As you've seen for yourself, Etolos is rapidly becoming unlivable."

"That's almost impossible," Riker said. "It would take months."

"Even if we could accomplish such a feat of transportation," said Picard, "what makes you think the Alajians will accommodate your needs?"

"Accomplishing that will be *my* job," Navirra said with brassy assurance. "Don't you know the definition of a diplomat, Captain? One who can tell you to go to hell—and make you look forward to the trip."

R'teep, captain of the most menacing raptor in the D'aveedi pirate fleet, looked forward to the trip home. His hold was filled to capacity after he and his crew had ambushed the lumbering Ta'Troshan freighter several parsecs from nowhere, on the far fringes of Sector Epsilon-485, and picked it clean.

Some pirate races preferred to blast their victims to dust after vanquishing them. But the D'aveedi considered it a point of honor to leave the lifeless hulks floating in space, a sort of calling card. So the Ta'Troshan vessel was left adrift, the corpses of her crew of four left where they'd fallen after R'teep's men boarded and slashed their leathery yellow throats.

The D'aveedi were humanoid, though they'd never be mistaken for human, with pug snouts and eyes mounted on cartilagenous stalks capable of springing out several inches, twisting in any direction, or retracting tightly into bony sockets. As his angular ship moved away from its dead prey, R'teep's eye-stalks were at full extension, wobbling about, joyfully independent of each other, drinking in the glory of the treasures taken this day. Lots to sell or trade, lots worth keeping as "investments" for the future.

And worth drinking to, R'teep thought during repeated swigs of the burning *zjveel* brew he'd fetched from his cabin. A day's work done, he could now drink himself into a stupor for the journey back to base camp. He was halfway to both when the shrilling of an alarm roused him up to the cramped foredeck.

R'teep forced his eyes to quit wavering and peered at the tiny viewscreen over the captain's bench where he saw pale tendrils of energy drifting lazily toward his ship.

"What is it?" he demanded of his lieutenant.

"A powerful force, Lord."

R'teep took a swipe at the lieutenant's head. "I know that, idiot. But it isn't even holding us in place. Doesn't look all *that* powerful. Is there a ship out there?"

"Must be, Lord."

"Then let's kill it."

"But it might be a warship. We have no shields—"

"Shields are for cowards," R'teep roared drunkenly. No self-respecting D'aveedi buccaneer wasted power on shields, not at the expense of speed and weaponry. The privateers' code called for cunning, craft, and quickness. Anyone who fell short deserved to die.

R'teep brought the raptor's weapons to full power and took the controls himself. His breath reeked of brew and his lieutenant, unfortunately all too sober, slid as far across the tiny cabin as he could.

"Captain, we've already had a victorious day. Let's go home and enjoy—"

"Shut up! Set course for the center of whatever's out there and go to full speed."

The lieutenant did as ordered and the privateer surged forward. R'teep thought he spied a target in his sights and he squeezed the triggers. Blue bolts of energy screamed from the battery of guns in the raptor's belly. Almost immediately, the bolts were twisted back on themselves by the deceptive strength of the surrounding force field. An instant later, the raptor's own weapon beams enveloped the D'aveedi vessel and blew it to bits.

Like some cosmic fog bank, the enigmatic energy field rolled on. There was no one left to mark its course as it headed into Sector Sigma-485.

Chapter Five

PICARD AND RIKER had barely sat down in a quiet corner of Ten-Forward when Guinan met them at their table with a tray and four glasses.

"One for the road, Commander?" she said, her voice low and serene as usual.

"Captain's idea," Riker grinned. He thumbed a gesture at the extra glass. "Did you think I'd need *two* for the road?"

Guinan joined them in the booth. "Deanna will be here in a minute, right?"

Picard's eyes narrowed. "How did you know that?"

Her only reply was a cryptic smile. A moment later, Troi approached the table, slid in next to Riker and thanked Guinan for the drink.

"Is your away team ready, Number One?" said Picard.

Riker's brow hitched skeptically. "Ready—but for what, I'm not sure. Are *you* ready for the Etolosans? Asking us to move their entire civilization—are they crazy?"

"They believe," Troi said.

"Believe?" Riker echoed. "In what—magic?"

"They have an unshakable faith in the correctness of their way of life."

"And," Picard said with a thoughtful sip, "they seem to have an equally unshakable belief that we will somehow be able to accomplish what they've asked of us."

"Is it possible?" Guinan asked.

"Not likely," said Picard. "Geordi is working on the problem, but . . ." He finished with a dubious shrug.

"Every man prefers belief to the exercise of judgment," Guinan said.

Picard frowned. "Didn't Seneca say that?"

"Not to me personally. I just happen to enjoy reading ancient philosophers."

"You're a bit of an ancient philosopher yourself," said Picard.

"Our problem isn't ancient philosophers," said Riker. "It's true believers. I don't like being lectured."

"Their attitude did verge on the sanctimonious," Picard agreed. "But the fact that we may find the Etolosans a bit priggish should not detract from the value of their work. They allowed Data to access their files, and their dedication and record of success are admirable."

"I wonder if the Alajians will agree," Deanna said.

Riker finished his drink. "I guess that'll depend on whether Alaj wants to buy what the Etolosans want to sell."

"You'll know in thirty-six hours, Number One."

Ozemmik pounded Retthew's desk so hard the seed dish rattled. "Why wasn't I at that meeting?"

"This is why."

"This is between us." Ozemmik hissed a calming

breath between his teeth and sat. "I'm your security adviser. I'm offended that you didn't think I could get through a meeting with these Federation people without bringing up our disagreement."

The prefex shoved the dish of seeds toward his friend. "Oh, you take offense too easily. You always have."

Ozemmik plucked up a couple of seeds with his fingertips. He placed them onto his tongue, drew them back between his lips and chewed. "Those things are really awful, Rett. I don't know how you eat them."

"Good for the digestion."

"Well . . . I'm just concerned with what's good for Etolos."

"I know that." Retthew wagged his head in concession. "Maybe I should have had you there."

"I'm on your side."

"I know."

"You need me."

"I know that, too," said Retthew kindly. "Give me your word that we'll have no more of your ominous warnings about violent opposition."

"I only warn you when you need to be warned."

"*I'm* the prefex here," Retthew said, flaring just a bit. "I sometimes think you forget that."

"Never—*Excellency.*" The title of respect was tinged with sarcasm. "I just don't like being excluded."

"I have your word?"

"You have it."

"Good," Retthew sighed. "That's settled. I feel better already. I really did feel badly having that meeting without you."

"Then don't let it happen again. After all, you *are* the prefex."

* * *

Geordi La Forge's engineering domain was quiet, the starship's heartbeat filling the large chamber with a soft glow and the sound of its pulse. The chief engineer himself provided the muttering as he hunched over his desk, shaking his head. He was so wrapped up in his work he failed to notice Wesley Crusher entering with Gina Pace, a pert seventeen-year-old with shaggy dark hair.

"Headaches, Geordi?" said Wes with sympathy.

La Forge snorted as he flung his arms up in frustration. "They've got to be kidding. Look at this."

Wes and Gina bent over Geordi's computer screen. "The evacuation of Etolos, huh," said Wesley. "Is it possible?"

"I'm getting tired of hearing that question," Geordi snapped.

"From the captain?" Gina asked.

"No . . . from me," said Geordi wearily. "I've asked myself about a billion times today. Unfortunately, I keep coming up with the same answer."

"No way," Wes concluded.

"That's it. And that's just not good enough." Geordi turned back to the computer. "Look at this—look at the volume we'd need to transport a couple of hundred thousand people, plus their belongings, plus all the animals."

Wesley's eyes widened. "That's a lot of ships."

"There aren't that many available ships in all of Starfleet—hell, in the whole Federation. I can't see any way those people could be relocated in less than the better part of a year."

Gina's big brown eyes squinted down as she peered at the jumble of statistics and schematics on the screen. "Isn't there any way we could stop the volcanic eruptions the way we did on Drema Four, when the *Enterprise* saved Data's little friend, Sarjenka?"

"That was different," Wes said. "Drema Four's geological instability had a specific cause. What's going on inside Etolos is part of the planet's natural evolution."

Geordi slumped down into his chair. "Besides, even if we could stop it, the Etolosans wouldn't let us. They don't believe in working against nature, even when their own existence hangs in the balance."

"Oh," said Gina. "A kind of environmental Prime Directive?"

"I guess so," Geordi replied. "So they want to be moved."

Gina's expression turned impish. "How many animals do you think we could fit on the *Enterprise?*"

Geordi and Wes both stared at her. The concept brought interesting images to mind: grazing herds on the hangar deck, flocks wheeling through imaginary holodeck skies, stepping around malodorous deposits left on decks everywhere. It didn't take long before Wes and Geordi both began to snicker.

"Who'd have to clean up after the elephants?" Wes wondered.

"And the phrase 'getting the captain's goat' would take on a whole new meaning," Geordi said. "Imagine the jokes about Picard's ark."

After another moment's contemplation, all three said, "Nahhh."

"I heard they've got some really rare animals on Etolos," Gina said seriously. "I'd love to see them. I'd love to have a chance to draw them. Which reminds me, when are you going to pose for me, Wesley Crusher?"

"Dressed or undressed?" Geordi asked in mock innocence.

"Geordi!" Wes hissed in mortified protest, blushing instantly.

"Just his face, Geordi," said Gina, still laughing as she enjoyed Wesley's obvious discomfort.

"I took art classes for a while," Geordi said, diverting scrutiny and giving Wesley's blush a chance to fade. He tapped the VISOR covering his eyes. "I thought this might give me an unusual perspective."

"Did it?" asked Gina.

"Yeah. Too bad it didn't give me unusual talent to go with it."

Gina sighed. "Speaking of classes, I've got an astrophysics lab to go to. See you guys later." She skipped out of Engineering and Geordi watched Wes watch her go.

"She likes you, Wesley."

Wesley shrugged with teenage diffidence. "I guess."

"She's cute, Wes. Go for it."

"You mean let her draw me?"

"Why not? I got to be pretty good friends with a model from my art class."

"Did you go out, like on dates?"

Geordi grinned. "He wasn't my type."

The *Enterprise* shuttlecraft *Onizuka* hung in space just behind the starship's warp nacelles. Data and Riker sat in the cockpit, while Lieutenant Rick Holzrichter of Security and Ensign Rachel Lopez of Environmental Sciences settled down in the aft cabin. Holzrichter was stout and sturdy, with short sandy hair and a boyish grin. Lopez was young, and looked younger, partly because of her tiny stature and partly because of her round face and wide dark eyes. She had a bronze-brown complexion and straight black hair pulled back into a French braid. Both had accompanied Riker on away teams in the past, and he'd found them skilled and reliable despite their relative youth.

He liked Holzrichter's thirst for a challenge, any

challenge, and his thoughtful decisiveness. Riker doubted any unexpected turn of events would catch him unprepared. As for Lopez, she'd topped her Starfleet graduating class, and she compensated for her youthful appearance with extra assertiveness. Recalling their first meeting still gave Riker a chuckle. "People may step on me," she'd said to him, noting one of the perils of being short, "but if they do, they'll *hear* about it." He knew she meant it both literally and figuratively.

"Enterprise to Commander Riker." The voice of Transporter Chief O'Brien came over the speaker.

"This is Riker."

"We've got the Etolosan coordinates, sir. Standing by to transport this Ambassador Navirra directly aboard the shuttle on your order."

"We're ready, O'Brien. Transport now."

A moment later, the rotund form of the Etolosan envoy shimmered into existence in the rear cabin. Riker greeted her and introduced the rest of the crew, then showed her to one of the contoured seats. "If you'll make yourself comfortable, Ambassador, we'll be getting underway. It's our pleasure to have you aboard."

"I don't doubt that," she said solemnly as she lowered herself into the seat. Only Riker caught the twinkle beneath her wrinkled eyelids.

Jean-Luc Picard sipped a steaming cup of Earl Grey in his ready room, pondering the mysteries of faith. Deanna had observed in the Etolosans what she'd termed unshakable faith. In the realm of reality, was there any such thing? Picard's own life certainly contained large dollops of faith, in his crew, his ship, the correctness of the philosophies underlying both Starfleet and the Federation.

I suppose I could characterize my confidence in those things as unshakable. Barring any totally unforeseeable changes in my knowledge about them.

There it was. The escape clause. Faith could be unshakable, relatively speaking, without being absolute. *How much easier life would be if we didn't have to maintain any skepticism at all about those things we most fervently wish to believe.* But reality, in Picard's experience, had the nasty habit of not accommodating such blind faith.

The Etolosans, however, saw things differently. And, for the moment at least, he too would have to attempt to see things their way. He finished his tea and strode out onto the bridge, motioning to Deanna Troi. "Counselor, I believe it is time for our safari."

She approached him near the turbolift. "Captain," she said quietly, "I could do this alone. With Commander Riker and Data gone, perhaps you should remain onboard."

"Noted. Unfortunately, strict adherence to protocol is not always possible. Besides, I don't think we'll be facing any immediate dangers on Etolos." Picard glanced at his security chief. "Mr. Worf, you have the conn."

With a grave nod of acknowledgment, the burly Klingon squared his shoulders and took his place in the command chair.

Picard and Troi stood facing each other inside the turbolift as it whisked them through the *Enterprise* to Transporter Room Three. "I know you don't like riding horses or similar animals, Counselor. But did you ever experience animals in the wild?"

"I've been to zoological parks on Betazed and other worlds. I enjoyed them, but only when the animals had room to roam freely enough that they did not feel they were captive."

"Didn't that make it difficult to actually see them?"

"Yes, but just knowing they were there—and happy—was enough."

"Hmm. We humans would imagine how the animals felt, where a Betazoid would know."

"What about you, Captain? Does your appreciation for animals include the untamed?"

"Indeed. For my twelfth birthday, my mother took me to the Serengeti World Wildlife Park in eastern Africa. Now, I'd grown up in Europe, which was lovely but hardly wild. And then I saw this vast landscape, which had been painstakingly restored over a hundred and fifty years to the way it was before civilization nearly ruined Africa."

The turbolift opened and they continued on to the transporter room. "And was it also difficult to see the animals?"

"Some were out in plain sight. As for the others? Like you, I knew they were there ... and it *was* enough." Picard smiled at the memory.

"You're trying hard to understand the Etolosans' commitment to their conservationism, aren't you?"

Picard's eyebrows twitched. He hated appearing transparent, even to a Betazoid empath. "It isn't so much their commitment to the principle I find troubling. It's their unwillingness to recognize the possibility that all this may *not* work out for the best."

The transporter room door slid open and O'Brien nodded at them as they stepped up onto the platform. "Coordinates set, sir."

"Energize."

The four-seat flyer banked steeply and dropped down through the dusky sky. Sedge handled the controls while Retthew sat next to him in the other front seat, swiveled about to face Picard and Troi in the rear. Through the flyer's clear bubble top, they had unobstructed visibility in all directions. This side of Etolos looked calm, with no volcanoes burping up molten material from deep within the planet, or flinging out choking clouds of ash. But after months of eruptions elsewhere, no part of this world remained untouched by the spreading gloom.

Sedge slowed and leveled off a few hundred feet above a bleak plain that extended from the sea on its south and east to jagged mountain ranges which crossed diagonally to the west and north, virtually cutting the plateau off from the rest of the island continent on which it lay.

"The mountains," Retthew explained, "made this the perfect isolated habitat for a whole variety of animals which originally came from relatively dry grasslands."

Picard strained for a glimpse of something alive. For a fleeting moment, he remembered the feeling he'd had while searching for wild things on his childhood visit to the Serengeti. In Africa, he'd known they were out there somewhere. And he'd felt the rush of life unseen, the heat of wild blood, the wind of freedom. Here, above this Etolosan savanna, he felt only the cold touch of approaching death.

"There, Captain!" Troi called, pointing out the left side. They all turned, and spotted a sparse herd of animals wandering along a streambed. Sedge took the flyer closer. The animals didn't notice, since it cast no shadow in the volcano-clouded twilight and the whisper of its engines was lost in the moan of the wind.

The animals were spindly legged beasts about the size of domestic cattle, with humps on their shoulders, complex antlers extending forward, and trunked snouts with which they scrabbled through the barren soil in search of food. Even from the air, it was clear that they were wasting away, their mottled hides hanging gauntly on protruding ribs and bones.

"They're called ondryx," Retthew said. "Native to the planet Kejor Six. There were three left—in captivity—when the Kejori asked us to save them. Within four years, we'd built a herd of five thousand. The Kejori had only a limited habitat left, so we gave them a thousand head and maintained the other four thousand here. Now, half of those have died. The rest have had to split up into small foraging groups. By nature, they're social animals, so you can imagine—"

Troi turned sharply to look out the other side of the flyer. "Captain, over there."

As she pointed, they watched one of the ondryx fall to its knees. It struggled to rise, its trunk flailing defiantly. Then it pitched forward, rolled onto its side and moved no more.

"I felt it die," Troi whispered. "Confusion . . . pain . . . but no peace."

At a nod from Retthew, Sedge turned the flyer north. It only took a few minutes to cross fifty miles of desolation and reach the mountains. The steep slopes there were thickly forested, but the trees had already been blighted by months of reduced sunlight. Most of their leaves were down, covering the ground with a dry mat of organic decay.

Retthew scanned the mountainsides, searching for something. He found what he was looking for—an orange marker flag flapping in a skeletal treetop—and directed Sedge toward a notch in the mountain's face just below the treeline. The flyer landed in a level clearing and Retthew slid the side hatch open, leading the others toward the marker.

"This is one of our greatest triumphs," he said, "and one of our greatest tragedies, if we can't relocate soon."

As they followed him through the woods, Picard imagined how dense the foliage must have once been. He'd climbed mountains on several worlds and knew firsthand how strong a sun could be at high altitudes. A stand of trees with their thick dome of leaves could offer shade as dark as dusk, cool relief on a hot day. But these branches were bare, and offered no protection from the glowering chill of a sunless sky.

They reached the marked tree after a short hike, and saw a huge animal corpse curled on its side. It was at least twice the size of the African elephants Picard had viewed as a boy, with a downy coat of gray-brown fur. The stench of rotting flesh had faded by now. It had been dead long enough to become dessicated, skin stretched over pelvic bones and a rib cage so large that a man could have stood inside with room to spare. The animal's neck was nearly as long as its body, twisted so the head was laying flat, face up. Compared to the creature's overall bulk, the head seemed incongruously delicate, with flared nostrils and a paired vee of horns growing just behind its nose.

Troi approached it, her mind a jumble of conflicting emotions: sadness, curiosity, and relief that she could not share directly the suffering of a beast already dead. Taken by the long blond lashes on its closed eyelids and the gentle curve of its mouth, she wondered whether it might have been gentle in spite of its size.

"This is . . . was a keegron," said Retthew. "They were native to Gamma Norik."

"Were?" said Picard.

Retthew nodded. "They'd been extinct for at least a century. The Norikan population needed the land for people. So this magnificent creature lost out after roaming that world for five million years. Same old sad tale."

"If it was extinct—" Troi began.

Retthew anticipated the question. "How did we bring it back to life? The Norikans found two keegron frozen in a glacier. They'd heard of our work and asked us to help. We found enough preserved genetic material in the frozen specimens to recreate the species."

Picard circled the keegron slowly. "Their food source—these trees?"

"Correct, Captain. Which is why this animal is dead. They're plant eaters, incredibly gentle, and friendly, too. You can ride on their backs and they won't raise a fuss."

"What about those horns?" asked Picard.

"For use in mock mating battles," Retthew said.

Troi couldn't take her eyes off the tranquil face. "Are there any remaining here?"

"We had the group up to one hundred and eight. As you might expect, they need quite a bit of range per animal in order to have sufficient food. Now we're down to nineteen."

"We've seen enough here, Retthew," Picard announced abruptly, turning back toward the flyer.

Retthew trotted to catch up. "Captain, I'd hoped—"

"You are attempting to manipulate our sympathies, sir," said Picard in a clipped tone. "And you are succeeding."

Retthew looked pleased, but before he could speak, Picard cut him off. "I do not want our decisions to be based on emotional appeals. From the outset, our inclination has always been to supply whatever aid may be possible."

"That is all we've been asking, Captain."

They reached the flyer, with Sedge and Counselor Troi trailing behind. "No, it is not," Picard shot back. Then his tone softened. "However magnificent and varied these animals may be, however rare and precious, you may be asking the impossible. And that we cannot do."

Chapter Six

"SO, TELL ME, DATA, what do you think of Ambassador Navirra?"

Riker leaned back in his cockpit seat as the shuttlecraft made its way toward Alaj. His android companion mulled the question. "Her record of diplomatic experience and accomplishments is quite impressive."

"I mean what do you think of *her?*"

Data seemed momentarily perplexed. "She is unlike most of the diplomats with whom we have had contact."

"How so?"

"That is difficult to say. I am not quite sure what she means by some of her statements."

Riker's eyes twinkled in amusement. "Such as?"

"Such as her comment that the shuttle might not be large enough for her ego. Is that not a term referring to a part of the human psyche as described by—"

"Yes, Data, yes," Riker said. "It's a joke."

Data cocked his head quizzically. "Psychoanalysis?"

"No, what Navirra said."

"Oh. Ahh." Data gave the subject an instant of thought, then said, "Did you hear the one about the psychoanalyst and the—"

"Never mind, Data. Mind if I go back and chat with our guest?"

"If I said I did, would you then remain here?"

"No."

"That is what I thought, Commander. In that case, I have no objection at all."

Riker unfolded his tall frame and stepped through the mid-ship hatch to the aft compartment, where Lopez and Holzrichter were engaged in lively conversation with the Etolosan emissary.

". . . not enough truth," Rachel Lopez was saying passionately. "Why can't diplomats be straight talkers?"

"Because, dear girl, truth is not a solitary endeavor. It takes two—one to speak and one to listen."

Holzrichter nodded. "And listening isn't always the same as hearing."

With a grand flourish of one gnarled hand, Navirra invited Riker to sit with them. As he did, he also poured himself a cup of tea from the steaming pot resting on a fold-out food tray.

"Don't let me interrupt," said Riker. "Sounds interesting."

"Ambassador," Lopez said, "why wouldn't the Alajians listen, *really* listen to you now?"

Navirra reacted with a wisp of a smile. "Three hundred years of reasons could not be enumerated on a trip of this brief duration."

"It doesn't make sense. They've practically ruined their world, and you could help them salvage it."

"Could," said Navirra, "is the operative word."

"Back on Earth," said Lopez, "my Sioux ancestors had a saying: 'We do not inherit the world from our parents, we borrow it from our children.'"

The old ambassador seemed genuinely impressed. "You had very wise ancestors. Did anyone heed their words before it was too late?"

"In the nick of time," Riker replied with a smile. "If I may be so bold, Ambassador—"

"Please do, Commander. I've always liked boldness in a man."

Riker smiled. Whatever happened on this mission, he was pretty sure traveling with Navirra was going to be a memorable experience. "What do you have to offer the Alajians that's worth a whole planet in return?"

"A fair question, Mr. Riker. And a fair trade—a planet for a planet."

"I don't understand."

"We get Anarra, their empty fourth planet, and we give them back Alaj."

"You mean by helping them clean it up," said Lopez.

"Exactly."

Riker looked dubious. "But that hinges on their admitting they've made a mess of their own world, not to mention accepting help from people they consider an enemy."

"Commander," said Navirra in a conspiratorial tone, "at my age, a long trip in a tiny space vessel is not my favorite activity. Do you think I'd be making this journey if we didn't have reason to expect a change in attitude by the new Alajian leadership?"

"No, I don't suppose you would."

With pained effort, Navirra shifted in her seat.

"Are you all right, ma'am?" Holzrichter asked with concern.

"Quite, quite. Just the usual aches and creaks. Had I known I'd survive this long, I'd have taken better care of myself. Back to your question, Mr. Riker . . . I do not undertake this venture without a treasure or two hidden in my skirts."

"In addition to offering Etolosan environmental expertise?"

Navirra's multiple chins compressed under a stately nod. "Indeed. Something the Alajians would not expect us to give . . . something we would expect them to accept eagerly."

"Something you'd care to tell us about?" asked Riker.

"In due time."

"The time has come," Retthew said, "to let you in on our secret, Captain Picard."

Descending through the charcoal sky, the flyer set down on a hill overlooking the government center and the rest of the capital city of Baradar spreading along the ocean shore. As they got out, Picard saw that they'd landed near three rustic buildings set into the hillside and designed to blend with the natural terrain under a cloak of trees and bushes. With so much Etolosan flora now dead or dormant, the camouflage effect didn't quite work. Retthew led the group toward the largest of the structures.

"What secret, Prefex?"

"You've had a hard time understanding why we're so confident that an agreement can be reached with Alaj. Is that a fair conclusion?"

"I suppose it is," said Picard warily.

"Probably the one unbreakable bond still remaining between Etolos and Alaj is our common origin," Retthew said as they entered the main building. The walls and floor were constructed of rough-finished boards. As in the official buildings Picard had visited on their first beam-down, the only ornamental item here was a nefittifi bust, this one carved into the top of a log standing on end in the entryway. "Looking at our two societies, you would not believe we sprang from the same roots. The Alajians have twisted Original Truth, believing it gave them license to treat the natural world—and other people—with cruelty and utter disregard. Yet, for reasons we Etolosans cannot begin to guess, they still honor the Sacred Symbol of Wisdom . . . the nefittifi."

"I explained the nefittifi's place to them, Prefex," Sedge said.

"Ahh, good. These little *kitas* we wear," said Retthew, touching the small pouch stitched onto his headband, "they contain tiny scrolls with the Original Truths written on them, the exact words of the Spirit."

"I see the *kita* is worn over the right ear," Deanna said. "Is there a significance to that?"

Retthew nodded. "When the Originator heard the words of the Spirit from the nefittifi, they were spoken into her right ear. I suppose our beliefs must seem strange to you."

"No stranger than ours would seem to you," Troi said reassuringly.

"Do the Alajians continue to share these beliefs?" Picard asked.

"If you strip an Alajian to his soul, he does—in spite of all the centuries of blasphemy and sacrilege. And the sacred symbolism of the nefittifi is part of that. Sedge was not entirely truthful with you when you asked him if any nefittifi remained on Alaj."

Picard's jaw stiffened. "Oh?"

"Our intelligence reports that the last nefittifi on Alaj has just died. And the Alajian government is keeping this a secret from their people."

"Why?" said Troi.

"Because the most sacred day of the year is approaching."

"Their year or yours?" Picard asked.

"Both," said Retthew. "The Feast of the Awakening celebrates the giving of the Original Truths to our ancestors. The political situation on Alaj is so explosive right now . . . if Curister Zeila appears at the feast parade without a nefittifi, it could be just the fuel her opposition needs to light the fire that ends her regime and her reforms."

Picard pursed his lips. "What do you know of Zeila and her government?"

"Enough to give us the hope that she may be someone we might be able to deal with. Which is why we would be willing to consider, as part of our negotiations, part of a comprehensive agreement, the possibility of giving them a breeding pair of nefittifi."

Retthew's sentence nearly strangled on qualifiers, but his meaning was clear. "You want to save Zeila's regime," Picard said plainly.

"Perhaps," said Retthew, "if *she* is willing to save our *world.*"

Picard turned away, and found himself facing the wooden nefittifi carving. Historically, such symbolic gifts had served as tokens of friendship between nations on Earth as well as between worlds, helping to bridge rifts separating all sorts of opponents. But had any animals ever before been so important that they'd transformed the impossible into the probable? Data might have such details somewhere in his vast positronic memory. Picard made a mental footnote for later inquiry. "Are we permitted to see these rare and reclusive animals?"

"We'd be honored to show them to you, Captain," Retthew said. "In anticipation of a possible agreement, we've already isolated two from the other six—"

Troi couldn't hide her surprise. "There are only eight in all?"

"That's right, Counselor," Retthew said.

"I told them how difficult it was to get them to breed," Sedge added.

Retthew's brows rose in emphatic assent. *"There's* a cosmic understatement. If nefittifi didn't live so long, we'd probably have none left. In the past hundred years, only *one* chetling has been born."

"Why don't they produce more offspring?" Troi wondered.

"Well, I'm not an expert. They're very sensitive to their surroundings. The smallest thing can upset their cycles. You'll meet our resident specialist, a young fellow named Robbal, and he can answer your questions in great—I might say excessive—detail," Retthew said, concluding with a chuckle. Then he became solemn again. "This way, please."

The starship officers followed Retthew, with Sedge behind. The passageway took them into a small room arranged like a shrine, with rows of glowing candles and a sacramental basin mounted above glowing coals. The basin was half-filled with a simmering vermilion liquid into which Retthew dipped a ladle. He poured it into a stoneware chalice and raised it to his lips. Then he murmured a prayer, took two small sips of the drink, and spilled the rest onto the wood floor. The floor was already well-stained from past entry rites.

"What does the ritual mean?" Troi asked.

"The wine is the blood of the universe," Retthew explained in a hushed voice. "What we drink signifies our sharing in that lifeblood. And what we spill signifies all the innocent blood shed needlessly

through the cruelty and stupidity of beings like us . . .
beings who should know better." He moved toward a
heavy security door across the chapel. "The nefittifi
are through here, adjacent to our most advanced bio
labs. We built a special enclosed habitat to protect
them from everything that's happening to our world
outside."

As Retthew set about opening the computerized
locking mechanism, Picard wondered idly if he and
Troi should genuflect or something similarly ceremonial. It wasn't often that a starship captain got introduced to so exalted a symbol . . . a living symbol that
could mean renaissance or terminus for not just one
world, but two.

The Ta'Troshan patrol ship turned and pointed its
blunt nose toward home, three days distant at comfortable cruising velocity. In the control chamber, the
commander watched with his red eye-slits as the
starfield wheeled across the oval viewer. Ta'Troshans
had leathery yellow skin, stumpy legs and pipestem
arms; and they were a jovial race, with voices like
lilting chimes. And they much preferred songs of
homecoming to the silence of space. With great joy,
the commander activated his communications console.

"Home base, we shall soon be there," he sang. And
then he sang some more.

The subspace signal of joy crossed the interstellar
void and arrived at Ta'Troshan home base on the
planet's rocky moon. But it was not a complete
message. The reception technician couldn't understand why the crystalline trills grew fuzzy and garbled,
as if something had first overlapped the signal—and
then overpowered it.

If the Commander had known anything was amiss,

his song gave no hint. But the transmission terminated abruptly, and the technician could not restore it. From the safety of his moon outpost, he could not tell that the transmitting ship had been swallowed up by a vast whorl of white haze, moving ever closer to the heart of Sector Sigma-485.

Chapter Seven

RETTHEW LED PICARD AND TROI through the portal and into a simulated woodland biosphere, complete with natural sounds and smells, as authentic as an *Enterprise* holodeck recreation. With one difference—this was real. Indoors, but real. A path meandered through the trees toward a footbridge spanning a stream.

After all the artistic renderings of the nefittifi, Picard wondered what the actual creatures would be like. How tall were they? He expected animals of intimidating stature and bulk. He considered asking Retthew and Sedge, but he rather enjoyed the tranquil hush of the woods and chose not to disturb it. He'd have his answers soon enough.

The group reached a clearing with a feeding station set up, where a young attendant poured a mixture of shredded leaves and assorted grains and kernels into a shallow pan. Even for an Etolosan, he was skinny, all elbows and knees as he loped over to meet his visitors. With his lopsided smile and the scraggly patch of fuzz on his chin, a not-yet-successful attempt at a traditional Etolosan beard, he had a certain gawky charm.

"Robbal," said Retthew, "this is Captain Picard and Counselor Troi from the Federation starship. This is young Robbal. In spite of his age, he probably knows more about nefittifi than anyone else on Etolos."

Robbal put down his food scoop, wiped his hands on his shirt and greeted each of them with a genial two-handed clasp. "Welcome to our little indoor world. I've never met anyone from Earth before." He held Troi's hands and her gaze with extra enthusiasm. "Or anyone like you."

"And we've never met a nefittifi before," Troi answered, smiling up at the young Etolosan towering over her.

It was a slightly embarrassed smile, Picard noted. He didn't have to be an empath to come up with a fair estimate of what Robbal was thinking as he gaped at Troi, eyes wide with innocent intoxication. Robbal finally let go of her hands only after a throat-clearing prompt from Retthew.

"Uhh, Robbal—"

"Yes, Prefex."

"Could you call them, please?"

Robbal nodded, then closed his eyes, tilted his head back, and made a series of soft popping sounds with his lips. Slowly at first, then speeding up to a syncopated rhythm.

Picard and Troi both concluded from Robbal's upturned face that the nefittifi were birds and they looked up themselves, glancing around, expecting to see a majestic airborne arrival. Instead, they heard an erratic approach of something on foot, alternately trudging and scuffling through the leaves and underbrush.

Robbal paused, licked his lips, then continued his call, the pops slowing to a tease, then racing into a musical frenzy. Finally, there came a reply from behind them. Picard and Troi turned and beheld, at the edge of the forest, the pair of sacred nefittifi.

Troi drew her mouth into a tight line. Picard's expression twitched as if someone had just waved a feather beneath his nose. As they stared at the creatures, it was all they could do to keep from laughing.

Starting at the head, the nefittifi did bear a passing resemblance to the heroic sculptures and grand paintings. They did have powerful curved beaks and moody eyes set deep under their brows. But those heads only stood waist-high to Picard and they were attached to potato-sack bodies without benefit of a noticeable neck. They had stubby vestigial wings and fragile stems for legs, leading down to comically oversized feet with four talons. The head and wings were covered in fine dark quills, while the rest of the body was softly coated in rich auburn down. Their faces were oddly expressive, and they were obviously thrilled to answer Robbal's call. With a clownish skip, they rushed to him and clung to his legs like toddlers greeting a parent, cooing and clicking and popping happily.

Picard guessed by the maternal look on Deanna's face that she found them endearing. But, in spite of all his experience with alien life forms, all his Starfleet training, and his innate sensitivity and open-mindedness, he could not shake one overwhelming reaction: *those are the most absurd sacred creatures I have ever laid eyes on.*

"This is totally unacceptable," stormed the tallest Alajian in the Forum Rotunda. White-haired, dressed in royal blue, he paced the chamber's speaking well with theatrical flourishes of his velvet cape. Three half-circle tiers of ornate desks rose around him, with two hundred other deputies seated there, both male and female, rumbling in agreement or dissent. Roughly half wore the same shade of blue as the speaker, while the rest wore gold robes or capes, as did Zeila, who noted—not for the first time—that almost everyone in the assembly was considerably older than she.

Zeila sat at the ruler's lectern, a bored look on her face. "Get on with it, Turchin."

Turchin froze as if stricken by the insult, then made a dramatic half-turn. "Is Her Honoress imposing a dictatorial time limit on comments by her respected opposition?"

"Would I do that to you, Turchin?"

He smiled unctuously. "Perhaps. Now, where was I? Ahh, yes." He resumed his pacing, his voice echoing under the frescoed dome of the government chamber. "The curister cannot be serious when she suggests deposing the Sacred Nefittifi as our most meaningful symbol. Such an act of heresy would be nothing less than a treachery against the whole of Alajian history. My fellow deputies, do you agree with her that our civilization is about to be cast onto the trash heap of history?"

A wave of jumbled voices rippled across the Forum, which Zeila silenced with five deliberately spaced slams of her gavel, so sharp they sounded like shots. "I raised a theoretical question, not a serious proposal, Turchin. Have you become so literal-minded in your declining years?"

The white-haired deputy reacted with a huff, but Zeila cut him off before he could reply.

"Sit," she commanded. "Old beliefs, stiffened with age like some members of this august body, are what brought Alaj to the brink of self-destruction."

Turchin bounced to his feet. "Many would disagree with that appraisal, Zeila."

"Then many are stupid, Deputy Turchin. The Sacred Nefittifi is endangered by what we and our ancestors have done to this world. Someday soon, they may be gone altogether. If we don't change, we *will* end up on history's trash heap. By the way, Turchin, nice turn of phrase."

Turchin chimed the ceremonial bell on his desk, the traditional way to ask for attention in the Presiding Forum. Zeila looked his way with a nod. He stood. "Assuming, for the sake of discussion, there is truth to your apocalyptic vision, what do you propose, Honoress?"

"Getting help."

"From whom?"

"Etolos."

Now the place really exploded. Even Zeila's own Gold party colleagues didn't know what to make of her statement.

"Is this another theoretical question?" Turchin shouted.

Once again, Zeila gaveled the assembly into submission. Turchin took advantage of the momentary calm, his voice booming out over the others as they subsided. "Etolos hates us and the hatred is mutual. What fantasy makes you think they would help Alaj?"

"No fantasy, Turchin. The existence of life on Etolos is being threatened by massive volcanic activity. They want to relocate. And they are interested in Anarra—"

"Anarra?" Turchin roared. "Our prize—"

"—which we never thought worth settling on our own. It's too cold and too savage for the soft-shelled people of Alaj," Zeila said. "We may be able to trade it for a renewed chance of survival right here on this world."

Turchin unleashed a barrage of sarcastic laughter.

"We haven't spoken to Etolos in three hundred years. Do you expect them to suddenly bring us *bawjen* pastries and tell us they love us?"

"We have all the pastries we need," Zeila replied evenly. "As for the centuries without contact, that's about to end."

Turchin's eyes narrowed to a suspicious glare. "We won't permit it—you don't have the votes."

"I don't need the votes. Not from this collection of timid followers. I was elected to be a leader, and that's what I'm doing. Etolos asked the Federation to mediate, the Federation asked me if we had any interest in the notion, and I said yes." Again, opposition voices began to rise and she stilled them with a preemptive rap of the gavel. "Just before this forum session, I received word from the starship *Enterprise* that a shuttle is on its way, carrying an Etolosan ambassador—"

Turchin strode forward to the speaker's well. "This is an *outrage!* This act of treason will not be allowed—"

"It will as long as I am in charge," Zeila said briskly.

"That," said Turchin, "may not be for long."

"Unless you plan to overthrow me or kill me, these talks *will* take place."

"He threatened you. Let me arrest him. *Please.*" Lef was almost begging as he followed the curister into her office.

"You take Turchin too seriously," said Zeila in a calm tone. "I learned long ago that it's much safer to be a moving target. And I move much too fast for Turchin and his lap-dogs."

The burly intelligence chief rolled his eyes in weary exasperation. "You move much too fast for me."

"You're the main reason we're going to succeed."

Zeila's praise caught Lef by surprise. "I am?"

"Of course you are. If I hadn't known about conditions on Etolos, I wouldn't have known this was the time to be bold."

Lef slumped into an armchair, hands covering his face. "Then it's all my fault. I'm the cause of your downfall."

"You're becoming tiresome, Lef. Get out and go to work."

He started for the door, then turned back to her. "Curister?" He was as worried as she'd ever seen him.

"What is it, Lef?" she asked kindly.

"Are you afraid?"

"Of what?"

"Of what might happen to you . . . to us . . . to Alaj."

"We already know what *is* happening, Lef. You and I do. Whatever else we might make happen, could it be any worse?"

His only reply was a fatalistic shrug.

"When I was a girl in school, I used to *love* making trouble. I still do."

Lef had a tough time grasping that. "Why?"

"You've never made trouble?"

"Not intentionally," he said glumly, thinking again how the information he'd gathered had caused Zeila to plot her current course.

"Then you missed out on a useful experience, Lef. The idea is planned chaos."

"What?"

"If you're the one who instigates it, you know it's coming and you're ready to take advantage when you throw everyone else onto their rumps. The difference is, back then I got punished. Now, I might just save this world."

If I don't, she thought to herself, *there might not be any world left to save.*

"She seems quite taken with you, Captain," Troi deadpanned.

The larger of the nefittifi nudged Picard's hand with its beak, then positioned its head so he could scratch it. Picard seemed considerably less taken with the nefittifi, extending one finger for a few half-hearted strokes.

Both animals were standing on a platform built for them to climb upon. There were several levels, but they preferred the perch which allowed them to make eye contact with people. Robbal sat next to the other nefittifi, which not coincidentally put him next to Troi, too.

"Are they birds?" she asked.

It was hard to tell who reveled more in attention from Troi, Robbal or the male nefittifi she was petting under its beak. "They have some characteristics of birds, obviously, but they bear live young like mammals, and they're photosensitive, almost like plants," he babbled, apparently bent on telling her everything there was to know about nefittifi in one breath. "Which is why it's so dangerous for them to live in this volcanic twilight out there. Their physiological functions slow in darkness and they enter a sort of hibernation, during which they don't eat. If the darkness lasted long enough, they would starve to death. Of course, we won't let that happen to these two or to the other six."

Robbal paused for a breath and Retthew jumped in. "They can be fragile, so they get constant attention. If one of them so much as sneezes, Robbal and the other caretakers give it immediate medical care."

"They don't really sneeze," Robbal murmured to

70

Troi, as if sharing a lover's secret not meant for Picard, Sedge, or Retthew.

"Figure of speech," the prefex said sternly. "When you take them to Alaj—"

"If we do, Prefex," said Picard.

"When. It will happen, Captain," Retthew insisted. "And when it does, the nefittifi will need an appropriate environment. Now that you've seen this—" He waved at the woods around them.

"The *Enterprise* has holodecks that can recreate any environment, real or imaginary."

Robbal's eyes widened in wonder. "That must be amazing."

"Perhaps you'll have a chance to see it for yourself," Deanna said.

"Captain Picard," said Retthew, "can these holodecks be made secure? As rare as the nefittifi are, I'm sure you can appreciate that their safety is of absolute importance."

"The holodeck can be secured," Picard said.

"Good. Security is one of our highest priorities here and—"

Retthew's voice was overwhelmed by the sudden thunder of an explosion. A blinding flash flared inside of the biosphere, and a shock wave knocked them all off their feet as dirt, tree limbs, and chunks of the domed structure itself rained down on them.

Chapter Eight

SECONDS AFTER THE BLAST, flames were already leaping from tree to tree, spreading like an indoor forest fire. In choking smoke and heat, Robbal helped Troi to her knees. She'd never realized how much noise a fire could make.

The two nefittifi were sprawled motionless on the ground. Robbal gathered up one in his arms and Troi cradled the other. She could feel its heartbeat against her body—at least it was alive. Picard and the others were quickly on their feet, crouching low, as they all hurried back over the footbridge to the heavy door through which they'd entered. Retthew opened it and they stumbled through to the outside passageway.

Troi desperately needed to sit and gasp fresh air but Robbal pulled her up as she slumped.

"No! They may die! Hurry up!"

Her lungs heaving, the injured creature still in her arms, Troi followed.

Picard, Troi, and Retthew waited in an alcove near the health lab, faces and clothing smudged with soot.

On the other side of a glass door, Robbal and his
assistants worked on the animals he and Troi had
carried to safety. Sedge had been dispatched by his
prefex to supervise fire-fighting and damage control in
the biosphere complex.

Retthew paced anxiously, while Troi huddled in a
private corner, hugging her knees to her chest. Her
face drained of color, her eyes gazed vacantly at some
distant focus. She didn't notice Picard approach.

"Counselor." He sat next to her on the couch and
spoke gently. "Are you all right?"

Finally, her eyes blinked and she turned with a
slight nod. "Yes."

Picard wasn't convinced. "Are you sure?"

"Yes, Captain. Really." She took a deep breath to
steady the quiver in her voice.

"Did you notice anything, any feelings, any
thoughts from anyone at all which might help figure
out who is responsible for this?"

She shook her head forlornly. "I was too caught up
in the emotions of the moment to notice anything
more removed. I am sorry."

"No need, Counselor." Captain Picard paused.
"You're concerned about the nefittifi."

She managed a wisp of a smile. "Practicing empathic psychology without a license, Captain?" The smile
faded. "Yes, I am. But I am also concerned about
Robbal. He regards those creatures as if they were his
children."

"He seemed to be in admirable control of the whole
situation."

"During a crisis," said Troi, "people are capable of
amazing inner strength. If either animal does not
survive, though, I am worried about how he'll react
once the emergency has past."

Just then, the glass door opened and a beaming Robbal stepped through, one nefittifi tucked under his arm. It was shivering and chittering nervously.

Retthew rushed over with obvious relief. "Robbal, they're all right?"

"He's a little upset, I can tell you that. But otherwise, this guy is none the worse for combat."

"What about the female?" Retthew fretted.

"She'll probably make it."

Retthew didn't like the sound of that. "What do you mean, probably?"

"She was hurt, Prefex. Having some trouble breathing, from all the junk that got down into her lungs. Give her a little recovery time, and I think she'll be fine."

The smart click of bootsteps approached, and a stone-faced official strode around the corner into the waiting area. His shaved head and beardless chin set him apart from the standard for Etolosan men.

"Ozemmik," said Retthew, "this is Captain Picard and Counselor Troi from the Federation starship. This is Ozemmik, my security adviser. Do you have anything to report?"

"First, how are the nefittifi?"

"Not too bad," said Robbal, stroking the animal nestled in the crook of his arm.

"Good, good," said Ozemmik. "We're lucky they're not dead. The bomb damage was worst—"

Retthew looked dazed. *"Bomb?"*

"Yes," Ozemmik replied impassively. "That's certain. The worst damage was in the northeastern quadrant of the complex, which is where the nefittifi usually spend their rest periods. Robbal, wouldn't they normally have been napping at this time of day?"

"Yes, sir."

"So, if you and these starship officers hadn't been

visiting, it's unlikely they would have survived the blast."

To Picard, there was something unsettling about Adviser Ozemmik. Considering the nature of the apparent attack, and the near-demise of this pair of sacred animals, his interest in their health had been all too perfunctory. Perhaps his stolid attitude could be ascribed to extreme professionalism. Perhaps not.

Retthew's face had turned even more ashen than usual. "Ozemmik, I want you in personal charge of the investigation. Do whatever you have to do to find out who did this. I want extra security around the nefittifi reserve and this complex. I want an impenetrable protective shell around them."

"Prefex, the security resources of the *Enterprise* are at your disposal," said Picard.

"We don't need outsiders to protect our treasures," Ozemmik said with frigid assurance.

Retthew's jaw stiffened. He was obviously angry about Ozemmik's casual dismissal of Picard's offer. But instead of a firm override of an insubordinate adviser, Retthew's objection came out as a timorous question. "You're not implying a lack of trust, are you?"

"I'm implying nothing. This is an internal Etolosan matter."

"Gentlemen," said Picard, attempting to smooth the ruffles, "our assistance would of course be supplemental to your own security measures."

Counselor Troi rose and stood next to Picard. "No intrusion or offense was intended."

"None taken," Retthew said quickly. "Ozemmik occasionally gets overzealous." But the security adviser's icy expression left no doubt he hadn't been mollified in the least. "This sort of violence simply doesn't happen here."

"It does now," said Ozemmik. "I gave you my warnings."

"Warnings?" said Picard. "What sort of warnings?"

"Very simple ones, Captain," Ozemmik replied. "I had reason to believe there would be violent opposition to the prefex's plan to negotiate with the Alajians and I told him so."

"We have no proof of anything," Retthew stammered. "No proof of any organized opposition, none at all."

Picard framed a careful response. "I see. This is, of course, an Etolosan matter, Prefex, as your security adviser has said. However, are you quite certain you do not wish to avail yourselves of our offer of additional security?"

"No," Ozemmik started to say, "we will not—"

Retthew cut him off. "Yes, Captain, I think we will."

"Very well. How can we be of service?"

"A small complement of guards to protect this facility. And to be absolutely certain these two nefittifi remain safe, I would like them transferred to your starship as soon as Robbal declares them fit enough to leave."

Ozemmik's displeasure flashed in his eyes. "Prefex—"

"You have an objection?" said Retthew.

The security adviser made an abrupt turnabout. "No, Excellency. You're correct to accept Captain Picard's offer. I, for one, will worry less about these two nefittifi if they're aboard the *Enterprise.*"

"Really? Well, I'm glad to hear that," Retthew said.

"I have just one proviso before I agree."

"And that is—?"

"In order to assure their safety, I want to escort

them to Captain Picard's ship and personally take charge of their security before and during transit—if they ever do go to Alaj."

Retthew appeared relieved. "If you don't think it's too much for you to handle, what with the investigation of the bombing here."

"It's not too much, Prefex."

"Then, if Captain Picard has no objections—"

"I do not think Ozemmik's presence on the Enterprise is necessary to assure the nefittifi's safety," said Picard, "but if his supervision will set your minds at ease, then he is quite welcome."

"Then that's settled," Retthew said. "Robbal, will they be able to travel soon?"

"I think so, Excellency. A few hours, maybe."

"Good. When they're ready, you'll go with them as their chief caretaker."

Robbal's face lit up. "Thank you, Prefex!" He grinned at Deanna. "You foretold the future, Counselor. You said I might see your ship . . . and your holodeck. Will you show it to me?"

"I think that can be arranged," she said affably.

"Counselor Troi," said Picard, "will you work with Robbal on specific facilities for the nefittifi during their stay aboard the *Enterprise?*"

"Yes, Captain."

Robbal curbed his delight and returned to professional considerations. "After this traumatic experience, I'd rather have them in a closely supervised environment, the safest place on the ship, someplace where I'd have fast access to medical equipment if there's any delayed reaction or relapse in their conditions."

Picard and Troi traded a glance. "That would be sickbay, Captain," Deanna concluded.

For just one hesitant moment, Picard scowled.

"Yes, I agree. While Robbal prepares the nefittifi for their journey, we shall prepare my chief medical officer for her, uh, unusual guests."

"Captain, you're kidding," said Dr. Beverly Crusher, rising out of her desk chair. "Deanna, tell me he's kidding."

"He is not."

Picard stood stiffly, arms crossed over his chest. "Do you have a problem with this, Doctor?"

"Do I have a problem?" she echoed.

"Beverly," said Troi, "you've had nonhuman patients in sickbay before."

"But they were intelligent beings. These whatchamacallits—"

"Nefittifi," Picard prompted.

"Right," said Crusher, "they're animals, you said."

"Sacred animals," Deanna reminded her. "And they are clean and relatively small. I really don't think they will cause any problems at all. Actually, they're kind of endearing."

"Then I assume the Captain didn't like them."

"Not very much," Troi said, suppressing a smile.

Not one to put up with *too* much disrespect in any one dose, Picard countered in a mocking tone: "You're not guilty of species discrimination, are you, Doctor?"

"Of course not!" Crusher huffed indignantly.

"Ah. Then you will welcome these nefittifi to your sickbay?"

"Will they be in a cage or something?"

Troi nodded. "There will be an enclosure."

"I just don't want these things underfoot. And I don't want to be cleaning feathers or fur or whatever they've got out of all my instruments, Jean-Luc. Is that clear?"

"Yes, Doctor," Picard said with brittle patience as he sidled toward the door. "Quite clear. And if you have any problems at all—"

"Your door is always open," Beverly guessed.

"Mine isn't—*hers* is," Picard replied, his thumb pointed at Troi. With that last word, he was gone.

The *Enterprise* shuttlecraft eased into orbit around Alaj. With Data supervising, Ensign Lopez set to work documenting the current environmental condition of the planet. En route, Navirra had shared some intelligence tidbits her government had collected indirectly over recent years, and Lopez's initial scan confirmed the worst. She glanced up from her science console at Riker looming over her shoulder.

"What's it like?" he asked.

"Unbelievable, Commander."

"Care to be more specific?"

"When I was at the Academy, I did this experimental project—make sure everything in an ecosphere that *can* go wrong *does* go wrong, and see how long it takes to kill every living thing on the planet."

Lieutenant Holzrichter blinked in confusion. "What's that got to do with Alaj?"

"Down on Alaj," Lopez said wryly, "they're doing my experiment. With one difference—mine was a computer model."

Riker nodded. "Theirs is real."

"Right, sir." As she tapped codes into her keypad, her braid switched back and forth like a horsetail. "There's not a major body of water that's not seriously polluted, the air is barely breatheable, there's nowhere near enough plant life."

"Are we in any danger going down there?" asked Riker.

Lopez shrugged. "Our sinuses might feel like we've been through a poison-inhalation survival test, and the air might eat the paint off the shuttle hull, but we should last long enough to come and go."

"Sounds like fun," said Riker. "Ambassador, are you ready for us to contact the Alajians? This is a rather historic occasion."

"Mr. Riker, I've been ready to make history more or less since I was born."

With a grin, Riker returned to the cockpit and activated the comm system. "Federation shuttlecraft to Alajian government. We have arrived to initiate negotiations between your planet and Etolos. Request contact with Curister Zeila."

The U.F.P. logo on the small viewscreen winked out, to be replaced by a cordial Alajian face with a striking head of red and black spiked hair. "I am Curister Zeila. And you are—?"

"Commander William T. Riker, first officer of the starship *Enterprise.*"

"Welcome to Alajian space, Commander. You have the Etolosan delegation aboard?"

"Yes, ma'am. Though the delegation consists of one delegate." He saw Zeila's brows arch with annoyance, as if the size of the delegation was an insult. "She is Ambassador Navirra, the most experienced diplomat on Etolos."

"We have heard of her," said Zeila, settling back.

"Then you understand that the Etolosans wouldn't send someone of her stature unless they were serious about their desire to see this preliminary phase of negotiations succeed, and lead to an agreement which will benefit both worlds."

"Yes, Commander. Are you to be the mediator?"

"For this early phase, I am."

"Are you prepared for hard bargaining and probably more than a few harsh words?"

"Starfleet trained me well, Honoress. And I've had some experience."

"I don't doubt that," Zeila said with a faint smile. "Actually, it's just as well that the Etolosans sent only one person, since I'm to be the sole negotiator for our side. Much simpler this way—no quibbling about who sits where and all that diplomatic detritus."

"I'm encouraged that you feel that way. We're ready to land and begin talks at your convenience."

"First, I'd like to greet my counterpart. Would that be possible?"

"Of course. Stand by." Riker went back to the passenger cabin. "Ambassador, Curister Zeila would like to speak with you."

Navirra nodded, and Riker engaged the comm panel closest to her seat. He noticed the old envoy revert to her most dispassionate poker face. *She's good.* "Curister Zeila, allow me to present Etolosan Plenipotentiary Navirra."

"Welcome to Alaj, Ambassador Navirra. Your reputation precedes you. I hope we'll have a productive meeting."

"Hope is vague, dread is precise," Navirra intoned.

Riker watched both faces as best he could. He wondered if Zeila had discerned the glint in Navirra's eye. He got his answer quickly.

"Does the word *szchuwoh'szcha* mean anything to you, Ambassador?" asked Zeila with that shadow smile playing at the corners of her lips.

The word evoked an involuntary twitch of Navirra's eyebrows. Riker wondered what could get that much of a rise out of her. "Data," he whispered, "translation?"

The android cocked his head as he did a quick language scan.

Navirra was chuckling now. "The old language is still one of our common links."

"There are a number of colorful translations, Commander," Data whispered back. "Twaddle, balderdash, bilge, bunk, bullsh—"

"I get the picture, Data."

"Let us hope those links will help rather than hinder us," Zeila said. "I know how to say that word in forty-two languages . . . and I can recognize it in quite a few more. I suspect you can, too."

"I think we understand each other," said Navirra with a ponderous nod.

"Then if Commander Riker will be good enough to land his shuttlecraft, we can see about saving our planets."

"Curister Zeila," said Riker, "we're on our way."

Chapter Nine

JEAN-LUC PICARD held the ship in the palm of his hand, a miniature sailing vessel perfect right down to its rigging. His admiration of his own handiwork was interrupted by the chime of the ready room door.

"Come."

The door slid aside and Counselor Troi entered, immediately noticing the ship model. "I see you've managed to find a little time to relax."

"Upon the orders of my ship's counselor and her co-conspirator from sickbay, I did find some odd spare moments here and there."

"Everyone needs an escape from stress, sir—even astonishingly stable starship captains. Dr. Crusher and I have to be concerned about your well-being as part of our duties on the *Enterprise.*"

His brows arched like a man who knew he'd been maneuvered by experts. "Not to mention your concern about how long it would take you both to break in a new captain should I ever crack under the strain," he kidded.

Deanna held out her cupped hands. "May I?"

Picard allowed her to hold the model and watched with a craftsman's satisfaction as she examined every detail.

"I don't think I'd have the patience to handle all these tiny pieces. I'm amazed at the workmanship."

"Thank you, Counselor."

"Is it a particular vessel?"

"It is indeed—the *Bon Homme Richard,* commanded by John Paul Jones in the American Revolution, circa 1779." She handed the replica back to him and he held it like a priceless jewel. "In one battle, the ship was badly damaged and Jones was ordered to surrender by the captain of the *Serapis.*"

Troi smiled to herself. She could tell by the look on Picard's face as he told the story that, for these few moments at least, he was *on* the deck of that ancient vessel, the sounds of cannon ringing in his ears, the smoke of battle rising around him, the salt spray of ocean waves stinging his face. *Yes, even starship captains need to escape.* "Did he surrender?"

"No. No, he didn't. Admiral Jones delivered the defiant reply, 'Sir, I have not yet begun to fight.'"

Troi's eyes shone with interest, reflecting Picard's own passion. "What happened?"

"Jones won the battle. He captured the *Serapis.*" Picard gently placed the model on its stand. "As soon as I find the time to put it in the bottle, it'll be finished. But that's not why you're here, Counselor. Please, sit down."

"Dr. Crusher has cleared a section of sickbay for her special guests. Their accommodations are ready any time they are."

"Good. Has Dr. Crusher accommodated herself to their presence?"

"I'm sure she will, Captain."

* * *

"Deanna, they're sort of homely," Beverly muttered within thirty seconds after the nefittifi enclosure had been beamed directly into a spare sickbay ward, along with Robbal. The animals were inside the large transparent structure, which stood nearly three meters high and four in diameter. The recovering female lay on her side on a fluffy nest-bed of soft grass and leaves, lolling in a medication-induced stupor as her nervous mate hunkered next to her, emitting a sort of scratchy sigh every few seconds.

"That noise could get to me after a while," said Crusher as she stepped up for a closer look, putting her face next to the strip of fine-mesh screening which girded the otherwise solid enclosure all the way around. The screen permitted not only sounds to flow in and out of the enclosure, but scents as well. Crusher took a whiff of the nefittifi and her nose crinkled in distaste. "Not a pretty smell, Deanna."

"Beverly," Troi sighed, "don't be difficult."

Bev's eyelashes batted in innocent protest. "Me? Difficult?"

"Only now and then," said Troi wryly. "This is only for a few days." The tall Etolosan approached them. "Dr. Beverly Crusher, this is Robbal. He is in charge of caring for the nefittifi."

Robbal greeted Beverly with his usual geniality. "I really do appreciate your allowing us to keep Kyd and Kad here in your sickbay. I guess Counselor Troi told you what they've been through, and I just want you to know how much better I feel knowing they're close to such wonderful medical equipment in case they should get sick, and I don't know if Counselor Troi mentioned it, but they can be pretty fragile under stress, which I'm sure contributed to their extinction on Alaj and has to be among the primary reasons why they seem to have so much trouble breeding."

Crusher gazed at Robbal in amazement. "All that in one breath. You must have astounding lung capacity."

Robbal blushed with a good-natured grin. "Once I get going, I sometimes forget to stop."

"Kyd and Kad," Crusher repeated. "Which is which?"

"Kyd is the male and Kad is the female."

"Do the names mean anything?" asked Troi.

"Just nonsense words," Robbal shrugged. "Somebody must have liked the sounds."

"You didn't name them?" said Crusher.

Robbal laughed out loud. "Oh, no—they were named long before I was born."

"Really," Crusher said. "How old are they?"

"Well, Kyd's about eighty-four and Kad's a hundred and twenty."

"Ahh . . . ," said Beverly knowingly. "An older woman."

That made Robbal laugh again, "I never thought of it that way, but I guess you're right. Counselor, do I still get that tour of your ship?"

"As promised. Now?"

"Let me just check out my little friends and make sure they're comfortable." Robbal opened a hatch and stepped into the enclosure. The male nefittifi, Kyd, immediately responded by making much happier noises.

Beverly draped an arm over Troi's shoulder. "Speaking of older women, Robbal's got a huge crush on you." Then Bev rolled her eyes. "But then you knew that, of course. Doesn't being an empath take all the mystery out of love?"

"Not really," Deanna answered lightly. "Knowing it's there and knowing what to do with it are two very different things."

* * *

Slicing through a sky smudged with rusty haze (that Ensign Lopez found both disgusting and fascinating), Commander Data set the *Enterprise* shuttle down in a broad plaza adjacent to the elegant building containing Alaj's Presiding Forum.

Riker slid out of his seat and ducked into the aft cabin. "Lopez, do you have enough to keep you busy for a while?"

Rachel Lopez nodded gleefully. "Oh, *yessir.* Alaj is one messed-up world, ecologically speaking. I can't wait to get a look at all that atmospheric gunk out there."

"I like a woman who likes her work. Holzrichter, hold down the fort here. Don't let anybody tow the ship away."

"Aye, sir."

Riker thumbed a control switch and the shuttle's hatch opened. He jumped down and reached back to assist Navirra. Data followed them out and Holzrichter closed the hatch.

Once outside, they took a look around. All the government buildings surrounding the plaza were constructed of sparkling white stone with gold trim, a garish pastiche of classical columns, domes, and spires. The dominant structure was the one housing the Legislative Forum and Curister Zeila's offices. Soaring above every other building on the square, its facade was the most ornate, and it was capped by a dome finished in a rainbow of stained glass. It struck Riker as resembling a faintly vulgar church.

Upon closer inspection of a retaining wall, Data noticed that the marble-like stone was turning yellow and pitted. Without applying much force, he broke a chunk off in his hand.

"The heavy concentration of pollutants," Data explained, "is eating away the surface of the stone."

Riker shook his head. "The place is rotting."

"I believe our welcome committee is arriving," said Navirra, pointing to an escort squad of a half-dozen soldiers in flamboyant blue and gold uniforms. A small woman in a gold cape led the honor guard—small, that is, compared to the guards behind her. She was about Riker's height and looked him directly in the eye.

"Commander, I'm Zeila. Welcome to Alaj."

"Thank you. This is Lieutenant Commander Data from the *Enterprise*. And, of course, this is Ambassador Navirra of Etolos."

Navirra and Zeila exchanged formal bows. "This way," said Zeila. The escort guard fell into step behind them as she led the group back to the main Forum, through huge doors of wood and colored glass, and into the cathedral-like lobby. The floors were polished black-stone slabs; scenic mosaics and rich tapestries decorated the walls. Riker guessed they depicted momentous events in Alajian history or important places around the planet.

It was Data who noticed one common element, the imposing head of a bird-like animal, either interacting with the people in the pictures or observing like deities from above. Navirra identified the animal for them—the sacred nefittifi.

Zeila took them to a vaulted conference chamber, with a long rectangular table dominating the space. The table stood on spiral-carved legs, and the top was inlaid with various woods and polished tiles. Even the chairs were made with elaborately carved pieces and velvet cushions.

Their world might be crumbling and choking, Riker thought sarcastically, *but at least they're going out in style.*

They sat at the table, Zeila at one end, Navirra at

the other, and Riker and Data in the center. Riker noticed that the refreshments were meager in contrast with the surroundings, just pitchers of water and platters of what looked like dried fruit. He also noticed that Zeila and Navirra mirrored each other in the relaxed but guarded way they'd settled into their chairs. Data activated his tricorder to keep an official record of the proceedings.

"Well," said Zeila amiably, "we in this room have the opportunity to alter the future course of history. I could go so far as to say, if we *don't,* there may soon *be* no future for either of our worlds."

"Would you say that?" Navirra parried. "I'm not sure I would."

Zeila's posture stiffened a bit. "Oh? Then I'm not sure you're being honest. We could dance around the issues, but that wouldn't serve either of us. We on Alaj have a very good idea of the conditions on Etolos. We know time is not something you have on your side. And the fact that you're here leads me to believe you know more about our problems than we would like you to know."

"Isn't it odd," Navirra said with deliberate meter, "how our two worlds are so intimate despite so many years of studied separation."

"Perhaps," said Riker, "people springing from the same origins must always be connected no matter how much time and distance they try to put between them."

"That's a theory we're about to test," Zeila said. "Let's get to it, Ambassador."

Considering the shared history of conflict between Alaj and Etolos, there was surprisingly little time wasted on disagreements of the bitter past. Riker was intrigued by Navirra's skill in staking out an Etolosan position based on one main principle: that Etolos was an equal of Alaj, not a prodigal offspring trying to worm its way back into the family fold.

Zeila accepted that with no quibbling. She was evidently a leader with a firm grip on reality—as well as one with long-term problems in need of short-term solutions. It didn't take them long to lay down a foundation built of real goals rather than bargaining chips.

"We want just one thing," said Navirra bluntly. "The fourth planet in the Alajian system, now known as Anarra. It remains unsettled by Alaj or anyone else?"

"It does," Zeila said. "Unsettled and undeveloped. And Etolos would relocate its entire population and society there?"

"That would be our plan, with the aid of the United Federation of Planets."

"And would Etolos then become a Federation member?"

"We would apply."

"And in all likelihood," Riker interjected, "Etolos would be approved."

Zeila nodded. "Good. We would prefer such a close neighbor to be a fellow Federation member. Now, even though Alaj has never developed Anarra, it is a valuable piece of planetary property. It would be shortsighted and unwise for us to give it up without retaining some interest in its potential wealth."

The old ambassador pursed her lips in disapproval. "We are not colonists, Curister. We are a free people. We would expect full sovereignty."

Riker sensed a bump in the road. "Perhaps some sort of mutually beneficial trade treaty could be worked out. Allow me to remind you that this is a minor issue compared to what else your two worlds have at stake."

"Commander Riker is correct," said Navirra. "This disagreement can be sorted out once we have settled larger matters. Permit *me* to remind you, Curister Zeila, that we can offer much to your world. If Alaj were a person, its medical condition would be grave indeed. In such a case, this person would be foolish not to obtain the best care and treatment available. Alaj is the patient, and Etolos is the master physician. Even we may not be able to save the patient . . . but we would certainly be more likely to try, in accordance with an agreement ceding Anarra to us. As neighbors, our close proximity would enable us to monitor the patient closely and better guide it back to health."

"Hmm," Zeila pondered. "This planetary treatment, as you characterize it—would it be the currency with which you pay for acquisition of Anarra? A direct trade?"

"No, that is not the arrangement we envision."

Zeila frowned warily. "And what do you envision?"

"Let me be clear about this. In return for Anarra, we would merely *consider* offering Alaj our environmental rescue services and expertise."

Now Zeila's eyes flashed in anger. *"What?* We give you a planet and you give us nothing?"

Even Riker was surprised at Navirra's audacity. He wondered where she was heading with this peculiar proposition. "That doesn't seem quite equitable," he said.

"Well," said Navirra, drawing out the word. "We would certainly be favorably disposed toward helping Alaj. But the art and science of ecological rescue is what we do, what we are as a people and a planet. Our services do not come cheaply. Let us not forget that what we do for Alaj will renew this befouled world of yours. Without us, your planet *will* become uninhabitable. It's merely a question of when. So, Anarra is the initial payment for which we *consider* saving your world. The services we would subsequently provide would give you something without which the Alajian civilization will shrivel and die—a revitalized, life-giving world. For that, we would expect something more."

"So what exactly are you saying," Zeila said, growing testy, "that you will help us in return for Anarra *plus* something else?"

"Substantial additional payments . . ." Navirra paused. ". . . or something of significant importance to us."

Zeila made no attempt to hide her annoyance. "Such as?"

"Make us an offer," said the crafty old Etolosan.

"Such as sovereignty over Anarra?"

Navirra permitted a shadow of a smile to tip one corner of her mouth. "That would be acceptable."

"Not to us," said Zeila, slapping her open hand on the table. "I don't see this as a fair trade at all. The honorable ambassador seems to have forgotten that *her* society on Etolos is the one threatened with imminent extinction. We deal planet for planet—Anarra in return for Etolosan help in saving Alaj from its own excesses. Etolos also wants complete sovereignty over its new world? We're willing to make that part of the deal—in exchange for something quite minor, something purely symbolic."

"And what might that be?" asked Navirra.

"Four nefittifi."

That sly smile touched Navirra's lips. "But we only have five. How can you ask for—"

"Szchuwoh'szcha," said Zeila with a matching smile. "We believe Etolos has at least eight. As won-

drous as your people are in renewing endangered species, you can certainly spare half of your total."

"Possibly, I could convince my government to include one sacred nefittifi in the arrangement."

Zeila shook her head firmly. "Not good enough. We need at least a breeding pair."

With a slow huff, Navirra said, "I will recommend that provision."

Zeila pushed back from the table. "Then I believe we have a sufficient basis for formal negotiations between our governments. Do you agree, ambassador?"

"Yes, I do, Curister. Considerable details need to be worked out on exact specifications, sovereignty, trade, how to implement measures to restore Alaj, the nature of future relations—but I see no major obstacles to peoples of good faith."

"Excellent," Zeila said. "Commander Riker, what's the next step?"

Riker rested his clasped hands on the table. "I will send a message to the *Enterprise,* which is waiting at Etolos. The prefex of Etolos specified that only he could sign a final agreement. The *Enterprise* will bring him here to engage in direct negotiations with you, if that's acceptable."

"Will the nefittifi be aboard your starship, too?"

Riker looked over at Navirra. "That can be arranged," she said.

"Do either of your worlds have a particular custom for sealing an agreement?" Riker asked.

"We do," said Zeila. She rose from the table, opened a lacquered cabinet and returned with four crystal goblets and a decanter. "As host, I'm pleased to provide a very special vintage of *kavleeah* wine."

As she poured the effervescent blue liquid, Data

scanned his memory. "Ahh—a beverage considered something of a delicacy on Alaj, fermented from the sweet berries of the *kavleeah* tree, which grows in an isolated region of the planet's southern hemisphere and must be harvested during a two-day period each spring."

"Grew in our southern hemisphere," Zeila corrected him, wistful regret in her voice. "That isolated region has become too dry for agriculture. By the time anyone realized it, years ago, the last *kavleeah* trees were dead, and no other place on the planet has the right climate and soil."

"To borrow the Curister's word," said Navirra dismissively, "that is *szchuwoh'szcha.* You have seeds?"

Zeila shrugged. "I suppose."

"We Etolosans can make almost anything grow anywhere," Navirra boasted.

"Then here's to a future of cooperative growth shared by your *two* worlds," Riker said hastily, hoping to smother any discord which might upset the fragile balance reached this afternoon.

Zeila and Navirra went along, and joined the toast. Data raised his glass at a prompt from Riker, and with the ring of clinking crystal, the deal was done.

"Well done, Number One," said Picard's voice over the shuttle comm speaker.

Riker leaned back in the padding of the cockpit seat. "You sound surprised, Captain," he said, feigning insult.

"I must admit I had not expected your expedition to proceed so smoothly."

"Neither did I," Riker chuckled.

"Well, perhaps you missed your true calling."

"William Riker, full-time diplomat? I don't think

so, Captain. *This* venture may have succeeded, but I still think of diplomacy as the art of saying 'Nice doggie' until you can find a rock."

"Is that original cynicism or borrowed?"

"Borrowed, sir," Riker admitted. "I came across it after you once scolded me to read more history."

"Oh?" Picard seemed pleased that his first officer had heeded that recommendation to broaden his horizons. "Who said it?"

"Will Rogers."

"Will Rogers?" Picard repeated. "He wasn't a historian. He was a humorist."

"My kind of guy, Captain," Riker said wryly. "Still, I'm glad that both sides here were serious about making real progress—though it does make me wonder."

"What about, Number One?"

"If they were that anxious to reach an agreement—as bad as *we* thought things were on both planets, they must be a lot worse."

Picard made a considering grunt. "Quite possible. I don't know about Alaj, but the situation here on Etolos is quite grave indeed. Which is why I would like you back aboard the *Enterprise* as quickly as possible to tackle the logistical nightmare of relocating the Etolosans."

"Then how about a change in schedule, sir? Instead of us waiting here for the *Enterprise,* what if we head back and meet you on the way?"

"My thoughts exactly, Number One."

"Great minds think alike, Captain," Riker quipped.

"That," said Data from the other cockpit seat, "would result in a rendezvous in nineteen hours and fourteen minutes . . . approximately."

"Make it so, Number One," said Picard.

"Aye, sir. See you in nineteen hours."

"—and fourteen minutes," Data added.

"Thank you, Mr. Data," said Picard. *"Enterprise* out."

Riker informed the others of the altered plan, eliciting a squawk of protest from Rachel Lopez. "Commander, I was just starting to get to the good stuff. Alaj is the worst real-life mess I've ever seen. But I need some more orbital time."

"How much?" Riker said, scowling like a miffed schoolteacher.

"Five orbits?" Lopez asked hopefully.

"One."

"Please, Commander, I need both equatorial and polar scans."

"Two then, one of each. Take it or leave it."

"Take it," she said. "You won't be sorry. I'll even have a report for you on the way back to the *Enterprise.*"

"Great. I'm in the mood for a horror story. Data, lift off when ready."

The shuttle pierced the grimy Alajian atmosphere and circled through the orbits promised to Ensign Lopez. Once again, as she soaked up real-time observational data, she felt like a passerby at an accident scene, repulsed by what she saw yet unable to look away for fear of missing some grisly detail.

Still, two orbits didn't take long, and the shuttle had soon left Alaj behind, heading across the gulf of open space between this system and Etolos. Following a couple of hours of computer correlation work, Lopez couldn't wait to share her findings with Riker and she practically dragged him out of the cockpit so she could do it face to face. Holzrichter and Navirra were something of a captive audience, while Data remained up front, splitting his attention between listening to Lopez's presentation and piloting the shuttle.

"Mess" seemed a fitting overall description of Alaj —pollution of water and air, dying forests, profligate use of nonrenewable resources, no apparent effort at management of renewable ones, a frightening loss of animal and plant species resulting in a dangerous reduction in bio-diversity. And on top of everything else—literally—was the problem of overpopulation.

"Best estimate," said Lopez, shaking her head in amazement, "Alaj can support two billion people. They've got *four*. The wonder isn't that so many indigenous life forms have died out—it's that *any* life still exists there at all!"

"Well, Ambassador," said Riker, "you Etolosans are going to have your work cut out for you."

"We've seen worse."

"Commander," Data called from up front, "there is something you should see."

Riker stepped forward, bracing a hand on the midship bulkhead and leaning through so he could see over the android's shoulder. Data pointed at his sensor screen. The grid showed an energy disturbance in the shuttle's flight path, visible through the front viewscreen as a hazy blotch in space.

"Where the hell did that come from?" said Riker.

"Unknown. It simply appeared."

"You mean it just turned on like a light?"

"That is probably not a scientifically accurate analogy, but it is a practical visual description."

Riker slipped into the empty cockpit seat and brought the shuttle to a halt. "What's that thing doing?"

Data checked the sensors. "It is still advancing toward us."

That wasn't what Riker hoped to hear. The energy disturbance was already uncomfortably close. "Analysis, Data. What is it?"

"In form, ionized gases resembling plasma . . . but that is only a partial characterization. It exhibits properties not normally associated with plasma, and does not match any phenomenon in recorded astrophysical data banks."

"Is it natural or artificially generated?"

"Impossible to tell, Commander. To obtain that information, we would have to enter the disturbance," Data said with more than a touch of curiosity.

Riker shot him a disbelieving look. "Inside that thing is the one place I do not plan to be. But I would like to know more about it. Keep scanning, and let's try a little evasive action."

The shuttle's drive nacelles glowed bright blue as Riker powered the engines back to maximum and the stubby craft heeled hard to the port side. Data kept a careful watch on his sensor readout.

"Intriguing," the android murmured.

"What is?"

"The body of the disturbance, for lack of a more precise term, continues on its apparent course. But a portion of it is reaching out toward us."

Riker blanched. "Is it catching up to us?"

"Yes—" Data was interrupted by a momentary flicker of the shuttle's interior lights and computer screens. When the power returned, it was definitely weaker than before. "It is also beginning to interfere with shuttlecraft systems."

"Can we get away?"

When Data answered, he sounded almost apologetic. "I do not think so, sir."

"Damn. That's not the right answer, Data." Riker hunched forward and gunned the shuttle to full power. For a moment, the ship surged ahead—then almost immediately faltered, like an old-style ground car stalling on a road. "What the hell . . . ?"

Imperceptibly at first, then with greater certainty, the shuttle was being tugged involuntarily toward the misty bulk of the energy disturbance looming ahead.

"Do we still have shields, Data?"

"Still functioning, sir."

"Since it looks like we're going for a little ride, channel engine power to the shields." Will Riker peered at the viewscreen, trying to fathom the radiant nimbus which had managed to surround the shuttlecraft so swiftly. "What the hell *is* that?" Then he glanced at Data. "You said the body of the disturbance is maintaining its course. Did you get enough of a fix to calculate its heading?"

Data's fingers skipped across his keypad. "Yes, sir. It appears to be heading for Alaj. And we are going with it."

"But going with what?"

"Sensors are operating only intermittently, but we may soon find out," said Data, referring briefly to his computer screen. "We are being pulled toward its center."

Chapter Ten

"PLEASE, CURISTER," Lef pleaded, "don't do this."

He stood in Zeila's office with hands spread plaintively before him, and he actually blocked her path through the door. He saw the anger in her eyes, but he'd decided before he came in that it would take more than angry looks to make him step aside.

"Everybody is telling me what to do," she muttered.

"I'm not telling you what to do. I just don't think this is the time for you to be visiting the marketplaces or the poor districts. It's not safe."

"This isn't Swatarra, Lef. This is right here in the capital."

"Oh, and that's supposed to make it better? Swatarra was your home province, and they still rioted. People without food or a decent place to live aren't going to be any happier to see you just because they're neighbors," he said without any effort to conceal his sarcasm.

"Do you know of any particular threat?"

The direct question caught Lef off-guard. "Uhh, no. No, it's just a feeling. When the facts leave blanks, I have to fill them in with common sense. It's part of my job. I thought it was part of the reason you gave it to me."

"You have your common sense, and I have mine," Zeila said shortly. "Your role is a well-defined one. Mine isn't. When common sense says I should remain barricaded here for safety, that's the time I most need to get out and show the most miserable people in the world that someone cares about them."

"You mean that's the time to distract them."

"In a way. There's a change coming. Soon. But we have to hold things together for a few more days, a few more weeks. I can't do that locked inside this damned office, Lef. You can come along, or you can stay. But I don't have that choice."

With that, she strode straight at him. And he yielded, as she knew he would.

But she almost wished he hadn't. It would have been a lot easier to do what Lef asked, to remain safe behind the walls of the forum center. Maybe she was a fool to think that her appearance at the street bazaar would accomplish anything at all. In better times— well, there hadn't really *been* better times since she'd been curister, only times when the end of Alajian civilization hadn't seemed quite so imminent. Following her election, her public visibility had usually been enough to defuse the anger running through city streets like storm-swollen streams, or sprouting in the countryside like the crops which had once grown in fields long since barren and parched.

In her first two years in power, Zeila had traveled all around her planet, preaching the gospel of renewal, promising relief that turned out to be unattainable. Half-measures had made no difference.

It had taken her two years to realize fully that Alaj could not simply be renewed. It would have to be remade. And that she could not do alone. Every Alajian would have to help.

And for the past year, that had been her message, delivered to anyone who would listen.

But farmers abandoning their withered land didn't care to listen. Perhaps they couldn't hear over the keening wind blowing their lives away with the top-soil.

Jobless workers in the cities didn't seem to hear, either. Maybe Zeila's words were lost in the void of silence surrounding factories hungry for fuel and raw materials.

Those who'd managed to hold onto wealth and prestige *chose* not to listen. They were too busy praying to gods of greed, begging protection for their privilege and power.

And wandering refugees in dusty camps didn't hear Zeila, either. Or they couldn't, not when they had to listen to the weak cries of their hungry children.

Sometimes, in private moments, the Curister of Alaj would ask herself, *Why bother?* What made her so certain that she could succeed where no one else had, when cruel common sense and the sights and sounds confronting her every day mocked that certainty? *I have no idea,* she would admit to herself. But not to anyone else.

The answer to those questions was actually absurd-ly simple. *If not this, what else would I do?*

To a casual observer, in spite of all of Alaj's troubles, the capital of Port Arabok had maintained some semblance of its normal bustling character, with heavy traffic both motorized and pedestrian. But a closer look revealed that the ground vehicles were old and battered, and many of those on foot carried all they owned in packs and carts.

The bazaar, snaking through several narrow streets

just a few blocks from the broad plaza and white buildings of the government center, was all that remained of Alaj's commercial district. With the old systems of trade and commerce broken down, whatever products were still available had to be gotten from peddlers who sold direct to anyone with money or something to trade.

As Zeila, Lef and their plain-clothes escort squad rounded the street corner and entered the Kovou marketplace, the Alajian leader thought to herself how this was one of the few places in the capital, maybe on the whole planet, with any vibrancy left to it. Those who came here still had some purpose in life. They were here to buy or sell, to trade or beg, even to steal if they could manage it. But they all had a reason to hope that by the end of the day they might be a little bit better off than they'd been that morning.

Lef saw things differently, however. "Every time I come through here," he grumped, "it's like the last eight hundred years never happened. Back into the Old Times."

"Is that so bad?" said Zeila, sniffing some skewered meat roasting on an open grill. She stopped at the meat-seller. "How much?"

The elderly woman tending the grill recognized her. "Twenty-five per stick, Honoress."

"Twenty-five! No one can afford that."

Others noticed the Curister, and a crowd began to gather. The peddler shrugged. "Meat's uncommon," she said. "Some are willing to pay. That's what it's worth."

"Well, soon it won't be so uncommon. And your prices will have to come down," Zeila bantered good-naturedly.

"So you've said. Do I look worried? I think I'll be dead long before that happens."

Before Zeila could respond, an explosion rocked the street. A few witnesses, as their last living view, saw an unattended peddlers' cart, thirty meters away from the Curister and her party, go up in a ball of flame and black smoke. The stone facades of the overhanging buildings acted like a conduit and channeled the blast up and down the street in a vortex of wood and brick, twisted steel, bodies, and blood.

The black cloud spiraled into the sky. Seconds after the roar of the explosion came the roar of silence. Then the screams of the wounded flooded the marketplace.

Lef lay facedown on the cobblestones, his cloak covered with splintered wood. He got to his knees, catching his breath, then staggered to his feet, his heart pounding in panic. But the panic was inside. Outside, he willed himself to stay calm. The members of his security squad were all down. Some were conscious and got up slowly. Of those, several were bloodied.

Where is Zeila? Lef's inner voice screamed. With a surge of clarity, he noted he'd been thrown about two meters from where he'd been standing by the force of the blast. Zeila must have been, too. He would not even permit the unthinkable to enter his mind. He never asked himself if she'd survived, only where she'd fallen.

The meat-seller's cart had been tossed on its side. The peddler herself was crushed under it, unmoving. Dead.

Where is Zeila?

Lef scrabbled through the rubble, kicking aside hunks of wood, stepping over bodies. Over pools of blood. He filtered out the cries for help. There was only one voice he—

"Lef."

He spun, his head whipping from side to side. The weak voice called again.

"Lef. Over here."

He found her, struggling to sit up, oblivious to the debris pinning her down as well as the dagger-shard of glass embedded in her thigh. Three of his guards made their way over to help. Lef lifted Zeila to her feet, but he knew her leg wouldn't be able to support her weight. The guards clasped hands to form a cradle-seat, and Lef set her down there. There was no way out of the demolished market except on foot. But he had to do something first.

"Hold her steady," he growled. He tore off a piece of his cloak and wrapped it around his hand. Then he grasped the glass in Zeila's leg and yanked it out.

She let out a short shriek of pain, then bit her lip and clamped her eyes shut. What little color remained in her face drained away. Then she opened her eyes and glared at him. "You enjoyed that, didn't you?" she breathed as he tied the shred of cloth around her leg to stem the bleeding.

"Only a little," Lef said, glaring back. At his quick nod, the escort guards carefully carried Zeila away from the devastated street.

"Lef," said Zeila hoarsely, blinking back a stab of pain.

"What?"

"I bet this is the last time you ever go shopping with me."

Lieutenant Worf and Chief O'Brien stood by the control console in Transporter Room Three, awaiting word from the bridge on beaming up the Etolosan prefex.

"I heard rumors we might be beaming more animals aboard," said O'Brien casually.

"Rumors," Worf sneered. "Gossip is for old women."

"I don't know. Sometimes the grapevine tells more than all the compu-memos combined. Maybe that's how old women live to be old women."

"It is still demeaning to engage in rumor and gossip-mongering," Worf said stiffly. "It is not honorable."

"Are you kidding?"

"Rarely."

"Worf, guys in the trenches have been trying to find out what the big wheels don't want them to know since the service began. If that's not an honorable tradition, I don't know what is."

The Klingon's ridged brow furrowed dubiously as he considered the concept, then dismissed it. "Subordinates should be content to wait until their superiors are ready to share such information."

O'Brien shrugged. "To each his own. But I'd think a warrior would want some idea of what's going to happen before it does."

Worf's expression darkened. *"LeSSov,"* he muttered.

"What's that?" O'Brien said at the same time as he considered dropping the whole conversation.

"Knowledge of tomorrow. It is not something Klingons seek."

"What about military intelligence?"

"Battle is different. *LeSSov* refers to personal matters. Klingons accept what each day offers, whatever the obstacles. To obtain excessive foreknowledge reduces the challenge in life and makes us weak."

"Oh. Then I guess you don't want to know what

Commander Riker and Geordi have planned for you after rugby."

There was a glimmer in Worf's eye and the barest flash of a smile. "No, I do not."

"Just testing."

The intercom tone sounded and they heard Picard's voice. "Bridge to Chief O'Brien."

"O'Brien here, sir."

"Prefex Retthew is ready to beam up. Is Mr. Worf there?"

"This is Worf, Captain. Shall I escort the prefex directly to the bridge?"

"Yes, Lieutenant. Mr. O'Brien, energize."

The turbolift door *whooshed* open and Retthew stepped out onto the bridge, followed by Worf who moved to his tactical station. Picard stood and greeted the Etolosan halfway up the sloping deck. "Welcome to the *Enterprise,* sir."

Retthew made a stiff bow. "Thank you, Captain."

"Ensign Crusher, take us out of orbit, ahead warp factor three."

"Aye, sir," Wesley replied crisply.

Picard extended a hand toward the conference lounge just off the bridge and ushered Retthew inside. They were treated to one of Picard's favorite views through the curved lounge windows, the mad rush of stars outside as the starship accelerated into warp. Retthew watched in admiration. "A magnificent vessel, Captain," he said as they sat at the long table.

"Yes, she is. I'm quite proud of her, and of my crew."

"Then I'm sure you can appreciate how I feel about the people of Etolos. Every man, woman and child is dedicated to our mission. They've placed their trust in me, Spirit help them," he said softly, shaking his head. "I'm afraid I'm not worthy of that trust. If I fail to reach an agreement with Alaj—"

Retthew swiveled out of his chair and paced along the lounge windows, his awkward gait matching his emotional discomfort. "This is not easy for me, Captain, this going to the home of our ancient adversary."

"Breaking with the past is never easy, for anyone."

"I'm not a bold man, Captain Picard," Retthew said. He measured the dimensions of his understatement and forced a hollow laugh. "I'm not a starship captain. I don't explore unknown realms. I'm not a leader. I'm a manager. Do you know what it's like for someone like me to suddenly face the horrible reality that what he's been managing has become *un*manageable?"

"Unsettling, to say the least."

"To say the least." Retthew sighed and sat down again, though he continued gazing out the viewports, mesmerized by the stars. "My whole life has been based on mastering the familiar. Etolos was long established by the time I came along. All I had to do was keep it going."

"That is exactly what you are doing," Picard offered. "You're just doing it in a slightly different way."

"Ozemmik makes fun of me because I've always relied on his public opinion polls to guide me. He says I lead by walking two strides behind the poll results. And he's probably right. But I'm out here on your ship, and there's no public consensus protecting me." Retthew turned, his eyes beseeching Picard for confirmation. "What if I'm wrong?"

"Prefex," Picard said, "you are doing your best for your world. No world could ask more than that."

* * *

The nefittifi had settled into their traveling quarters fairly comfortably by the time the *Enterprise* set out for Alaj. Dr. Crusher observed that the animals seemed to have simple needs—food, tranquillity, a soft place to nest. Those needs were met by the enclosure and the attentive care given by Robbal. But they seemed happiest when an extra element was added—companionship. When they saw Robbal coming, they'd let out little anticipatory trills. When he went into the cage with them, they went into raptures of popping that subsided only when he sat and stroked them as they cuddled up alongside him.

Perhaps it was that old maternal instinct, but Beverly found her attitude toward her sickbay guests softening a bit as she watched them. Maybe Deanna had been right. Maybe they were endearing after all, though the faintly musky odor wafting through the cage screening still made her nose twitch. But it did seem less pungent than her initial sniffs.

Beverly heard the waiting-room door slide open and Wesley came in, with Gina Pace in tow. *It's an unpardonable sin to embarrass your son in the presence of a girl, so I can't say this out loud,* Beverly thought, *but they do make a cute couple.* However, all she said was, "Hi, Wes. Hi, Gina."

"Hi, Mom."

"Hi, Dr. Crusher," said Gina. She had her sketchpad tucked under her arm. "Could we see the nefittifi?"

"As long as their caretaker doesn't mind," Beverly replied, getting up from her desk and leading them into the adjacent ward, where Robbal was entering some data on an electronic clipboard. He looked up and greeted them with his characteristic grin. Beverly couldn't remember the last time she'd seen anyone so happy so much of the time. "Robbal, this is my son

Wesley, and his friend Gina. They came to visit your charges. Is that okay?"

"Oh, sure. Nefittifi love company."

The two teens moved close to the enclosure, where the animals appeared to be asleep, nestled close to each other.

"Ooops," Wes whispered. "We didn't mean to disturb them."

Robbal waved off Wesley's concern. "Don't worry, they're very sound sleepers, almost like babies. I remember when I was a little child and I'd fall asleep on the way home from a trip, and my father would carry me in when we got home and put me into my bed and cover me up and I'd never wake up until morning. Was Wesley like that, Doctor?"

Beverly's mouth curled into a long-suffering mother's smile. "Yes and no. I always had the feeling Wes was awake even when he was asleep. He'd repeat things he could only have overheard when he'd been sleeping. It was positively spooky."

Gina snickered and Wesley blushed slightly. "Mom," he moaned.

"Someday you'll have a child of your own to embarrass."

"Yeah," Wesley retorted, "and that will make you a grandmother."

"No hurry, Wesley," Beverly said, raising a hand in surrender.

There was a rustling from the cage and the nefittifi shook themselves awake. Their mournful eyes blinked several times and they looked around for their guardian. Robbal opened the cage door and popped at them. They popped back and waddled over to nuzzle his hand, and Robbal introduced them by name.

"Can you actually understand them?" asked Wesley.

"Not like having a conversation, but I've got a pretty fair idea of what each sound means in their context, so, yes, I'd say we do communicate. Would you like to give them their wake-up snack?"

Gina answered instantly. "Yeah!" She grabbed Wesley's hand and they circled the enclosure together. Robbal gave them some rough-textured wafers and demonstrated by holding one in his open palm.

"Do they bite?" Gina suddenly asked, sizing up the animals' powerful beaks.

"No, and they're very gentle. Holding the snack that way lets them pick it up without accidentally snacking on a stray finger at the same time."

Gina hesitated, but Wesley held his hand out to the smaller one, the male. Kyd plucked the wafer up, crunched it in his beak, swallowed it and gazed at Wes with a satisfied gurgle. Gina then fed the female, though Kad moved feebly compared to her mate.

"Can I pet him?" said Wesley.

"Sure. They like to be scratched under their beaks."

Wes wriggled his fingers against Kyd's chest, and the nefittifi responded with a vibrating variation on the popping noise it had made earlier. There was no doubt that it was happy. "Mom," Wesley said, "I don't know why you thought they were ugly."

Now it was Beverly's turn to blush. "Wesley," she hissed, "that's not what I said. Robbal, that's not what I said. I never said they were ugly."

"She's right, Wes," Gina agreed. "I think the word was homely."

Beverly winced, but Robbal didn't seem offended. "Forget it, Dr. Crusher, you're not the first person to say things like that, and even I know they're not exactly the most beautiful animals ever created and if you've got a sensitive nose it might take a little time to get used to their scent. But they're pretty wonderful little creatures, and they win over most people all on their own, without me talking endlessly about their good points." He paused for a quick breath, and noted Dr. Crusher's dubious expression. "Ahh, I can see you're not quite convinced, but I think they'll grow on you, and I think you'll miss them after they're gone."

"Did it take you a while?" Wes asked. "To like them, I mean?"

"Yes, it did. We grow up on Etolos with all sorts of magnificent paintings and sculptures of the nefittifi all around us, so we're not exactly prepared for the less-spectacular reality," Robbal chuckled as he took Kyd out of the enclosure and sat with the animal on his lap.

"How did you get to be such an expert on them?" Gina wondered.

"There wasn't that much competition for the job. There are much more exciting areas of study on Etolos, learning about animals that have much larger populations and breed a lot more frequently. But the nefittifi is so important to our society and there are so few of them and there's so much we haven't figured out about them that I just thought this would be a good thing to keep me busy for my whole life." Then he laughed out loud. "We Etolosans think of ourselves as the biggest bio-experts in the known galaxy, but there've always been so few nefittifi to study and they have babies so infrequently that we don't even know how to tell when they're pregnant until about five minutes before they give birth. That's one of the things maybe I'll be able to change."

"Robbal," said Gina, "would you mind if I draw a picture of you and Kyd?"

"Not at all. If we sit still long enough, he'll just fall asleep. Come to think of it, so will I."

*　*　*

The *Enterprise* shuttlecraft drifted through the radiant fog of the energy disturbance, without engine power, unable to maneuver or break free. Riker had already sent three distress calls out to the *Enterprise* or any other ship which might hear, with words carefully chosen to warn as well as summon help.

As he shifted in his seat, he was all too aware of the possibility that the shuttle transmissions had been smothered by the disruptive energy field. There was a very good chance no one would pick up the signals. More than likely, the shuttle was on its own as it moved toward . . . *toward what?* He felt a bit like a fish on a line. *Does the fish know where it's headed?*

They were waiting for something to reveal itself, but had no idea what they'd find and no way to estimate how long the wait might be. On top of everything else, Riker was frustrated by their inability to counter the energy disturbance's effects on the shuttlecraft or to predict which function might be the next to shut down. There was only one certainty: system by system, the shuttle was failing.

"Commander," said Data as they sat in the cockpit together, "you appear restless." The android gave a moment's consideration to his choice of words. "Is that the correct characterization?"

"Yes, it is, my friend," said Riker with a fractional smile. "When I know there's an imminent danger, the quicker it gets here the happier I am."

Data cocked his head quizzically. "Even if, hypothetically speaking, confrontation includes a likelihood of injury or death?"

Riker nodded. "Human reactions to grave danger generally fall into two categories. Some people figure if they can put off dealing with it, it might go away. And others say, if there's no escape, let's just get it over with."

"Does the first attitude demonstrate cowardice while the second displays bravery?"

"I don't think it's that simple. Somebody else—"

"Such as whom?"

"A hypothetical somebody other than me, Data, might figure that buying time might give him a chance to think of better strategy or even a way out of the danger. And sometimes, when you know what the danger is, I'd agree with that."

"But this is not one of those times," Data concluded.

"Not as long as we don't know what's reeling us in. The sooner we know, the sooner we can deal with it . . . or cash in our chips." Riker decided he needed to stretch his legs and he slid out of his seat. "Time to visit the troops," he said, ducking into the aft compartment.

Navirra and Holzrichter were seated together, engaged in a spirited chess match on one computer screen, while Lopez continued to work on her backlog of environmental information gathered at Alaj. Riker peeked at the chess battle, which looked too close to call.

"Who's winning?"

Neither player looked up.

"Your young Mr. Holzrichter is quite a competitor, Mr. Riker," Navirra offered.

"Nobody gets through Starfleet Academy without learning the art of strategic thinking, Ambassador Navirra," said Riker.

"Well, sir," Holzrichter said, "the ambassador could teach Starfleet a thing or two. That's for sure."

"Enough of this mutual admiration society," Navirra rumbled. "The time has come for . . . for . . . ." Her voice faltered and she swooned forward, jerking herself upright just before she pitched out of the seat. Both Riker and Holzrichter reached out to steady her. Her head lolled as if she'd suddenly been drugged.

"Ambassador," Riker said urgently, crouching next to her, "are you all right?" He raised his hand, flashing three fingers in front of her face. "How many fingers am I holding up?"

"Three," she said weakly, struggling to focus.

Without warning, Riker's footing gave way and he flopped unceremoniously onto his rump. His head spun as a nauseous wave rolled through his gut. His vision blurred and he fought to keep heavy eyelids open.

Holzrichter was kneeling next to him. "Sir, are you—" But before the young security officer could finish his sentence, he keeled over.

Now Riker felt a strong grip on his arms, lifting him to an empty seat. "Data, the others?"

"They are all unconscious."

"What's . . . what's happening?" Riker's words slurred together and his tongue felt heavier than his eyelids. *Have to stay awake.*

"I do not know, sir."

For a moment, Riker blanked, followed by a return to a murky state of awareness. "Data . . . are you—"

"I am fine, sir. So far."

"I don't understand. Data . . . you have to . . . have to stay—"

Riker slumped and the android eased him back into the seat. Data was alone, and his magnificent positronic brain occupied itself with an absurdly basic question: was this sudden solitude temporary . . . or permanent?

Chapter Eleven

COMMANDER DATA WAS NO DOCTOR, but he did have an encyclopedic knowledge of the physiology of assorted humanoid species. He also knew the purpose and basic operation of most Starfleet medical equipment, including the emergency pack stowed aboard the shuttlecraft. Removing the medi-kit from its storage niche in the bulkhead, he switched on the medical tricorder and set it for basic brainwave scans.

He moved from one inert body to the next, wondering idly what Dr. Katherine Pulaski might have thought of the notion of Data practicing even this rudimentary form of medicine. During her year of service aboard the *Enterprise,* Pulaski had started out regarding Data as an ambulatory machine unworthy even of being referred to by the pronoun *he.* To her, Data had been an *it,* and it had taken her some time to adopt the mere courtesy of pronouncing his name properly.

It was not in Data's makeup to feel insulted or slighted by Pulaski's attitude; as an android, he could not *feel* anything resembling human emotions. But when Pulaski had finally come around to accepting him as an intelligent being and not a piece of hardware, he'd somehow found that change satisfying in a way he could not explain empirically. Oddly enough, he took pleasure in his inability to understand that satisfaction and decided that, perhaps, it represented one tiny step toward becoming more like his human shipmates.

The condition of his current shipmates remained unchanged. The tricorder detected some chemical differences between the Etolosan and Earth-human brain, but those minor variations didn't alter the conclusion he drew from the overall readings: the energy field in which the shuttle was mired had a disruptive effect on their biological brains, sending electrical impulses skipping wildly about instead of tracking in orderly fashion. The result was a form of unconsciousness that resembled deep sleep.

There was nothing he could really do for them, and he returned to the cockpit, resuming the only useful function he could fulfill at this point—observation. With shuttle sensors either suspect or totally inoperative, his senses and memory were the only means of recording this experience for later reference.

He wondered if the energy field would impair his own accuracy, and he had no idea when or if he might also succumb to its effects. As long as he remained conscious, he would do his best to observe every possible detail despite the knowledge that his next moment of awareness might be his last. Whatever happened to him, there was always the chance that someone finding him could retrieve part or all of his stored impressions.

So Data watched.

The shuttle coursed slowly and steadily through

space, and the patterns of the energy disturbance seemed to change at random. So far, Data was unable to detect any consistency, and without sensors he couldn't really attempt any analysis. Sometimes, space around the shuttle danced as the power of the field interacted with particles of matter and gas floating into its path. And sometimes, the swirls of energy simply spun in aimless spirals.

One corner of Data's subconscious was occupied with something widely removed from scientific observation. *What would a human feel in this situation?* he wondered. *Alone, facing total uncertainty—very possibly facing death. Far from home. The concept of a home seems to have great importance to humans. To some, the birthplace is home. To others, it is where they are now, a meaningful place not because of geographical location but because of feelings which this homeplace arouses. Those feelings often grow out of relationships. I do not have feelings, yet I do value relationships with my fellow crew members. Perhaps I have never really had a home. Or, perhaps the* Enterprise *has been my only true home.*

Data recalled an old human proverb: *Home is where the heart is.* Humans, he had noticed, seemed to put great stock in such proverbs, though Data often had difficulty sorting out their essence. In this case, he did not have the organ in question, though he did have assorted micro-pumps propelling a variety of liquids through his body. And as he'd drunkenly reminded Captain Picard on one occasion, *If you prick me, do I not leak?*

Still, strictly speaking, he had to conclude regrettably that like the tin woodsman of an ancient children's tale, he had no heart.

His philosophical musings were abruptly interrupted by a physical jolt racing through his body. His torso stiffened. His yellow eyes blinked five times in rapid succession, then froze into a glassy stare. Five seconds later, his functions resumed.

"Interesting," he murmured. "I may not be immune to the effects of this energy field. It is distinctly possible I may be rendered as nonoperational as if I, in fact, had a heart."

Robbal clasped his hands over his heart as he gazed at Troi across drinks in a private corner of Ten-Forward. "I can't help it, Counselor. It happened the first time I saw you," he said, flashing a goofy grin. "It was almost enough to make me speechless, and I think you've already noticed that's something I rarely am."

Deanna sat primly, her hands folded in front of her, an embarrassed smile playing at the corners of her mouth. Robbal's moony gaze never strayed from hers, and she found that a sweet change of pace from many of her experiences with the opposite sex. Males of most species, she'd noted with her trained powers of observation, could scarcely refrain from undressing with their eyes any female they found attractive. But Robbal's pure affection reminded her of—

Oh my stars, she suddenly realized, *he reminds me of Will the first time we met . . . so afraid he'd make a fool of himself, and so head-over-heels that he couldn't help it.*

"Have you had many romantic relationships?" she asked simply, keeping everything else to herself.

"No. I was always a little afraid of women."

"But you're not afraid of me?"

Robbal laughed. "Terrified." He took a deep breath. "At least tell me you're flattered."

"Oh, I am."

"Then tell me you're tempted," he said, his hand snaking across the table to snare hers.

"Robbal," she scolded, yanking free.

The young Etolosan heaved a theatrical sigh. *"But —we lead separate lives, and we're two ships passing in space, and you have your work and I have mine, and you're much older than I am—"*

"Not *that* much older," Deanna said quickly, pretending to be insulted.

"Did I miss anything?"

She laughed. "No, I think you covered all the standard reasons."

He stood up and backed away from the table. "We haven't reached Alaj yet, Counselor. And I haven't given up." He turned with a gawky flourish and headed for the door.

"You're grinning like a schoolgirl," said Guinan, appearing out of nowhere. She slid into the seat Robbal had just left, handing Troi a fresh drink in a tall glass.

Deanna's expression betrayed the slightest shred of guilt over how much she'd been enjoying Robbal's attention. "He's adorable, and it's nice to be chased once in a while."

"Chaste, or chased?" Guinan asked in a sly tone.

"Both," said Deanna with a Mona Lisa smile.

Guinan noticed a new arrival at the bar. "Fresh customer," she said, getting up.

Troi turned and saw that the new customer was Ozemmik, the bald-headed Etolosan security adviser who'd kept pretty much to himself since coming aboard for the journey to Alaj. Picking up her drink, she approached him at the bar. Guinan had already served him a glass of sparkling gold liquid.

"May I join you?" Troi asked.

"Sure," he shrugged.

"Is everything on the *Enterprise* to your satisfaction?"

"I suppose."

Not quite as verbal as Robbal, she thought. "Then you found the sickbay facilities secure enough?"

"Sufficient. Main thing is, we're off my planet. With only me and two other Etolosans aboard, I don't have much to worry about."

Troi nodded in understanding. "I guess you can trust that Retthew and Robbal pose no danger to the nefittifi."

"Never trust anyone, Counselor," he said with the briefest of frosty glances.

"Never?"

"Never."

"But you've known the prefex since you were both children, haven't you?"

"I see you've done your research."

"That is part of my job," she said pleasantly, raising her guard at the same time and hoping he wouldn't notice.

"Mine, too," Ozemmik said, his tone matching hers in a subtle duel. "I know you're a highly trained expert in psychology. Wouldn't you agree that you can know someone forever and not know him at one key moment?"

"I suppose that is possible, depending on the individuals involved and the specifics of their relationship."

Ozemmik's lips curled into a chilly smile. "You're thinking that a truly observant person shouldn't regard a friend with such suspicion. Either he's a friend or he isn't."

"That is not for me to judge. We all have our own standards."

He paused for a thoughtful sip. "You're not easy to pin down, are you, Counselor."

121

"Are you accusing me of being evasive?"

"Not at all. Just cautious. A wise tactic. Up to a point. As long as it's not a signal of uncertainty."

Troi sipped her own drink. "Do you find it easy to be certain?"

"Most of the time. For instance, I'm certain that desperation can stress a person beyond the breaking point . . . force him into behavior he'd never even consider otherwise."

"And is that what you think Retthew has done?"

Ozemmik's brows arched in mild surprise at her directness. "Why would you say that?"

"I'm aware of your opposition to negotiation with Alaj."

"Retthew is my friend, and the prefex of Etolos. I work for him. I'm loyal to my planet, probably to a fault."

"Is there anything you wouldn't do to protect Etolos?"

"Not that I can think of." With a last swallow, he emptied his glass and stepped away from the bar. "It's been a pleasure chatting with you, Counselor."

Deanna watched him leave the lounge. Something about Ozemmik set her teeth on edge, and it annoyed her that she couldn't say precisely *why* he unsettled her so. But she would definitely talk to Captain Picard about him.

When Robbal entered sickbay, he found Wesley in Dr. Crusher's office, watching the nefittifi on the monitor screen at his mother's desk. The male, Kyd, preened and primped before his unresponsive mate. She lay on their nestbed, only occasionally raising her head.

"Hello, Ensign Crusher."

"Hi, Robbal. I came down to visit them, but the

door was locked and you and my mother weren't here. So I just thought I'd watch them for a while."

Robbal moved to the door leading to the nefittifi ward and released the security lock. "I told them I didn't think this was necessary," he said with mild irritation. "'They've got to be protected,' Retthew says. Who on this ship is going to threaten them? But do they listen to me? No. I'm just the surrogate mother, that's all."

Wes followed the Etolosan inside and they watched through the enclosure wall. "She seems kind of lethargic."

"And he seems kind of disappointed," said Robbal as Kyd's little dance petered out and he slumped down next to the female. Robbal opened the enclosure door, petted Kyd and gently removed Kad. The male coughed out a few distressed snorts and shifted anxiously from one foot to the other. His snorts became a scratchy whine.

"He's not happy," said Wesley.

"No," Robbal agreed as he examined the female nefittifi in his arms. "They're monogamous creatures and they get pretty upset when they're separated, and he knows she's sick."

"What's wrong with her?"

"Mmm, I think she's a little feverish." Robbal picked up a hypo from an examining table and gave her a short injection. "She's still shaky from the bombing on Etolos. They're nervous little beasts. Why don't you pick up Kyd and hold him for a bit while I hold her, and I think he'll settle down."

Wesley hesitated. "You're sure it's okay?" At Robbal's nod, Wesley reached into the cage and was surprised to have the lonely nefittifi practically jump into his hands. With a grin, he picked the creature up and braced Kyd like a baby against his shoulder. As predicted, the nefittifi calmed down almost immediately, even uttering an occasional contented pop from deep in its throat.

"You're very good with animals, Wesley."

"Thanks. I've always liked them, ever since I can remember. Hey, they seem to like the sound of my voice."

"They do like voices. Maybe that's why I talk so much," Robbal chuckled. "Tell me more about you and animals. How did you get introduced to the wonders of creatures that don't speak your language?"

"Well, I guess it started when I was a little kid and my mom used to read me bedtime stories. The ones I remember the most were about animals. Let's see— one writer was named Owon Jolai. She was from a planet called Keroven, and she wrote a whole series of stories about a world where animals from all over the galaxy lived together. And then there were a bunch of ancient Earth books about a character named Dr. Dolittle. I can't even remember who wrote them, but I remember Dr. Dolittle took care of all kinds of animals, including some imaginary ones, and had lots of adventures with them. He could talk in any animal language and, when I was little, I thought that was great."

Robbal gave Wesley a couple of the snack wafers and they fed the nefittifi. "Those books sound wonderful. I'd love to read them sometime."

"Before you leave the *Enterprise,* I'll find out the titles for you. We probably have some of them in the ship's library computer. They're pretty much classics." Wes laughed at another recollection. "When I was first old enough to understand that my mother was a doctor, I just automatically expected her to be like Dr. Dolittle and take care of animals."

"What happened when you found out she took care of people?"

"I was really disappointed. I must've been about five, and I tried to talk her into a career change."

They both laughed at the shared memory. "Wesley, how is Gina doing on her picture of me and Kyd? She promised it to me as a souvenir of my trip on your starship."

Wes looked dubious. "Uhh, I just hope it's done in time. Gina's a really good artist, but she's an incredible perfectionist. I'll hurry her up for you."

"Thanks. I'm sure she'll listen to you. She really likes you."

Wesley blushed. "So everybody tells me."

Robbal leaned close, his voice dropping confidentially. "What do you think of Counselor Troi?"

"Counselor Troi?" Wes repeated in confusion. "Um, she's a good counselor. She helps the Enterprise run a lot more smoothly."

"No, no. I mean, what do you think of *her?*"

As Robbal's eyebrows waggled for emphasis, Wesley caught on, and his blush deepened by several shades. "Oh." Ensign Crusher tried to choose his words carefully. After a few thoughts about Troi's deep dark eyes and the perfect curves under her tightly tailored uniform, that attempt crumbled. "I think she's gorgeous. I also think she's out of my league. *Way* out," he sighed wistfully.

"Do you think she's out of mine?"

Wesley stared at his companion. "Huh?"

"Tell me about her. Tell me everything."

"Are you sure you're telling me everything, Deanna?" Beverly Crusher taunted playfully.

"Can't I have any secrets at all?" Troi complained.

Both women were flat on the padded floor of an exercise room, dressed in workout togs, kicking alternate legs straight up toward the ceiling to the bouncy beat of recorded music.

"What are friends for if not to pry into your personal life?" Crusher quipped. "It sounds like Robbal was ready to propose to you."

"I wouldn't go that far," said Troi with a laugh.

"And how far *would* you go?"

Troi snickered at the double entendre. "Ha, ha. It's just innocent flirtation. For both of us. He is very sweet, though. You have to admit that."

Crusher sat up and reached for her toes, flattening her torso parallel to the floor with each stretch. "Yes, he is. And tall."

Troi laughed as she watched her friend jealously. "How do you do that? You make it look so easy."

"I guess I'm genetically flexible. Wesley seems to like Robbal a lot."

"Everyone who meets him likes him. And how are you and the nefittifi getting along?"

"Okay, I guess," said Crusher. "I'm not sure I'd want one as a pet—"

"Which isn't likely considering their sacred status and the fact that there are only eight left in the galaxy."

"In that case, they're not bad little guests. Though Robbal seems worried about the female. She still hasn't recovered from the shock of that explosion on Etolos."

Both women stopped to rest. "Will she be all right?" Troi asked with concern. "Because it appears that those two animals will play a key role in any settlement between Etolos and Alaj. If the Alajians accept these nefittifi, they are going to expect them to be healthy."

The door of the exercise room opened and Captain Picard came in. "Are there many health benefits to be gained from just sitting on the deck, Doctor?"

"Not funny, Jean-Luc," Beverly said. "You know, *you* could use a little more exercise time."

"Is that a prescription?"

"Just a professional warning."

"I shall consider myself warned. Counselor, you wanted to speak to me?"

Troi and Crusher both got to their feet. "You didn't have to come all the way down here, sir."

"I was passing by. Now, what was on your mind?"

"It's about Ozemmik, Captain."

"What about him?"

"I almost hesitate to bring it up, since there is nothing specific to which I can point."

Picard gestured encouragingly. "I have learned to trust your feelings, Counselor."

Troi frowned, trying to frame her misgivings with some coherence. "Captain, Ozemmik is a man who believes he knows all the answers. And he freely admits that he would stop at nothing to protect Etolos."

"The same could be said about Lieutenant Worf and this ship," Beverly offered. "Isn't that part of the mind-set of someone in the security business?"

"I am not sure," Troi said, frankly perplexed. "And I do not approve of everything Worf does, or the way he does it. But he doesn't have to perform to my standards, Captain. He has to perform to yours."

Now Picard looked puzzled as well. "I'm not following you, Counselor."

With a small sigh, Deanna made another attempt to clarify her thoughts. "Worf is part of a chain of command. And although he can be overly aggressive and surly, he has never given any indication that he would not follow your orders even under the most dire of circumstances."

"Agreed," said Picard. "If I had any doubt of that, he would not be in a position of authority on this ship, or any other. But we're not talking about Worf."

"That is true," Troi said. "I had a conversation with Ozemmik in Ten-Forward, and I cannot say with any assurance that he considers himself bound by any chain of command."

The captain's mouth compressed into a thin line as he mulled Troi's statement. There was little doubt he found it troubling. "Hmm. Technically, any disobedience on Ozemmik's part is the problem of the prefex of Etolos. But we must be concerned if Ozemmik poses a threat to this peace mission. Do you believe that he does?"

Troi shook her head. "I wish I could be definite, Captain. But I can't. Comparing him to Worf again, I have never sensed that Worf is reckless. Ozemmik may be."

"A loose cannon," Picard murmured.

"Possibly. He has a very independent mind. Even as part of a greater whole, he views himself as separate."

The captain leaned against the padded back of a gymnastics horse. "Are you saying he has his own agenda?"

"Not in the sense that he is dedicated to anything other than the preservation of Etolos and its people."

"Is he hiding something?" asked Dr. Crusher.

"I couldn't tell. On the one hand, he's almost proud of his clearly stated disagreement with Retthew's strategy for peace. But on the other hand, I cannot be sure if his opposition extends beyond that."

"Counselor," said Picard, "would you recommend my apprising Prefex Retthew of your doubts?"

"Yes, Captain, I would."

"Well then, I shall do so. If there's anything else you notice and think worthy of—"

Picard was interrupted by the hailing tone of the intercom and Wesley Crusher's urgent voice. "Dr. Crusher to sickbay—*immediately!*"

Beverly strode to the comm panel on the wall. "What is it, Wesley?"

"It's the nefittifi—some kind of seizure. Robbal's working on her, but we need you."

Beverly glanced at the captain and spread her hands in a helpless gesture. "I'm a doctor, not a vet."

"You're a healer," said Picard flatly. "There's a life in danger. Do what you can to save it."

"On my way, Wesley." With that, Crusher was gone at a gallop.

Chapter Twelve

DR. CRUSHER RUSHED INTO SICKBAY to find her son helping Robbal, who was inside the enclosure examining the female nefittifi.

It didn't take an advanced degree to see the animal couldn't breathe, its chest heaving and an alarming sucking noise coming from its throat.

"Wes, clear that table," Beverly ordered, jabbing a finger toward the nearest examining bench, now covered with assorted supplies for the nefittifi. Wes did as he was told, as his mother squeezed into the cage with Robbal, the sick creature and its fretting mate. She gave the distressed animal a cursory exam, then shook her head. "Robbal, get her out of here. We need some room."

Crusher clambered out of the cage, then tugged on her lab coat over her leotard. As Robbal gently set the animal down on the treatment table, Crusher watched the bio-function monitor. She had no idea what readings might be normal for this strange little creature, but she could tell these levels were erratic and sinking. She leaned close. "Let's get to work."

Still in her workout clothing, Troi accompanied

Picard directly to Retthew's quarters. When the door to the VIP cabin slid open and he saw their solemn faces, his own expression edged toward panic.

On the way here, Picard had made up his mind to deal with one problem at a time, and the nefittifi's health crisis took precedence. Troi's qualms about Ozemmik would have to wait for later discussion.

"Something is wrong, Captain?"

"I'm afraid it is. Dr. Crusher was just summoned to sickbay."

Retthew looked stricken. "The nefittifi?"

"We don't know how serious it is," said Troi softly, hoping her reassuring tone would keep Retthew calm. It didn't.

"Robbal was present," said Picard, "and Dr. Crusher went to offer immediate assistance. Whatever the problem, the nefittifi is receiving the best of care."

"But we knew you would want to be there," Troi added. "We'll take you."

"Thank you."

Wesley met them as they hustled into the outer sickbay office. "My mother said to have you wait out here."

"But I have to know what's happening," Retthew protested. "Captain, please!"

Picard placed a restraining hand on Retthew's shoulder. It occurred to him that the much taller Etolosan could probably barge in if he chose to, but Crusher's orders were to be obeyed. "Prefex, they need to be able to concentrate on their patient. There's nothing we can do in there."

"Captain," Wes volunteered, "if the prefex wants to watch, he can do it here." He motioned to the viewer on his mother's desk and waited for Picard's approval.

The captain nodded. "Visual only, Ensign." He didn't want Retthew overhearing medical jargon which might be misunderstood.

"Aye, sir," Wes said, turning on the small viewer.

Retthew moved as if in a trance and hunched close to the screen. He was a man clinging to his last hope.

Picard tapped his uniform communicator. "Doctor, we are in your office. Can you give us a status report?"

"Too early to tell, Captain," came the reply over the speaker. Crusher's voice was rock steady.

"Then we won't disturb you." Picard admired her *sangfroid,* but knew her well enough to expect nothing less than icy poise under pressure.

"Thank you, Captain. We'll let you know as soon as we do. Crusher out," she said, intentionally closing the channel.

The voice of authority, Crusher thought. *One of the most useful tricks a doctor can learn . . . buys you time without scaring the hell out of people when you haven't got the slightest idea what you're doing.*

She passed her diagnostic probe over the nefittifi's shivering body, then referred to her display screen showing a diagram of the animal's innards. "There," she said, trying to ignore the unceasing wails of the terrified male locked in the enclosure. "The breathing tubes are almost completely occluded. Is this a common ailment in these animals?"

"Not uncommon," said Robbal. "But not usually this bad. I've never treated it."

"Is there a prescribed treatment?"

"Not that I know of."

"I thought you were the expert," she said, not unkindly. A particularly grating screech from the other nefittifi made her wince.

"Doctor, nobody knows a whole lot about these animals."

"Well, then, we're about to learn by doing. Computer, display blood analysis." A graphics chart appeared on a portion of her viewer. "Damn. Robbal, we have to sedate it. I've got a whole range of drugs to choose from, but if I pick the wrong one—"

She didn't have to complete the sentence. He knew what she meant. His mind raced through everything he knew about nefittifi. Then he slowed his mental review, afraid of rushing right past a solution. In a tiny corner of his head, a small voice mocked him: *Some expert!*

He looked up. Crusher had a hypo in her hand, hovering over the nefittifi. The male, Kyd, kept up his pitiful keening.

"Wait," Robbal blurted. "They're sensitive to light and dark."

"How sensitive?"

"In low light or darkness, they enter a state of deep sleep."

"But I've seen them sleep in broad daylight."

"That's voluntary. With light deprivation, it's involuntary. Their bio-functions drop fifty to sixty percent."

Crusher put the hypo back on the tool tray. "That might do it. Computer, reduce lighting to nocturnal." Almost immediately, the room lighting dimmed and assumed a red hue. They waited. It took almost a minute, but the nefittifi's eyes fluttered shut as its bio-readings began to drift downward, then leveled off. As she and Robbal exchanged triumphant grins, Beverly realized she'd been awarded a bonus as well: the frazzled Kyd had also fallen into stone-like slumber in his cage.

"Now what?" Robbal asked.

"Now, this." Dr. Crusher's practiced fingers chose an instrument from her tray and thumbed the switch. The tool glowed a pearly blue and hummed to life. She adjusted the control wheel and the hum increased in pitch, then rose into silence. Crusher pressed it against the nefittifi's chest and moved it slowly up and down. She repeated the treatment four times, and examined the cutaway schematic of the creature's body on her computer screen. She cross-referenced with another monitor chart. Finally, with a satisfied nod, she shut off the device and set it back on the tray. "That should do it."

"What did you do?" asked Robbal in wonder.

"Application of concentrated hypersonics to break up the material clogging her lungs and breathing passages. I think she'll be fine. But why don't we leave the lights off for a while and let them both get some rest."

"I concur, Dr. Crusher."

"You *are* an expert, Robbal. I couldn't have done it without you. And now for the best part of being a doctor."

"What's that?"

"Telling the family the patient will be fine."

As they left the dark ward for the bright office, Beverly reminded herself to smile. For Robbal, as usual, a cheery expression was pretty much automatic. Retthew jumped to his feet, and he and the starship officers waiting with him seemed immediately, if conditionally, relieved.

"Well?" said Picard, looking to his chief surgeon for a prognosis. She deferred to her young colleague.

"Kad is all right now, thanks to Dr. Crusher, but it *was* touch and go for a while, and I was afraid we were going to lose her, I really was, but we pulled her through, and it was because of Dr. Crusher's professionalism and skill, and I'm happy I was able to help even a little bit, because it was *incredibly* inspiring to watch her work," he told them in a single breath.

As she listened to Robbal embellishing their work with a patina of heroism, Beverly suppressed the urge to laugh. *Let him enjoy it. He deserves it.*

Retthew collapsed into a chair. "Thank you, Doctor," he mumbled. "I don't know how Etolos can ever repay you."

"I was just doing my job," Crusher replied, "and it was Robbal who supplied the key piece of information we needed. You're very lucky to have him taking care of these animals."

Her accolade made Robbal beam proudly.

"Then the nefittifi *will* be healthy by the time we reach Alaj?" Picard asked.

Crusher nodded. "It should be, Captain—I mean *she* should be. The problem was a stress-induced reaction to the incident on Etolos, and it just kept getting worse. But we took corrective action. Now, I'm no expert on these animals, so I can't give guarantees."

"Do you mean to say there could be a relapse?" Picard said with a frown.

"If there is, I think it will occur soon. She'll be under close observation for the next few hours—"

"I'll take a shift," Wesley volunteered.

"If anything does happen," Beverly said, "now we know how to deal with it. But I'd be surprised if there was any recurrence."

"Please, Doctor," said Picard, "no more surprises."

When he opened his eyes, Will Riker was more than a little surprised—first, to be alive and conscious, feeling no ill effects other than a monumental throbbing inside his skull; and second, to find that the shuttlecraft was apparently no longer in motion.

He was less surprised, actually not surprised at all, to find his first sight to be the concerned face of Lieutenant Commander Data, hovering maternally over him, illuminated only by the shuttle's red emergency lights.

"Well, you're a sight for sore eyes," Riker said, his throat dry and raspy. He winced and leaned forward in the seat, rubbing the back of his neck. "Make that a sore head."

"Are you all right, Commander?" Data had the medi-kit diagnostic probe poised in one hand, the medical tricorder in the other.

"You tell me."

Data ran a quick scan, concentrating at Riker's forehead. "Brain activity appears to have resumed normal patterns."

At the reference to brain activity, Riker's expression clouded. "Why? Was it abnormal before?"

"Do you remember blacking out, sir?"

Riker had to think hard for a second. "Yes, I do."

"That is good. It indicates retention of last memories and suggests that there is no loss of function." As he spoke, Holzrichter and Lopez stirred back to life. Data stepped over to repeat the precautionary scans. "After you lapsed into unconsciousness, you all had critical reductions in brainwave activity, far greater than in normal sleep or even biostasis."

"Sounds serious," said Lopez, her voice groggy.

"It was," said Data. "I did not know when or if you would recover, and I was apprehensive about possible permanent damage. But there is none, at least none detectable by this basic medical equipment."

Riker got to his feet, swaying on rubbery knees and bracing himself with a hand on the seatback until his dizziness subsided a few moments later. He moved over to Navirra, who was just coming around. "Ambassador." Her eyelids fluttered, but failed to open. He leaned close to her ear. "Ambassador, can you hear me?"

"Of course I can, Mr. Riker," she rumbled, her eyes still closed. Finally they opened, blinking to restore some semblance of focus. "Pleased to see you, as well, though I'd appreciate a less intimate view."

Riker straightened up. "Your wit remains intact, Ambassador."

"It's usually the first part of me to wake up," the old Etolosan said as she gingerly tested her stiff joints. "Might I ask where we are?"

"My question, too," said Riker, directing his attention to Data. "Did you stay conscious the entire time we were out? Which reminds me, how long *were* we out?"

"Two hours, forty-two minutes. And yes, I did remain conscious, though I had a few momentary dysfunctional lapses. And we are inside a vessel."

They all stared at Data. "We're *what?*" said Riker.

"Inside a vessel—a very large vessel at that."

Riker stumbled up to the nearest viewport to take a look. Data was right. The shuttle and its occupants were indeed inside what seemed to be a dimly lit cargo bay, considerably larger than the *Enterprise*'s own hangar deck.

"When you say 'very large vessel,'" said Riker, "what are we talking about?"

"Any estimate would be based on my visual observations only, and would quite likely be inaccurate." At Riker's nod, he continued. "I would say it is at least fifteen times the size of the *Enterprise,* and as much as three thousand times the volume. There were no markings which I could identify."

As he absorbed that information, Riker glanced around the cabin. "Data, is anything in here working?"

"Major systems are out. Back-up life support is operative. And while waiting for you to regain consciousness, I passed the time repairing and recalibrating tricorders. Two are now operative, as are two phasers. Also, our communicators appear to be functioning."

Riker's lips thinned into a displeased line. "Well, better than nothing. I'm curious—do you have any idea why this energy field scrambled our brains and the shuttle's innards but it didn't seriously affect you?"

"Evidently, my circuitry is better protected."

"Why did *we* recover at all?" Lopez wondered.

"I cannot be certain," Data said, "but I believe there are at least two contributing factors. First, for an organ so complex, the human brain has a remarkable ability to compensate for certain interference. And in addition, it appears that the interior of this vessel in which we are now contained is screened from the effects of the exterior energy disturbance."

"Data," Riker said, "were you able to make any other useful observations about this ship or the energy field?"

"Perhaps. Once we were caught in its grasp, the energy field seemed to make no adjustments."

"What do you mean, adjustments?" asked Riker.

"One example would be the navigational deflectors on the *Enterprise,* which are operative at all times but compensate as needed to protect the ship from variable concentrations of interstellar matter and energy.

"The energy disturbance we just encountered, on the other hand, reacted to our initial presence and then maintained itself at a continuous level of power. This could indicate that it emanates from an automated system of considerably less sophistication than the navigational deflectors standard on a starship."

"So what you are saying," said Navirra, "is that this spacecraft may be exceedingly large but not very advanced."

"That is quite possible," Data said.

Navirra nodded, almost to herself. "Hmm . . . which raises the question of who would build such a vessel and why?"

"Not to mention why we got dragged aboard it," Holzrichter muttered.

Riker folded his arms across his chest. "Data, has anyone tried to contact us?"

"No, sir. Nor was there any response to signals I sent via our communicators. With one exception, our presence aboard this vessel has been virtually ignored."

"What exception?"

"After the shuttle was brought into this storage bay, we were scanned by some sort of sensor beam."

Riker's eyes narrowed, an expression combining annoyance and confusion. "And that's it?"

"Yes, sir."

"Could that scanner also have been some sort of automated system?"

"That is possible, sir, but I cannot be certain."

"Commander Riker," said Holzrichter, "request permission to explore our surroundings."

"Rick, we don't even know if there's a breatheable atmosphere out there," Lopez reminded him. "And if shuttle systems aren't working, we don't have any way of finding out."

"There is a way," said Data. "I do not require a breatheable atmosphere. I could take a tricorder outside the shuttle and sample the immediate environment."

"Do it, Data," Riker decided. "Rick, break out the respirator masks."

"Aye, sir." The stocky security guard opened a storage compartment and handed out compact breather masks which fit over the nose and mouth. They were designed to provide emergency oxygen in case the shuttle was ever forced to land on an inhospitable world. When the masks were in place and tested, Riker stood by the hatch. "Data, be careful. Take no chances. We need you in one functional piece."

"I shall bear that in mind," the android said as pleasantly as if he were strolling through a doorway on the *Enterprise* instead of stepping into the belly of a captor ship.

Riker opened the hatch and Data climbed out. The hatch shut behind him and he moved warily away from the shuttle, its running lights glowing around it like a halo. He pointed his searchlight into the gloom and activated the tricorder, sampling the environment and surveying the landing bay's interior volume.

Dust and smoke danced in the light beam as it sliced through the darkness. The bay was huge, in keeping with the scale of the whole vessel, dwarfing the tiny shuttle as it sat in the middle of this vast cavern.

Data's communicator chirped and he heard Riker's voice. "Report, Mr. Data."

"The atmosphere is breatheable for humans, Commander, though with only fourteen percent oxygen rather than the twenty percent to which you are accustomed. I read no elements harmful to humanoid life.

"The dimensions of the bay are approximately three hundred meters square by fifty meters high. The walls are constructed of a metal alloy which is not familiar." Sweeping his light along one perimeter, Data found what seemed to be a set of large bay doors, sealed tightly. Did they lead further into the giant ship, or out to space? There was no way to tell.

"Have you found anything resembling an open door with an exit sign?"

"Not as yet, sir. Shall I continue to explore?"

"Return to the shuttle, Data. I don't want you roaming out there alone. If we're going to check this place out, I want to do it in teams."

"Agreed. That would be both safer and more productive." He retreated toward the shuttlecraft. "Strange," he murmured.

"What is?" Riker asked.

"That we have been brought inside this vessel and otherwise ignored."

"Maybe that one scan convinced them we're too insignificant to pay attention to us," Riker mused, his tone betraying some insult at that notion.

"Or," said Data, "perhaps we are so securely imprisoned that they have no *need* to pay attention to us."

Inside the shuttle, there was a moment of strained silence and an exchange of uncomfortable glances. "Data," Riker finally said, "that is *not* a comforting theory."

Chapter Thirteen

LEANING ON A lacquered black cane, Zeila hobbled through the vaulted lobby of the forum building, taking new pleasure from familiar tapestries and mosaics as she passed them. The day before, as she lay dazed under the rubble of the marketplace, she hadn't been sure she'd ever see anything again. For the first time in her life, she'd been forced to face squarely the real possibility that she might die at the hands of her own people before she could complete her plan to save Alaj.

Had she been standing a few meters closer to the booby-trapped peddler's cart, she would no longer be here to mull over such abstract concepts. Regardless, whether by dumb luck or cosmic plan, she'd survived the attempt on her life. Reducing circumstances to their basic components—as she preferred to do—a leader in her tenuous position had two choices: hide, or resume the march to wherever she'd been headed.

For Zeila, the choice was easy.

So she marched, as best she could, back to her office. And found a large obstacle blocking her chosen path.

Lef.

The burly intelligence deputy had staked out the doorway to her office like a soldier guarding a critical pass in the midst of battle. He did not look like someone who would easily yield.

"Honoress, what are you doing here?"

"I work here," she said dryly, noticing several fresh scabs on his face where he'd been cut by the flying debris the day before. "What are you doing here? Don't you work someplace else?"

"I knew you'd come in today."

"Oh, and when did you figure that out?"

"The moment the doctor told you to stay off that leg for at least two days."

"Well, Lef, I could do that if you'd let me go into my office where I could sit down."

"Curister," he scolded, "you were told to rest. You shouldn't be on your feet."

Zeila sighed. "You're right. I do feel weak. In fact . . . I feel very weak."

Lef took a concerned step toward her.

"I feel like . . ." Zeila's breathing grew shallow and she swayed. "I feel like . . . like I might faint." She folded, and Lef darted forward to catch her before she hit the floor. With a strained grunt, he got her upright, propped her slender body against his chest, and fumbled at the old-fashioned door handle with his free hand. He managed to get it open, then clumsily lifted Zeila, nearly tripping over the cane still snagged on her wrist. He brought her inside and gently set her down on the deep cushions of her couch.

The moment he straightened up, her eyes opened and she flashed a mischievous grin, highlighting the tapered white scar on her chin. "That's one way of getting you to let me into my own office. Did you have trouble picking me up because I'm getting fat, or because you were *also* hurt yesterday?"

He glared at her with a mixture of embarrassment and anger. "I'm not hurt."

She rested her injured leg on a footstool. "The hell you aren't. Did a doctor tell you that?"

"I didn't go to a doctor."

"Go to one."

"I hate doctors," Lef said, pouting like a sulky schoolboy. "I always have and I always will."

"You brought me to a doctor quickly enough yesterday."

"You were hurt. Bleeding. And by the way, you're not getting fat."

"That's a relief," she said as Lef began to pace, something he did so frequently in her office that Zeila fully expected he'd eventually wear a rut into the deep carpeting. "So why *did* you come here this morning? Was it just to stop me from coming in?"

"No. I knew I'd fail at that."

"Well, then, what?"

"No rules in a knife fight," he mumbled.

"What?"

"I said, no rules in a knife fight. Remember when you said that to me?"

"Sure. What about it?"

"You didn't say what happens when your opponent uses a much deadlier weapon."

They were interrupted by a knock at the door. "Come in," Zeila called. The door opened and there stood Deputy Turchin, her outspoken nemesis from the Presiding Forum. Though she tensed reflexively as he oozed into her office, her face froze into a neutral expression. "Turchin. To what do I owe this pleasure?"

His bristly gray brows rose solicitously. "I stopped at your home to pay my respects after I heard about the bombing incident, and your housekeeper said you were here. I couldn't believe it. You must be quite shaken by—"

"Shaken yesterday, settled today," she replied with forced affability.

"We may disagree on many things, Zeila, but I admire your courage . . ."

For a fleeting moment, Zeila entertained the possibility that Turchin's expression of admiration might actually be sincere.

". . . and all night I thought about how tragic it would be if you didn't heed this warning you received so violently yesterday."

A very fleeting moment, she thought.

"Turchin, this 'warning,' as you so daintily put it, was a crime against the Alajian government. Criminals aren't heeded, they are punished."

"And whoever committed this act of terrorism *will* be punished," said Lef.

Turchin, who was even taller than Lef, smirked at the intelligence deputy's pronouncement. "What makes you think you'll ever capture those responsible? Do you think they're going to wear signs identifying themselves? They got away, and they have many sympathizers who would gladly hide them. Zeila, you must be more careful. I would regret your death."

"Oh, how kind of you," she said sarcastically.

"I would, for two reasons. Assassination is not a preferable means of changing the government. And my party does not wish to take over until you have definitively and finally failed."

"Then I hope you're prepared for a long wait."

"No need," Turchin said. "All Alaj wishes you a speedy recovery."

"Not all. But thank you, and good day."

A moment after Turchin had gone, Lef cut loose a scorching string of curses. "That bastard! He comes all the way here to threaten you!"

"I don't care about his threats and you shouldn't either."

Lef stared at her in disbelief. "He has ties to the bombers. I'm sure of it."

"I think you give him too much credit for bravery, Lef. Turchin is not prone to radical action. But if you think otherwise, get me proof and you can arrest him. Until then, he's worthy of no attention at all."

Lef stopped near the large windows overlooking the main plaza and gazed outside, his back turned toward Zeila. "What about me?"

"Hmm?"

"Am I worthy of attention?"

"Of course."

"Then scrap this negotiation, Honoress. Please— before it goes too far. Maybe during another time this would be the right course to take. But with all this instability around the world . . ."

"Another time?" Her tone was gentle. "Lef, if we don't do this now, we're going to run *out* of time."

"Whatever happens, we can adapt. We've always been able to—"

"This world will not be able to support life," said Zeila, struggling to her feet and limping over to him. "This is our last chance to change our ways. Lef, look at me." She placed a firm hand on his shoulder and turned him until they faced each other. "You know I can't retreat now."

He nodded, his eyes hollow and sad. "I . . . I just worry about you. That's all."

"Is it?" she said, gazing up at him with a smile that

was warm, not mocking. "What's this really about, Lef?"

"It's my job to protect you," he said, looking away. "To preserve your government." He closed his eyes and took a long breath. Then he looked directly at her. "Turchin *says* he admires you, but I . . . I really do, Honoress . . . Zeila."

"You almost never call me by name, even though everyone else does."

"I believe in protocol. And propriety."

"Are you getting improper with me?" she said lightly. She cut him off before he could respond. "Why do you admire me?" she asked.

He gave her a look of incredulity, as if his reasons should have been obvious. "I know all about your background. I know your parents died before you were fifteen. I know how poor you were, and I know about all the scholarships you won. I followed your rise through the government . . . and I prayed you would ask me to serve you. I know that leaders like you—*people* like you—don't come along every day." His voice trailed off in embarrassment. "I . . . I've never met anyone like you. Your compassion, your strength—"

"Getting pretty personal here, aren't we?" she quipped.

"I . . . I'm sorry, Honoress."

"Don't be," she said, moving closer until their bodies pressed together.

"If we weren't who we are . . . I mean, if you weren't curister and I wasn't just a deputy," he stammered. "If . . . if you . . ."

Zeila clasped his hand. With her other hand, she tilted his head down. Then she brushed a kiss across his lips. "Maybe we shouldn't have done that," she said, swallowing as she looked away. "Maybe we shouldn't do it again." She turned back, a glimmer in her eye. "Then again, maybe we should."

Sunset cast golden light across Troi's face, and Robbal smiled at her. They sat together on a bench at the rim of a deep gorge. Five streams rushed down from the forests and hills above and behind them. The cliffs at the top of the gorge formed a nearly complete ring of rock, and five distinct waterfalls cascaded down to a single river a thousand feet below. Rainbow mists danced in the twilight, rising all the way up to the overlook.

"You were right," said Robbal happily, his words rushing as fast as the tumbling streams. "It *would* be impossible to describe how beautiful this place is, and I know we've got nothing like it on Etolos. I don't have any idea what this planet Anarra might be like, but somehow I doubt many worlds have anything quite like this, and I do thank you for sharing it with me—well, *sort* of sharing it with me—I can't believe all this is the inside of the *Enterprise* holodeck, which is absolutely amazing, though not as amazing as those waterfalls, since *those* are natural, or they would be if we were really there."

With a laugh, Deanna touched an outstretched finger to his lips. "Slow down, Robbal. Sometimes I get out of breath just listening to you."

"Sorry." With noticeable effort, he maintained a lengthy pause, then added, "See? Just one word."

"Plus four. But it's a start."

He turned to take in all the natural beauty around them. "Is this park near your home on Betazed?"

"No, but we went there frequently."

"I just have one complaint about it."

Troi looked surprised. "You do?"

"Mm-hmm. The name. Couldn't they have thought of something more poetic than Five Falls?"

"I don't know—I think simplicity is sometimes best."

Robbal watched the mists swirling up from the gorge and lapsed into uncharacteristic silence. When he spoke again, his voice was subdued. "Can I tell you something?"

"If you like."

"It's not cheerful."

"That's all right. You're one of the happiest people I've ever met. That's one of the reasons others enjoy your company. But no one can smile all the time."

"Today, in sickbay, I really thought we were going to lose Kad. I felt so helpless. It made me realize how much I *don't* know about nefittifi."

"Does that bother you?"

"A little. So when all this is over, I'm going to work even harder to figure out everything there is to know about those little guys. I'd love it if someday, on Etolos or Anarra, or wherever we are, there are thousands of them roaming around the woods, just like there used to be on Alaj in ancient times. And I'd love it if that happened because of something I discovered about them."

He was smiling again, but it was a different kind of smile, from much deeper in his soul. Troi leaned over and gave him a quick peck on his fuzzy cheek, then stood and took him by the hand. "Come," she said. "There is something else I'd like to share with you."

His smile suddenly faded, replaced by frightened hesitation in his eyes. "Uhh, Deanna. I . . . I know I've been flirting, but I . . . uhh. I never *actually* thought . . . I mean, I don't think I could . . . I don't think I'm ready."

As she picked up the meaning in his jumble of thoughts and words, Troi's eyes widened with astonished realization, and she nearly burst out laughing. "Robbal, I didn't mean we should make love."

"You didn't?" he squeaked.

She shook her head and her fingers brushed his cheek. "I just wanted to take you to Ten-Forward for Guinan's special Koquesian ice cream."

Robbal hid his face in his hands. "I am so embarrassed."

"That condition is rarely fatal, and Koquesian ice cream is the perfect cure—especially with hot fudge."

He lowered his hands, revealing a sheepish grin. "I have a lot to learn about nefittifi—and women, too."

They headed for the holodeck exit. "Robbal," said Deanna, "you may know more than you think."

"About nefittifi, or women?"

"Both."

The chime at Retthew's cabin door was a welcome intrusion. He'd been hunched awkwardly over the desktop computer screen, and he'd had quite enough of reviewing briefing notes on the upcoming negotiations with Alaj. "Yes, come in."

The door slid open and Captain Picard entered. "I hope I am not disturbing you, Prefex."

"Not at all, Captain. I'm glad for the company. Please, sit down."

Picard sat in a comfortable chair adjacent to the desk. The Etolosan shut off the computer and offered his visitor a drink from a pitcher on a nearby tray. Picard declined.

"The reason I've come is . . ." Picard's voice trailed off as he searched for an appropriate way to broach a thorny subject. If the situation were reversed, and someone had come to tell him something unsavory about one of his officers, he'd want the messenger to be direct. But Retthew had given the impression that he did not thrive on confrontation.

Although, Picard thought upon further consideration, *he is here on this ship. Perhaps my excessive circumspection is unnecessary.* "This is difficult," he began again.

"I can see that, Captain. Just say what's on your mind."

"Very well. Do you trust your security adviser?"

"Ozemmik? Yes, I do. Why? Is there some reason I shouldn't?"

"I have reason to believe he may pose a threat to your mission of reconciliation."

Retthew responded with a frosty stare. "Captain Picard, I've known Ozemmik since we were boys."

"I am aware of that."

"Ozemmik has his quirks, but I would never question his loyalty to Etolos."

"It is not his loyalty to Etolos which is in question," Picard said with stiff determination.

"Then what *is?*"

"His loyalty to you."

"Captain, people who don't know him can misinterpret what Ozemmik says. He doesn't always choose his words with diplomatic care. What did he tell you?"

"It isn't what he told me. I did not even speak with him."

"Then who did?"

"Counselor Troi."

Retthew's attitude grew increasingly defensive. "So these suspicions of yours are based on hearsay?"

"Counselor Troi's reports are not hearsay, Prefex. She is not only an extremely proficient expert in psychology, she also happens to be half Betazoid. She is empathic. And she believes he does not feel bound by his subordinate status."

"That may be so, Captain, but he would never, *never* do anything to harm our world."

"That may be so, Prefex. But his opinion as to what will or will not harm Etolos may be at considerable variance with your own."

The Etolosan leader simply did not want to believe what Picard was telling him. "Are you saying he's going to do something to disrupt the negotiations? Even if that were his true intention, it wouldn't be possible. He will not be with me when I meet with Zeila, and he knows that."

Picard tried a different approach. "He has said he does not agree with your decision to pursue these talks, has he not?"

"That's true. But if he planned something underhanded, don't you think he would have kept his opposition secret? That's what I would do if I were him. Wouldn't you?"

"Not if I had a reckless streak in my personality. Counselor Troi suspects Ozemmik possesses that trait."

"Ozemmik is independent, Captain, not reckless," said Retthew with renewed calmness, as if he'd already decided not to fret over Picard's warning. "I value that independence, because it gives him the backbone to tell me even those things I'd rather not hear. I appreciate your taking the time to relate Counselor Troi's concerns, but I don't believe they are warranted."

"That is, of course, your prerogative," Picard said as he stood to leave. "Good night, then."

"Captain."

Picard paused at the open door.

"I'd trust him not only with my life," Retthew said solemnly, "but with the future of my whole world."

Picard responded with a nod. But as the door shut behind him, he thought: *Let's hope it doesn't come to that.*

There were just a handful of late-evening patrons scattered about Ten-Forward when Troi and Robbal arrived. They picked up a couple of servings of Guinan's special ice cream, spotted Dr. Crusher, Wesley, and his friend Gina at a table and joined them near the observation windows.

"We were just talking about you, Robbal," said Wesley. "Mom was saying how calm and cool you were when you were working on Kad."

"Wes," Beverly admonished, "you're embarrassing him."

"That's okay," the lanky Etolosan said. "I've embarrassed myself plenty already tonight. A little more won't hurt." He spooned some of the ice cream into his mouth. "Mmmm. This *is* good!"

"Can I embarrass you, too, Mom?" said Wes.

"Not if you value your future."

Wesley cupped one hand alongside his mouth and stage-whispered: "She likes the nefittifi and she's going to miss them when they leave."

Troi looked pleased. "I knew you'd come around."

"They're kind of odd," Beverly said, "but I guess they *are* endearing."

"There's something I don't get," Gina said around a mouthful of ice cream. "How did they become a sacred symbol?"

Robbal shrugged. "How does anything? Just being in the right place at the right time, I suppose. I've heard about stranger symbols than ours, like on Pojed Seven, for instance, their main religious icon is an insect—and not an especially interesting one, at least from my point of view."

Wesley nodded. "I remember reading about the civilization on Harok. They worship light, and prisms are their holy symbols."

"And on one of the planets Etolos worked with, Gamma Breeg," Robbal said, "they worshipped something called a *hokazzesch.*"

"What's a *hokazzesch?*" asked Gina, wrestling with the pronunciation.

"It's sort of like a feline worm, about so big," Robbal said, holding his hands a couple of feet apart. "They bite, and they smell a *lot* worse than the nefittifi, Dr. Crusher." He finished his plate of ice cream and stood up. "Well, it's been a long day. If you all don't mind, I think I'll look in on Kyd and Kad and then go to sleep."

"I think I'd better be heading home, too," Gina said. "I have to get up early tomorrow and finish your portrait, Robbal. It *will* be finished, I promise. Good night, everybody." She headed for the door with the Etolosan.

On the pretext of stretching his long legs, Wesley also stood up. "I'm kind of tired, too, Mom. I think I'll call it a night." He hurried to catch up with Gina and Robbal as they reached the corridor. "Gina, we're going in the same direction. Maybe I'll walk you home?"

"Okay."

Robbal gave them a wave as he headed the other way, and they called their good-nights after him.

"Robbal," said Wesley as an afterthought, "how long will you be with Kyd and Kad?"

"At least fifteen minutes or so."

"Maybe I'll stop in after I drop Gina off."
"I'll be there."

The sickbay ward serving as home for the nefittifi was dark and quiet when Robbal came in. Kyd and Kad were asleep inside their enclosure, curled close together for warmth and comfort. Robbal smiled broadly as he gazed at them. Simply being around them always made him happy. Nothing he'd ever experienced had quite the same effect, though being around Deanna Troi was running a close second. He was really going to miss her when the *Enterprise* was gone.

With a shudder of embarrassment, he replayed that little holodeck scene. *What an idiot . . . how could I have thought she was planning to seduce me? Spirit! I'm just lucky it was her. At least I can trust her to keep the secret of just how stupid I can be.* He sighed as he looked at the nefittifi nestled so contentedly. "If only she *had* wanted to seduce me. I could've died a happy man. Oh, well. Sorry to wake you up guys, but I have to check you out. Computer, daylight illumination, please."

The computer obeyed, and Robbal opened the cage and lifted the sleeping nefittifi out, hugging them under his arms until they began to wake up. Then he set them on the examining table, Kyd standing and Kad on her back. Kyd watched with almost human interest as Robbal ran the diagnostic probe over the female's abdomen, consulting the computer display chart. Drawn by the colors on the screen, Kyd ambled across the table for a closer look.

"What do you think, Kyd? Do those readings meet with your approval?"

The nefittifi opened his beak and let out a happy chortle.

"Glad we concur, Doctor. I think—"

He felt something press against his neck, and in little more time than it takes to blink, he slumped into oblivion. The medical probe fell from his fingers and clattered across the floor. Kad rolled onto her belly to see where he'd gone, and Kyd uttered a cautionary squawk.

Strong hands lowered Robbal into a limp heap on the deck—the same strong hands that had injected him so deftly.

The hands belonged to Ozemmik.

Chapter Fourteen

As QUICKLY AND SILENTLY as he'd ambushed Robbal, Ozemmik moved to the examining table and grabbed the female nefittifi. At the rough touch of unfamiliar hands, however, she began to squirm—and Ozemmik found that a three-foot-tall animal weighing fifty pounds could kick up quite a struggle. As he wrestled with her, the small hypo he'd used to inject Robbal slipped from his fingers. And Kyd's tentative vocalization rose to a full-throated yowl.

Ozemmik muttered an oath as he scrambled across the floor, clutching the writhing nefittifi and reaching for the syringe. Just as he grabbed it, the door opened. He froze in his crouch and looked up to see Gina Pace standing in the doorway.

"What are you doing?" she asked warily. "What's going on?" Then she noticed Robbal's body lying on the floor.

Fortunately, Ozemmik did *not* notice Wesley Crusher sneaking in behind him—not until Wes brought a sturdy medical scope down across the back of Ozemmik's skull with a satisfying thud. Ozemmik crumpled and the terrified nefittifi wriggled free, skittering across the floor until Gina scooped her up into a comforting embrace. Kyd was still screeching from the examining table. Wes tapped his communicator.

"Security to sickbay—*on the double.*"

Worf was the first to arrive. By the time he did, Wes and Gina had Ozemmik securely bound hand and foot, and Robbal was off the floor and on a sickbay bed. Both were still unconscious. With a quick glance, the Klingon security chief sized up the surprising scene—and could not even begin to piece together what had taken place.

"What happened?" he rumbled.

Before either teen could answer, Picard strode in, stopped short, and gaped. "What the devil happened here?"

Then Beverly Crusher rushed in a second later, and looked horrified. "What *happened?*"

All that brass intimidated Gina and she retreated behind Wesley, who opted to address the captain directly, and did so with considerable aplomb, starting with the group snack in Ten-Forward. Picard hurried him along.

"Yes, sir. As I said, I was walking Gina back to her family quarters when she decided she also wanted to say good night to the nefittifi. As we approached sickbay, I heard one of the animals sort of screaming and that didn't sound right. Robbal had explained what their different sounds mean and I knew they were scared by something. So I checked the computer monitor and saw Ozemmik in here."

"Doing what?" asked Picard.

"He had Kad—that's the female, sir—and he was handling her roughly. Whatever he was doing, I knew it had to be unauthorized. So I sent Gina through my mother's office to distract him, and I came around through the connecting ward, snuck up behind him, and hit him with this." He held up the medical bludgeon.

"Ensign," said Picard, "why didn't you call security immediately?"

"Yes, Wesley," his mother echoed, her tone laden with disapproval, "why didn't you?"

"I didn't think there was time. I know how important the nefittifi are to this mission—and to Etolos. If I hesitated, I was afraid Ozemmik would have had time to hurt them, or kill them."

Picard had the offending hypo in his hand and gave it to Beverly. "Doctor, find out what is in that. Wesley, you took a big risk by acting on your own—"

"Begging your pardon, sir," Gina cut in. "But it wasn't as big a risk as it seems. Wesley figured just catching this Ozemmik in the act might be enough to stop him. And if he did go ahead with whatever he had planned, we could have signaled Lieutenant Worf then."

"That's right, sir," Wes said. "I thought the most important thing was to stop him before he harmed the nefittifi. Once we did that, because we had the element of surprise on our side—"

"—and because there were two of us—"

"—I felt pretty sure we had sufficient time and options to act without putting ourselves in immediate danger."

Picard pursed his lips in reflection. "You both have my personal commendation on your actions. It is quite likely that you did in fact prevent Ozemmik from inflicting any harm on these animals."

Worf took the medical scope from Wesley and hefted it, impressed by its weight. "There may be a place for you in security."

"Security?" Wesley mused. "Hmm. I never thought about—"

"Over my dead body," Beverly said sharply. "No offense, Worf."

The burly Klingon gave a neutral shrug.

Dr. Crusher's analysis revealed that the hypo contained two drugs, one to knock out a humanoid and one potent enough to cause death if administered to the nefittifi. Picard ordered Ozemmik moved to the brig and departed sickbay to make his grim report to Retthew.

With the chaos cleared, Beverly summoned Counselor Troi to sickbay to tell her what had happened. Shaken by the near-tragic turn of events, Deanna sat quietly at Crusher's desk, her emotions a jumble of anger, guilt, and relief.

"I *knew* Ozemmik couldn't be trusted," Troi said, her words tinged with bitter frustration. "I could have prevented this."

"Deanna, you did what you could."

"I should have done more."

"Like what?"

"I should have done more to convince the captain that Ozemmik was dangerous."

"You convinced *him*. He just couldn't convince Retthew."

"Then I should have gone with him. *I* should have convinced Retthew."

Beverly stepped over to the food synthesizer niche. "Two cups of orange spice tea, hot, one with lemon. You did your job, Deanna." The tea cups materialized and she brought them back to the desk.

"Not well enough," Troi said sadly, sipping carefully from the steaming cup.

Beverly sat opposite her friend. "You're a ship's

counselor. It's a damned tough job, and you do it exceedingly well. But you're not Q—you're not omnipotent. You do have limits."

"I don't like having limits, not when they endanger my friends and this ship."

"Tough. Neither do I."

"Is that supposed to make me feel better?" Deanna asked with wry resignation.

"I'm a doctor, not a miracle worker."

"Welcome to the club. Is Robbal awake yet?"

Crusher shook her head. "Just as well. The drug Ozemmik used on him was pretty strong stuff. The longer he sleeps it off, the better he'll feel when he does wake up." Exercising a little physician's intuition, she put her tea down and led Troi into the adjacent ward.

"He'll be all right, won't he?" Deanna asked.

"He'll be fine."

With a maternal touch, Troi brushed her fingers across his cheek, then started when his eyelids fluttered open.

"Was it good for you, too?" he said through a medicated haze.

Troi couldn't help laughing. "Spectacular."

"Must've been . . . I can't remember a thing."

"I'll tell you later. Dr. Crusher wants you to rest now."

He licked his dry lips and Deanna helped him to a sip of water. "Okay. But . . . Kyd and Kad—"

"They're fine. Go to sleep now. I'll be here when you wake up." She bent over and placed a light kiss on his forehead. Then he closed his eyes.

"Would you believe I've got the public opinion polls to back me up?" said Ozemmik lightly from the cot inside his brig cell. He reclined there, quite self-satisfied and thoroughly unconcerned.

On the other side of the force field stood Picard, Worf, and Prefex Retthew. Retthew's slumped shoulders and puffy face evidenced the emotional pummeling he'd been forced to absorb.

"Why would you do this?" Retthew's voice was utterly dispirited.

"I had no choice. You gave me no choice."

Retthew shook his head as if he'd been slapped. "How did I give you no choice?"

"You wouldn't listen to reason."

"Were you planning to kill the nefittifi?" Picard asked.

"Yes," Ozemmik said without hesitation.

Retthew couldn't believe what he was hearing. *"Why?"*

"I hated the idea of killing them when we have so few left. But if their deaths might prevent you from carrying out your foolish plan, the sacrifice would be acceptable."

Picard rubbed his tired eyes. His last sleep period seemed like days ago. "Did you also engineer the explosion at the nefittifi biosphere?"

"I did. No terrorists could ever have breached my security perimeter," Ozemmik said evenly. "I'd hoped I could stop your treason before you ever left Etolos, Retthew."

Ozemmik's disdain infuriated Picard, but the captain kept his temper under control. "What if Retthew and the rest of us had been killed in that bombing?"

"What if you had? That was never my intention—although, in retrospect, that might have been the most direct way to deal with the problem."

"I think we've heard enough," Picard said, angry disgust seeping into his voice. He turned to Retthew.

"Ozemmik will remain in our brig until we return to Etolos. At that time, we shall turn him over to your criminal justice authorities. Is that acceptable, Prefex?"

Retthew didn't reply right away, then gave Picard a dazed nod. "Uhh, yes, Captain."

"We'll be arriving at Alaj in about six hours, and the first round of talks will be early in the day. I suggest we all try to get some rest."

"Yes, some rest," Retthew mumbled.

"Lieutenant Worf, please escort the prefex to his quarters."

"Yes, sir." Worf motioned toward the exit and Retthew shambled after him.

Picard stayed behind, glaring at the prisoner.

"Something on your mind, Captain?"

"I was just thinking about how many times the course of history has been derailed by a lone fanatic determined to destroy what others are brave enough to build."

"What about lone heroes who save their people from weak-willed appeasers?"

"Is that how you see yourself?"

"My self-styled opinion doesn't matter."

"What does matter?"

"The judgment of history."

"I doubt history will judge you kindly."

Ozemmik shrugged casually. "If I'm right and Retthew is wrong, I'll be remembered as a martyr. That is, if there are any Etolosans left to remember. Me . . . a martyr. Hmm."

"I will do whatever I can to see that does not happen." Picard turned and left the brig.

Retthew tried to sleep, but couldn't. As exhausted as his body was, his mind would not rest. After a couple of hours spent either staring into the darkness of his cabin or tossing and turning, he got up, dressed and found his way to the starship's brig. As soon as he stepped up to Ozemmik's cell, the security adviser sat up on the cot and looked at him.

"You couldn't sleep either," said Retthew.

"I was sleeping," Ozemmik lied.

"Tell me the truth."

"About what?"

"You know." Retthew spoke in a numb monotone.

"You can't come right out and say it, can you?" Ozemmik taunted.

"Say what?"

"Accuse me of betraying you."

Retthew shifted uncomfortably. "You betrayed all of Etolos."

Ozemmik jumped to his feet and advanced to the fringe of the force field sealing him into the cell. "I betrayed *you!* Deal with it!"

"I can't!" Retthew shouted back, fists suddenly clenching and anguish twisting his face. "I trusted you . . . I thought I knew you."

"No one ever knows anyone else well enough to trust completely. But you never learned that lesson, did you?"

"If you disagreed with policy—"

"You still don't get it. This is more than policy. It's character. I didn't want to do all this, but you didn't leave me any choice—because you didn't have the strength to accept the truth."

"Tell me the truth," Retthew repeated. *"Your* truth."

"Quite simple, really. Alaj can't be trusted."

Retthew shook his head. "How do you know?"

"I know. Any deal with them betrays the heroes

who built our world out of the ashes of the Great Exodus."

"If we don't act now, everything those heroic ancestors built will be gone. You know that."

"Mm-hmm. But you propose saving our bodies at the expense of our souls—at the cost of what we *are.*"

"This isn't theological theory, Ozemmik, this is reality. Does the purity of your beliefs have room for that?"

"Purity is what saved us. Etol and the rest of the exiles based our entire civilization on that premise. Purity is what makes us different from Alaj and all the other stupid civilizations who squander their natural treasures. Purity is what makes us special."

Ozemmik's words sent a shiver down Retthew's spine. From somewhere deep inside, he felt a combative surge. Maybe, after all these years, he'd finally found the Spirit within himself. "You idiot! Our *work* is what makes us special. If we perish, no one else will do that work with the same dedication. *No one!* No one else will defend nature and creation the way we do. No one else will bind her wounds and preserve her when those stupid beings declare mindless war on her!"

"Plenty of Etolosans don't agree with you."

"That's their choice," Retthew shot back. "My way, at least we'll be around to argue about it."

"A leader serves his people."

"No. A leader *leads.* For the first time in my life, that's what I'm doing. Etol and the heroes of Totality gave us a rare gift—a second chance to fulfill our destiny."

"Not at the price of our ideals."

"You see things as absolutes, Ozemmik. You always have. But reality is rarely absolute."

"So, you suddenly fancy yourself another prophet?" Ozemmik ridiculed.

"Damn right I do. If this works, I'll be giving our descendants the same second chance our ancestors gave us. And, yes, it's true that if we fail now, we fail for all time. But if we don't even try to find a solution, that failure is a foregone conclusion." Retthew turned toward the exit.

"Rett, what about your sworn duty as prefex to uphold the past?"

Retthew stopped and glanced back over his shoulder. "Our duty, Mik," he said, "is to survive."

For the first time in his life, Retthew didn't give a damn what anyone else thought. For the first time in his life, he felt free.

Chapter Fifteen

To WILL RIKER, the concept of being a captive was not especially frightening. Imprisonment was assuredly not his preferred state of existence, but he'd been there before. And no one had ever promised this line of work to be free from danger. Through school and experience, Riker had become adept at the two basic techniques of handling such situations: survive until someone comes along to get you out, or extricate yourself.

"Why might someone capture you?" they'd asked green young cadets in Starfleet Academy lecture halls. A certain percentage of the galaxy consisted of nasty beings driven by nasty motivations. But a couple of centuries of alien contacts had demonstrated—sometimes with unfortunate results—that the precipitating factors in most conflicts were fear and misunderstanding. And the best method of dealing with fear and misunderstanding was communication.

At best, talking to your opponent could clear the path for mutual cooperation. At worst, it might enable you to find out just who was about to kill you, why they wanted to kill you, and how they planned to do it.

For Riker, the most frustrating aspect of captivity came when you tried to talk, and nobody heard. Or, if they heard, they didn't reply. This was one of those occasions.

During the hours since the shuttle had been sucked inside this giant vessel, repeated attempts to contact whatever life forms might be aboard had proven futile. So had the combined efforts of Data, Riker, Holzrichter, and Lopez to repair major shuttle systems. The higher-function circuitry of the on-board computers had been impressively scrambled by their lengthy exposure to the mysterious energy disturbance outside the big ship, and those systems were showing no signs of recovery now that they were inside.

Riker presided over a review of the repair status. The unanimous conclusion: grim.

"Maybe so," Riker said with forced cheer, "but we're alive and we're healthy. If whoever is running this show won't come to us, then it's time for us to go find them."

Holzrichter nodded eagerly. "I like that, sir. Maybe they'll take some notice if we stir up a little trouble."

"Careful what you volunteer for, Lieutenant," Riker said with a twinkle in his eye.

"I agree with Mr. Holzrichter," Navirra said. "We've been ignored long enough. It is high time we find out just how imprisoned we really are."

"My thoughts exactly, Ambassador," said Riker. "Data, I want you and Ensign Lopez to stay here with the ambassador. Keep trying to resuscitate shuttle systems. Holzrichter, you and I are going to find some chinks in their armor," he said, pointing his thumb outside the shuttlecraft.

Equipped with phasers, tricorders, lights, and a tool kit, Riker and Holzrichter climbed out into the dark hangar bay. They headed for a wall and examined it closely as they moved along.

"What are we looking for, Commander?"

"A way out. Or maybe a way in."

"In?"

"Into this ship. If we can't figure out how to escape, then I'd like to pop in and surprise the folks in charge."

"Sounds like a reasonable approach, sir," said Holzrichter. "I wasn't thrilled with the idea of spending my last days locked inside this cosmic closet."

Riker ran a hand over the smooth metal wall, sweeping his search light from the floor up to the ceiling fifty meters overhead, looking for anything resembling a hatch, a door, or a maintenance access panel. At the same time, Holzrichter panned his powerful beam slowly over the entire bay.

"Commander, what do you think this space was used for?"

"Probably a hangar deck. Look at this." Riker focused his lamp on a construction seam running from the base of the wall up into the gloom.

A moment later, the cavernous deck was filled with a bass vibration so deep and powerful that it felt like a quake and forced them to cover their ears. Then a harsh voice boomed out from everywhere at once.

"Prisoners, your time of judgment has passed. You have been sentenced, and the sentence will be carried out when we reach our destination."

As suddenly as they began, the voice and the throbbing bass tone were gone.

"Who are you?" Riker called up into the dark reaches of the hangar bay, trying to sound firm without being belligerent. "Why are we being held as prisoners?" He waited for a response. Nothing. "We are representatives of the United Federation of Planets. We are on a peaceful mission. We request further communication with you." Again, he waited, and again there was no response.

"I don't get it, sir," said Holzrichter.

Riker shrugged. "It could've been some kind of automated security warning. They don't seem overly concerned about us wandering around in here."

"Maybe they don't think we can get out."

"We'll see about *that,*" said Riker.

They moved on, and met with no interference at all as they continued their exploration. Finally, about midway along their second wall, they found what Riker was looking for—a grate—one that blended so gracefully into the wall that they nearly passed it by. It covered some sort of vent shaft, a shaft, Riker noted, that looked large enough for a man to crawl through.

Riker set his light down and took out a prying tool with a tapered edge. He wedged it under the seal surrounding the grate and pried. It didn't budge. He tried again, applying all his strength and finally the grate yielded. Holzrichter attacked the other side with a matching tool, and they had it off in no time.

They both retrieved their search lights and peered inside the tube-like shaft. Riker took a half-step up and touched the curved wall. "Some sort of molded material, like a plastic." Bending to a crouch, he stepped all the way into the tube and bounced gently to test its strength. The material had some give, but it made no alarming noises and rebounded to its original shape. "Seems like it'll support our weight. Ready for a little reconnaissance?"

"Yes, sir."

Riker touched his communicator. "Data. Can you see us?" He waved his light as a signal.

"Yes, Commander."

"We found what seems to be a ventilation shaft. We're going inside to see if it leads anywhere interesting. Can you track our communicator signals on the tricorder?"

"Yes, sir. But are you not concerned about the source of that brief announcement earlier?"

"Not especially. All they did was yell at us. They haven't made any attempt to stop what we've been doing."

"What if you should get into difficulty?"

"Then you're in command, my friend."

"And what shall I do?"

"Same thing we're doing now—improvise."

Data's head tilted as he pondered Riker's word of advice. He then fine-tuned the tricorder's reception of telemetry from Riker's open communicator.

"Have you ever, uhh, improvised before, sir?" asked Lopez.

Data thought for a moment. "I do not believe so. It seems I am not programmed for it."

Lopez nibbled her lip as she measured Data's statement. "Hmm. Improvisation is just . . . tap-dancing." She noticed his brow furrow in puzzlement as he glanced down at his own feet. "That's a figure of speech, sir," she added hastily.

"Ahh." With that hint, Data's pale eyes brightened. "Decision making without advanced analysis or planning. Spur of the moment. Ad-lib. The old soft-shoe?"

Lopez grinned and danced a quick shuffle-step.

Riker sneezed, and the sound reverberated inside the vent shaft with startling intensity. He scratched his nose with the back of his hand, a strategy that not only failed to relieve his nasal itch but in fact made it worse. The shaft was dirty and dusty, and he succeeded only in waving additional dust particles into his face. He sneezed again, then stifled a second sequel through sheer determination, and leaned against the grimy wall for a moment of recovery. Somewhere in the distance, he heard the sound of water dripping and felt as if he were in some ancient urban sewer.

"How far have we gone?"

Holzrichter checked his tricorder. "About a thousand meters, sir."

"Great," Riker said with a huff of annoyance. "For all we know, this tube goes from one end of this ship to the other without any outlet."

Holzrichter dropped from an uncomfortable crouch and rested on his knees, then aimed the tricorder ahead. "Interesting."

"What?"

"About thirty meters ahead, sir. The material of the shaft changes from this stuff to a metal alloy like the walls of that hangar deck area."

"Well, let's see if that means anything." With that goal in sight, Riker took the lead and picked up the pace.

"Uh-oh," said Ensign Lopez, staring at the tricorder.

Up in the cockpit, Data heard her and withdrew his head and arms from the shuttle's electronic innards. "Is something wrong, Ensign?"

"We just lost Commander Riker's signal."

Jean-Luc Picard strode from his ready room to the bridge turbolift and stepped inside. "Prefex Retthew's quarters," he said as the door slid shut. The pod accelerated smoothly.

Retthew had been through so much already on this

brief journey that Picard was reticent to confront him. But he had to have an answer to a question that had been festering ever since the *Enterprise* first arrived at Etolos: *Why was it so damned important for the Etolosans to move to a planet belonging to their ancestral enemies?*

The turbolift deposited him close by the VIP cabin. He'd asked Counselor Troi to meet him there and she was waiting. Picard pressed the door chime. A moment later, the door opened and they went inside.

Retthew sat motionless in an armchair. The lights glowed a restful blue, and classical music played softly in the background. Picard recognized the lilting melody. "Mozart's *Eine kleine Nachtmusik,*" he said.

"Please, sit down. Yes, I discovered him in your ship's music library. A man of breathtaking talent."

"Indeed," said Picard as he and Troi sat in chairs facing Retthew. "A child prodigy. Tragic, though. He died quite young."

"Since I'm not going to have a chance to listen to all his music during my stay on the *Enterprise,* would it be possible for me to obtain a copy of his works?"

"Certainly."

"I'll see to it, Captain," said Troi.

"Prefex," said Picard, "we are sorry to disturb you, but there is something I feel must be discussed."

"I'm at your service, Captain."

Picard noticed a tranquillity in the Etolosan's voice. *The peace of the just,* he wondered, *or of the condemned man?* "Thank you. Have you given any consideration to an alternative plan for your world?"

"Alternative?"

"Yes. If I were superstitious, I might conclude that your peace mission is jinxed. It is quite possible your worthy effort to settle old differences with Alaj will not be successful."

"Should that happen," Troi said, "your people will still need a new world on which to live."

"What are you both saying, then? That we should allow the Federation to move us someplace other than to Anarra?"

"At least consider the possibility," Picard said.

"Captain, Anarra is the nearest suitable planet. Your own surveys show that the next nearest uninhabited world with the proper climate is a hundred times farther away. Think how that would complicate the logistics that your own engineer already called nearly impossible."

Picard's posture stiffened. "If you and the Alajians cannot reach a mutually acceptable compromise—"

"We have no choice," said Retthew. "No other plan *requires* the settling of an ancient feud that split a civilization. This is about more than saving *my* world."

Picard grew wary. "It is?"

"Do you believe in destiny?"

"Many of our societies believe in a godforce," said Troi, "or some power of nature which created the universe. And some do believe in some form of fate, or destiny—"

"Or the guiding hand of one omnipotent God-Spirit?" asked Retthew with a passion they'd not seen in him before. "Well, I believe that all these unfortunate incidents have happened for a reason. Everything—from our volcanic disaster to Zeila's rise to power on Alaj, right down to your Ensign Crusher being there to stop Ozemmik from killing the nefittifi."

"And what is that reason?" Picard asked tentatively.

"In spite of all that happened, in spite of being banished centuries ago by the ancestors of today's

Alajians, *that* world is still our birthworld. It's the place from which we sprang."

"But you are not negotiating for possession of Alaj," said Picard.

"No," Retthew sighed. "That really is impossible."

Troi squinted slightly. "Then I am not sure I understand what you're saying."

"Let me offer a hypothetical situation. Say you'd each been banished from your homeworld. You couldn't return. How would you feel then if you found out that Earth was about to destroy itself, Captain? Or your world, Betazed, Counselor? Wouldn't you still feel something for the place which had given you birth?"

"I suppose we would," Picard admitted.

Troi's expression indicated agreement. "Your reason for all this, then—for insisting from the very start that you *had* to negotiate with Alaj—"

"Without us, the world of our origin is doomed . . . it will be scoured of life. We Etolosans are the only thing that can save Alaj. If we can't live there again ourselves, think how much it would mean to us to know that we preserved it. And if we and the Alajians can come to an agreement, someday we *might* be able to return to an Alaj restored by our love and work. Is it really so hard to understand why we must try for this special peace?"

"No," Picard said softly. "It is not hard to understand. But it may be hard to accomplish."

Riker and Holzrichter had discovered that the round ventilation tube fed into a slightly larger maintenance shaft. It was built solidly out of the metal alloy detected by Holzrichter's tricorder, and it tilted up at an incline steep enough that the hike would have been a tough one, except for a narrow floor strip of textured material providing passable traction. Like the outer vent tube, this shaft seemed to have fallen into disuse long ago, with wires, ductwork, and conduits sagging from their moorings and brackets.

"There's got to be a way out of this," Riker muttered.

They followed this new branch for another five hundred meters and found an access hatch which opened easily. Riker and the young security guard exchanged wary looks as the first officer poked his head through the opening for a quick glance. What he saw was an interior corridor, just as dark and empty and silent as every other place they'd been in this vessel.

Riker clambered through the hatch and Holzrichter followed. They shined their lights in both directions and found that the corridor seemed to extend without apparent end. Riker activated the voice channel of his communicator.

"This is Riker. Data—"

There was no reply. Holzrichter tried his and got the same result. "Sir, if we can't get through to them, then they've lost our signal, too."

Riker nodded. "We'd better get back and let them know we're all right."

"If they're still there," said Holzrichter grimly. "They may not be picking up our signal because—"

"No time for pessimism," Riker said, cutting him off.

Data sat quietly in the shuttle's pilot seat. Rachel Lopez paced nervously in the small aft compartment, finally irritating Navirra enough that the old diplomat spoke up: "Sit down, young lady, or pace outside."

"Sorry," Lopez said sheepishly. "I'm just worried

about Riker and Holzrichter. We should have heard from them by now. Commander Data, please let me go look for them."

"I do not think that is the sort of improvisation we should attempt. If something has happened to them, it would not be wise to risk losing another crew member. Nor is it wise for any one of us to search for them alone."

"Then what do you propose, sir, just sitting here?"

"For the time being."

Lopez flopped into an empty seat. "You were programmed for more patience than I was, Commander," she grumbled.

When they arrived at the junction with the original vent tube, Riker tried his communicator again. This time it worked and he heard Data's calm voice.

"We were concerned about you, Commander Riker."

"Must be something about the structure of this ship that blocks signals. But we found a way into the main part of the ship." He reconsidered the certitude of that conclusion. "At least we think it's the main part of the ship."

"Are you going farther inside, then?" asked Data.

"We will, but first we're coming back to the shuttle. I just wanted to let you know we were okay. We should be there in twenty minutes or so. Riker out."

Scuttling back through the dark vent tube, Riker and Holzrichter reached the open access grate and hopped out. Then they were halfway to the shuttle when the deck began shuddering and the same basso vibration as before filled the vast hangar bay. Then they heard the harsh voice: "Prisoners, the time of destiny approaches. When this vessel reaches the conclusion of its journey, so shall you."

"What destiny?" Riker shouted, with less concern for good manners than before. "What destination are you reaching?" He expected no reply and got none. With a diffident shrug, he and Holzrichter went on to the shuttlecraft.

Data opened the hatch and they climbed up and in. Once inside, Riker and Holzrichter could see by the cabin lights just how filthy they'd become, with smudges all over their uniforms and faces.

"We are mighty glad to see you two," said Lopez as she handed small towels to both of them. "You really gave us a scare."

"That wasn't our intent," said Riker, wiping his hands and face. "Besides, we knew *we* were fine. But we *didn't* know how you were. Anything interesting happen while we were gone?"

"Negative, sir," Data replied. "Nor were we able to restore any major systems."

"You heard both messages?" Riker asked.

The android nodded. "And felt them. Impressive volume."

"And yet that's all it was—loud enough to make us listen, but without any follow-through. I kept waiting for some being big enough to match that voice to come along and pick us up by the scruffs of our necks."

"Me, too, sir," said Holzrichter. "The last time I had that feeling, just waiting to get caught, was back at the Academy when we went on midnight raids—"

"Raids?" said Data, looking confused. "But Starfleet Academy is not a military institution."

Riker, Holzrichter, and Lopez—graduates all— traded smirks. "Uh, they weren't military raids, Data," Riker said.

"Oh. When we return to the *Enterprise,* will you explain these raids to me?"

"I suppose I could do that."

Lopez had a wicked glint in her eye. "I want to be there when you do, sir."

"Permission granted, Ensign. Perhaps you should do the explaining. I heard you were quite the midnight raider yourself."

"If the prize was cute enough," Lopez replied coyly.

"Mr. Riker, what did you find out here, other than grime?" asked Navirra, gesturing outside.

Riker gave a succinct report of their journey through the bowels of the big ship. "We've got no idea where that empty corridor might lead, but I think it's time we found out."

"Very odd," said the ambassador with a contemplative snort. "Here we are, supposedly prisoners, but no one stops you from creeping about this ship. And then you find no one aboard, and no signs that anyone's been about this section of the ship for Spirit knows how long."

"There's got to be *someone* aboard," said Lieutenant Holzrichter.

"Perhaps," Data said, "this portion of the vessel is simply not in use. With a ship as large as this one, that is possible. That may be why we have been confined here."

Riker leaned against the bulkhead. "A sort of quarantine. That voice mentioned a destiny, and the conclusion of a journey. Data, when we first encountered that energy field, you said it was on a rough course for Alaj."

"If you are going to ask whether that is still the case, I am afraid there is no way to be certain. In the time we have been inside this vessel, it could have changed direction and we would not know."

Riker nodded. "I realize that. But, just for argument's sake—"

Data cocked his head quizzically. "You wish to argue with me?"

"Figure of speech, Data. Say this ship didn't change course. Say it continued on the same heading at roughly the same speed. Can you estimate when it would reach Alaj?"

With a couple of blinks of his yellow eyes, Data made his calculations. "Within those parameters, and allowing a margin for error of approximately twelve percent, this vessel could be arriving at the Alajian system within the next two hours."

Riker's jaw tightened. "Then we've got that much time to find the people controlling this ship. If they *are* headed for Alaj, I've got a hunch they're not making a friendly visit."

His face clearly stamped him as one who had sprung from the same stock as the people of Etolos and Alaj, with the same prominent bone structure around the cheeks and brow, the short muzzlelike shape of the mouth and nose. But he was very, very old. His skin had the texture of mottled parchment, stretched so gauntly that he resembled a living skeleton. An unruly fringe of silver hair capped his severe countenance and spilled over his ears and collar.

He gripped a gold comb in his gnarled fingers and raked it obsessively through the beard extending down to the middle of his chest.

"Danid, don't you ever stop tending your facial hair?"

The question, in a snide tone, came from a disembodied voice, deep, expressive, and gender-neutral. Danid's eyes, nearly hidden under the folds of aged lids, blazed with quick anger. "Just because you don't have a beard—hell, you don't even have a *face,* damned Nole, damned, damned computer."

"For whom are you preening?" Nole taunted. Its voice echoed from all parts of the giant ship's control bridge. Danid never turned in any particular direction when conversing with it.

The old man's frail frame spun halfway around in the center of the otherwise empty bridge, his mouth gaping wide and filling the chamber with a burst of mirthless laughter. "For you, Nole! For you, my friend and companion!"

The laughter ended as abruptly as it began. Danid fell dizzily into a thronelike chair in the middle of the triangular bridge. There was a semicircular console in front of his seat, with other panels arrayed along all three walls—arrayed before empty crew seats. Unlike the parts of the ship Riker and his crew had explored, this chamber gleamed as if had been spit-shined moments earlier. Danid remained slumped in his chair, motionless, his eyes staring blankly.

"Danid."

The computer waited for a response. When Danid failed to answer, the computer's voice took on an anxious edge. "Danid, don't do this to me. Not now, not when we're so close."

The old man blinked out of his fog. "Worried I'll leave you alone?"

"Of course not," Nole huffed dismissively.

"Liar, liar, liar," Danid chanted.

"So I'm a liar. So what?"

"So admit that you don't want me to die."

"I admit it. Why do you like to humiliate me?"

Danid shrugged. "It's something we can do together, Nole."

The computer emitted a rude sound.

Danid wandered about the bridge, glancing at control panels and read-out screens. Then he turned to the large viewer displaying an outside image of star-strewn space. His eyes were drawn to a bright speck in the center. "Our home star, Nole."

"Yours, not mine," said the computer. "I've had no home star for two hundred years."

"Well, I have had none for *four* hundred years, fancy that."

"Your people, Danid. Not you. Can't your old brain grasp that distinction?"

"There is no distinction," Danid insisted. "Not any more. I *am* the Bekeem. Does that bother you?"

"Not at all. It's what you're planning to do that troubles me."

Danid waved his hands angrily. "Oh, no, you don't!" he screamed. "I've had my fill of your fits of ethical regret! There's nothing wrong with what I've planned."

"There is to me. It goes against everything I was created for."

"That is too damned bad," Danid retorted.

"I was created to nurture and protect—"

Danid clamped his hands over his ears. "I don't want to hear this anymore—"

Nole simply increased the volume of its voice. "—and you are asking me to help you destroy."

"You were also created to serve. You will serve me. I'm not asking you to be a party to destruction. I'm telling you to be a party to the deliverance of justice. And destruction is the justice they deserve."

"I don't want to discuss this anymore," Nole said. "Let's tend the garden."

Danid sighed. "All right. That always makes us both feel better." The old man hobbled toward a door that slid open when he reached it. He continued down a long corridor, then descended a tightly spiraled set of metal stairs, going down three levels. A short connecting corridor led to an arched entryway. Those doors slid aside and Danid stepped through into the garden deck.

To any newcomer, the scene would have been breathtaking—a vast domed cylinder, at least a kilometer across and several in length, with a clear latticework canopy vaulting high overhead, open to the stars. What the cylinder contained was at least as startling as the structure itself: a broad tract of hills and fields, a slice of countryside cruising through interstellar space.

Danid strolled down a gentle hillside path and soon reached a meticulously maintained plot, hoed into careful rows, with a variety of crops sprouting in lush columns.

"We've done fine work, Nole," said Danid with warm satisfaction. "You've given them just the right balance of sunlight and rain."

"Thank you," the computer said with a touch of pride, its voice echoed in the huge cylinder, sounding eerily like the voice of a god. "I have an evening shower scheduled now. Would you like me to postpone it?"

Danid shook his head. "Oh, no! Let it rain now. Let it rain on *me*," he said with the eagerness of a child. Turning his face up toward the stars, he spread his hands in anticipation. He felt the first drops, like kisses on his cheek. Then they came faster, rushing together until they ran down his face.

My land, Danid thought. *The only land, the only world I've ever known.* But he decided that it was much too late to get maudlin about his fate. He knew who was to blame, and he was on his way to deliver justice . . . long-delayed, but final.

Chapter Sixteen

IN THE SHUTTLE'S AFT CABIN, Riker gathered the equipment he wanted—extra search lamps, some tools, and two sturdy utility ropes—and stowed it all in an emergency pack, which he then slung over his shoulder. "Data, Lopez, you're with me. Holzrichter, you stay here and guard Ambassador Navirra and the ship."

The young security guard made no effort to hide his disappointment. "But, sir, I was hoping for another shot at—"

"I know you were. But this is where I need you. Both the ambassador and this shuttlecraft are extremely important."

"I won't embarrass us all by asking which is *more* important," Navirra interrupted with a droll smile. "Besides, Mr. Holzrichter, this gives us another chance at chess warfare."

"Stay on your toes," Riker warned. He opened the hatch, jumped down, and started across the broad deck. Data followed close behind. But when tiny Rachel Lopez clambered down and saw how huge the hangar bay was, she stopped and gaped.

"Wow," she said in an awed whisper. "This place is big enough for a three ring circus."

Riker looked back with a smile. "I hadn't thought of it in that way, but you're probably right."

"An unusual reference," Data observed.

"Not for me. I worked with a circus a couple of summers," Lopez explained as she trotted to catch up.

"So you must have an adventurous outlook on life," said Riker. "Are you ready to find out if the grass is greener on the other side of the hill?"

"Sir," Data said, "you did not say you had encountered grass and hills. Or is that another figure of speech?"

"It is," said Riker. "But on a ship this size, who knows?"

Jean-Luc Picard strode onto the bridge and circled to his command seat in the center of the lower level. Counselor Troi was in her usual place to his left. But the seat to his right, normally occupied by Riker, was conspicuously empty.

"Strange not to have Number One on the bridge," Picard murmured to Troi.

"Less than an hour to rendezvous," she said.

Picard glanced up at the tactical station over his shoulder. "Lieutenant Worf, hail the shuttlecraft, please."

"Yes, sir." The Klingon sent the comm signal, expecting a quick answer. "Captain, I am getting no response," he said with a glower of concern.

"Are we close enough for a long-range sensor scan?"

"Yes, sir."

"Make it so, Mr. Worf."

Worf nodded gravely and extended the starship's sensor sweep to its maximum reach. "A ship as small as the shuttle would not be detectable at this range, sir, but we are picking up no other unusual readings."

"Hmm." Picard leaned back in his seat, tugging at the hem of his uniform tunic. "Mr. Crusher, increase speed to warp five. Mr. Worf, continue long-range sensor scans and report anything of relevant interest the moment you see it."

A few minutes later, Worf looked up from his tactical console. "Captain, we are receiving a distress call from the shuttle. It is a recorded message."

The atmosphere on the bridge edged up a palpable notch in intensity. At such junctures, Picard always made a special effort to exude implacable calm. "Let us hear it, Lieutenant."

Riker's voice came over the speaker, nearly as calm as Picard's had just been. "To the *Enterprise,* or any other vessel within range. This is the Federation shuttlecraft *Onizuka,* en route from the Alajian system to the planet Etolos. We have been drawn off-course by an unidentifiable energy field. Please assist . . ."

And there the message ended.

"Mr. Worf, open a channel."

"Channel open, Captain."

"Enterprise to shuttlecraft *Onizuka.* Distress call received. Are you able to respond?" As Picard expected, there was no reply. He looked up at Worf. "Can you determine if that message actually came from the shuttlecraft?"

"Impossible to confirm, sir. The shuttle is not within sensor range."

"Was it actually Commander Riker's voice?" asked Troi.

"The computer verifies that," said Worf. "But there is something else, Captain. Computer analysis on the message as received indicates an abnormal frequency response curve—a variance of point-oh-two-five-three-five off the shuttle comm system norm."

Troi shifted her puzzled glance from Worf to Picard. "What does that mean?"

"It means," Picard said grimly, "that the message may very well have originated from Commander Riker and the shuttle, but the version we heard could possibly have come from an entirely different signal source."

"Someone else recorded Will's message and then played it back to us later?"

"That could be the case," Picard said, with the full realization that this scenario carried no good implications. The shuttlecraft and its passengers were in trouble. That was the only certainty. As to the how, when, where, and why of the shuttle's apparent disappearance, they were all questions that badly needed answers. But where to begin?

Worf contributed a starting point. "Something new on long-range sensors, Captain. An energy disturbance."

"Description."

"Difficult to get a definitive reading at this distance," said Worf, "but it seems to consist largely of ionized gases, similar to plasma . . . yet different. It is unlike any phenomena we've previously encountered."

"Is it a natural phenomenon?" Picard asked.

"Unknown, sir. But its location matches the point of origin of the shuttle distress call."

"Could the shuttle be inside it?" said Troi, her brow furrowed anxiously.

"That is a possibility we shall have to investigate," Picard said. "Mr. Worf, can you determine a heading for that energy disturbance?"

Worf nodded. "It appears to be on course for the Alajian system."

It didn't need to be said aloud, but everyone on the bridge knew the stakes had just gone up immeasurably. "Feed coordinates to Ensign Crusher," Picard ordered. "Ensign, set an intercept course. Bridge to engineering."

"Engineering—La Forge here, sir," Geordi said over the comm speaker.

"Warp seven, if you please, Mr. La Forge."

"Just give the word, Captain."

"Mr. Crusher, engage."

The starship surged ahead and Picard retreated to his ready room for some quiet thinking. He was caught in the middle of a diplomatic quandary of the most delicate kind, and he was now well aware that the Etolosans regarded their contact with ancestral enemies as some sort of holy imperative. If this new emergency caused a delay in arrival at Alaj, the Alajians might cancel negotiations altogether.

But this was no casual detour. The missing shuttle carried not only his first officer—the Federation representative who had mediated the initial round of talks—but also the Etolosans' most important ambassador. There was no choice but to divert the *Enterprise* for a search.

And, if Picard needed additional justification, there was one more ominous factor: if Riker's shuttlecraft had indeed vanished, it was quite possible that the force responsible might pose a threat to Alaj itself . . . to the *Enterprise* . . . and even to the Federation.

Safe at the core of his ship's protective field, Danid sat back in his bridge throne with a satisfied smirk on his muzzle. He tugged his gold comb through his beard and hummed tunelessly.

"Why did you do that?" his computer asked.

"Insurance."

"Against what?"

Danid clucked his tongue impatiently. "Interference."

"By what or whom? The initial distress call never got beyond our shield perimeter. No one could have heard it."

"But some ship called *Enterprise* was supposed to meet this shuttlecraft sometime and somewhere. If that other ship arrives and doesn't find it, they'll probably start searching."

"I understand," said Nole. "You sent out the recorded signal to draw this *Enterprise* to us . . ."

"—where it will be captured . . . or destroyed, before it can call on more help. One way or the other, it will *not* keep us from our holy task."

"This is really disgusting," Lopez griped as she slogged through the cramped ventilation tunnel behind Data and Riker. For once, being short was a blessing; while they had to stoop low, she could maintain near-normal posture.

"Don't tell me you also thought Starfleet service would be clean work," Riker said with a laugh. "If anybody had ever told me years ago that I'd get swallowed up by a living oil slick, or munch on Klingon gagh and Rokeg blood pie, I might have chosen another career."

"Would you really have, sir?" asked Data.

Riker shook his head. "Nahh."

"Neither would I," Lopez said. "I can't imagine doing anything else. How about you, Commander Data?"

"If I had an imagination, in the human sense, I do

not think I could imagine pursuing any other career either."

"You *do* have imagination," Riker said. "Ever since I've known you, I've seen you imagine what it would be like to be human. Every time you explore some new aspect of human behavior, that's exactly what you're doing—imagining."

Data considered that for a moment, and a pleased expression crossed his face. "I suppose that is correct, Commander. Do you recall the incident at Starbase 173, when Commander Maddox tried to force me to submit to disassembly?"

"Please, Data," Riker groaned, "I'd rather forget about that."

"Why?" said Lopez as they reached the metal access shaft angling up from the vent tube, and began climbing that branch. "They wanted to disassemble you, sir? How come I never heard about this?"

"It happened about a year before you joined the *Enterprise*," Riker said. Then he lapsed into silence.

"Well? Is somebody going to tell me about it?" Lopez prodded.

Riker finally gave in. "Oh, hell, I guess I will. Starfleet wanted to find out what makes Data tick—"

"Literally," Data added.

"Why?" Lopez asked.

"They wanted to be able to build more like him. The only trouble was, Data himself would not have existed anymore, not as the Data we already knew."

"What did you do?"

"I refused to cooperate," Data said softly. "Starfleet then ruled that since I was not human, I had no choice in the matter. So I resigned."

"Wow!"

Riker chuckled. "That sure shocked the hell out of everyone. There was one catch, though—Starfleet wouldn't *allow* him to resign. They considered him property, property that had no rights."

"Captain Picard would not accept that," Data recalled.

"This is a great story," said Lopez. "What happened then?"

"A hearing was convened," Data said, "to determine whether I could in fact be forced to submit to Starfleet experimentation."

"This is the part I'd rather forget," said Riker, ducking low as they crawled under a loose conduit sagging down.

"Why, sir?"

"Because," Data said, "Commander Riker was the prosecutor."

Lopez's jaw dropped. *"What?"*

The group entered an expanded section of the access shaft, the first place through which Riker and Data were able to pass in a crouch.

"I had no choice," Riker said apologetically, pausing to stretch the kinks out of his back. "There were no judicial officers present, so Captain Picard was appointed to defend Data and I had to argue Starfleet's side."

"You were an excellent prosecutor, sir," Data reminded him.

"Data, I almost got you dismantled."

"Yes, but had you not agreed to take part, there would have been no hearing and a summary judgment would have been handed down, comdemning me to positronic oblivion."

"So the Captain won the case?"

Riker let out a short, rueful laugh. "Bless his soul. Data, was there a point in torturing me with all that?"

"Yes, sir. We were discussing the process of imagining ourselves in other careers than Starfleet. At the time I tendered my resignation, I genuinely believed I would have to leave Starfleet in order to preserve my existence. Yet, I could not . . . imagine . . . any other function I would rather perform. That experience helped me define myself."

Before long, they'd reached the top of the inclined shaft and Riker shoved open the hatch. The three officers emerged into the corridor's eerie darkness and stood there for an uncertain moment.

"Well," said Riker, "does anybody have any good ideas about which way to go?"

"Eeeny, meeny, miney, moe?" Lopez suggested as she pointed in alternate directions.

Data gave her an inquisitive glance. "I am not familiar with that terminology."

"I'll explain it when we tell you about the midnight raids," Lopez said.

For no particular reason, Riker chose a direction and the others fell into step behind his lantern beam. "We better find something soon that gives us a hint about where we're going. We don't have the time to wander aimlessly. Phasers on stun. Stay close, and stay sharp."

Captain's Log, Supplemental:
The *Enterprise* is approaching the edge of the energy field, which is starting to affect the function of ship's sensors. Readings are becoming increasingly unreliable. Our repeated attempts to communicate with the missing shuttle—or any other vessel that might be inside the field—have been unsuccessful.

Picard convened a staff strategy session in the conference lounge, with Engineer La Forge, Security Chief Worf, Dr. Crusher, and Counselor Troi in attendance.

"I have a grave decision to make," said the captain, his clasped hands resting on the table. "Do we have sufficient reason to believe that this energy disturbance did indeed have something to do with the disappearance of the shuttlecraft? And does it represent a threat to Alaj? Opinions?"

Geordi La Forge spoke first. "Granted, the evidence is circumstantial, sir. But I don't think it's just coincidence that Commander Riker's distress call came from the same coordinates as the energy disturbance."

Worf nodded. "In addition, Captain, Alaj is a Federation member. We are bound by oath to protect it."

"And do you believe this energy field to be a threat, Lieutenant?"

"I do, sir."

"Guilty until proven innocent?" Troi challenged.

"I agree with Deanna," Beverly Crusher said. "It hasn't done anything hostile."

"The shuttle may be trapped within it," Worf rumbled.

"We don't know that," said Troi. "And even if it is, we don't know the condition of the ship or its passengers. They could be fine."

"That may be true," Picard said, "but the fact remains that this disturbance has the power to affect the function of this vessel. Even if those effects are unintentional, that power in itself constitutes a threat to the *Enterprise,* and potentially to Alaj as well."

"I still do not think that warrants an aggressive stance on our part," Deanna said, with a pointed glance at Worf.

"Agreed," said Picard. "But it does warrant the strongest possible defensive posture if we are to explore inside that energy field."

Dr. Crusher plainly did not like the sound of that. "Inside it, Captain?"

"I believe we have little choice. It is up to us to ascertain just what this thing is and whether it threatens Alaj or other worlds. If Alaj is indeed its destination, then we still have some time to analyze it and take action to stop it, if we decide such action is called for. But if we merely retreat in front of it, observing from a distance, we may find out nothing. And we will certainly run out of both time and options. Counselor, have you received any impressions at all since we've been in its vicinity?"

"No, sir. All I get is a sort of background buzzing. It is possible my senses are being affected by the energy field itself."

"I see. Mr. La Forge, divert all nonessential power to the shields. Afford us as much protection as you can. Mr. Worf, maintain yellow alert status. We are taking the *Enterprise* inside this thing, whatever it is."

"This is spooky," Rachel Lopez whispered as she entered the vacant chamber, with Riker and Data just behind. Their three beams of light swept the musty space, revealing some simple tables, chairs and double-deck bunks. "This reminds me of poking around haunted houses when I was a kid."

Data's eyebrows went up. "Haunted? Habitation by spirits of the dead? I thought humans generally did not believe in such things."

"Sir, kids aren't humans," Lopez said with an impish smile. "Just ask their parents."

"So human children believe in ghosts?"

"Not exactly," Lopez said. "Sometimes they like to pretend they believe just so they can do things like explore haunted houses."

"Is there a purpose to this activity?"

"A purpose? Not really. Sometimes it's just fun to be scared," said Lopez.

"It is?"

"It was for me," she reminisced. "I was always the smallest kid, so they'd throw me in first. They thought I'd be terrified, but I loved it. It was so exciting, not knowing what things might go bump in the night."

"Hmm. Intriguing," Data said. Then he turned to give his full attention to the open space before them. "Judging by the furnishings, whatever passengers once traveled in this ship must have been humanoid."

"But where are they?" Riker wondered. "And how long have they been gone?"

Lopez wiped one finger along a tabletop, tracing a trail through a heavy layer of dust. "We haven't seen a single hint that anybody's been here in years . . . maybe not *ever*. Really spooky."

They resumed their careful exploration of the giant vessel, continuing down the long corridor until they found another open hatchway. Riker leaned in with his light and peered up a narrow access tube with a ladder bolted to the wall. "It seems we can't get down from here."

"Maybe there is no down," said Lopez. "Maybe this is the bottom of the ship. And don't most ships have their command decks up top?"

Riker nodded. "I can't recall one that didn't. Data, scan your records of interstellar ship design."

Data's chin tilted slightly as he checked through his memory core. "I have no record of an interstellar design with a bridge or command center on its lower levels. However, my file on this subject includes only those designs known to the Federation. Therefore, we cannot draw an unimpeachable conclusion that *no* interstellar vessel has ever—"

Riker raised a hand to stop him. "I'm willing to play a hunch that this ship is not the exception. I'd say we've got no place to go but up."

Riker took the lead, glad to find that the rungs were nonskid and deep enough for Starfleet boot-toes, and that the handrails had finger grips grooved into them. Data waited until Riker had gone up a couple of meters, then followed. Lopez waited in turn, listening to the creaking of ancient metal straining under their weight. The sound did not please her, but she noted that the ladder was built in sections. If the climbers left enough space between them, the stress on any one section shouldn't be too extreme. And if those old ladder sections could hold a big man like Riker and an android, Lopez reasoned, her one hundred pounds shouldn't make the difference.

That reasoning held for five decks. At each one, Riker stayed on the ladder and poked his head out. Each deck looked as deserted as the first one they'd explored at length. Each time, he chose to forge ahead.

When Lopez reached the fifth deck, with Riker two decks ahead of her and Data one above, she leaned into the open hatchway and then continued the climb. She'd nearly reached the next access hatch when she heard the singular sound of fatally fatigued metal giving way.

Faster than she could react, the ladder section she was on tore away from the wall like a piece of tape peeled off by an unseen hand. She and the ladder teetered backward. From somewhere in the darkness above, she heard Riker call her name.

For just a heartbeat, the three-meter ladder section

seemed frozen in mid-air, top mountings detached, bottom half still holding. In that instant, her eyes darted in a frantic search for something to grab on to.

The next highest section was out of reach—

—the wall behind her was slick metal with no handholds—

—the access hatch to the next deck was closest, but she couldn't reach it without leaping—

—and she couldn't leap without pushing *off* something. The swaying ladder section she clung to was the only candidate for springboard, *if* those bottom mountings would just hold—

Lopez braced, her leg muscles coiled—

—and the mounting bolts below sheared away. With a short scream, she and the ladder section fell. . . .

Chapter Seventeen

TWISTING HER BODY IN MID-FALL, Rachel Lopez made a grab for life.

As she flashed by one of the hatch openings in the wall of the access shaft, her fingers hooked over the hatchway's bottom rim, wrenching her shoulders with a force that made her yelp in pain. But her grip held, breaking her fall.

Two light beams played across her as she hung there, trying to catch her breath. Every muscle in her back screamed.

"Lopez!" Riker shouted. "Are you all right?"

She managed an affirmative grunt, then mustered the strength to pull herself up over the hatch sill. Pain exploded through her shoulders and arms, and she blinked back tears welling in her eyes. *Couple of inches more, Rachel . . . couple of inches more . . .*

Riker called down again. "Can you make it?"

Struggling, she got her stomach as high as the threshold, then shifted her weight and toppled through the opening and out onto the deck. She let her head fall back against the sill.

"Made it," she called back feebly. It was too dark to

see, but she could feel soreness spreading through her arms and back.

"We'll come back to get you," Riker said.

"No!" Lopez got to her knees, letting her arms hang loose in the position that caused the least pain. "Both of you get off that ladder, Commander. If one section broke away—"

"Okay," said Riker. "We're getting out on the seventh deck. We'll drop a rope down and pull you up."

"Okay."

Lopez wiped stray tears off her face and willed her heaving lungs and racing heart back to normal. She listened to the scuffling of feet from the shaft, then heard the rope bounce off the metal wall as it dropped toward her, dangling in the open hatch.

"Just loop it under your arms," Riker yelled down. "Don't climb. Let us do the work."

She did as he instructed, then stopped at the opening. She took a deep breath and poised with one foot up on the sill.

"Commander Riker, I'm ready."

She wrapped her less-damaged left hand around the rope, felt a tug, and surrendered. Using her feet to keep from slamming into the shaft wall again as they hauled her up, she realized with a queasy twitch of her stomach that she'd fallen farther than she'd thought —not one but *two* decks before she'd caught herself.

The hands that reached out to her were cool to the touch—Data's hands. She felt herself being lifted through the deck-seven hatch as if she weighed no more than a doll.

Data set her down on her feet. "Are you all right, Ensign?"

Lopez nodded wryly. "Nothing a week in sickbay wouldn't cure."

"That circus work you mentioned," said Riker, "what was it?"

"Mostly trapeze, sir. My introduction to free-fall."

"At least you weren't scared of heights."

"Actually, I *was,* before the circus training," Lopez said as she slipped free of the rope. "That was one of the reasons I took up acrobatics. Pretty crazy, huh?"

"Not after today. If we ever get back to the *Enterprise,* maybe you can give us a proper demonstration. For now, though, I suggest we try finding an alternate route through this ship."

Lopez blew out a relieved breath. "Amen to that, sir."

For the starship *Enterprise,* there was only one route—deeper into the baffling energy disturbance. Geordi La Forge, at his engineering station on the outer ring of the bridge, devoted all his attention and considerable skills to maintaining the deflector shields wrapping the ship in their protective cloak— one form of carefully modulated energy keeping another, unexplained form at bay.

Chief engineers had to be practical by nature, able to take the most arcane concepts and crystallize them into some useful shape. Not one in a hundred could do that job as well as La Forge. But the best engineers were much more than nuts-and-bolts fix-it wizards; they also possessed insatiable curiosity about phenomena that stubbornly defied explanation.

Even when those phenomena might be deadly.

So, even as he monitored the *Enterprise* shields, making hair's-breadth adjustments with a deft touch, one corner of Geordi's mind couldn't help wondering about the energy dancing around the big starship. He couldn't dispel the urge to reach out and hold it in his hand, and he couldn't wait to unravel all its secrets.

But his theoretical musings were bumped aside by the sudden flickering of lights on the bridge and the red-alert klaxon. The *Enterprise* shuddered, pitching to starboard as its automatic guidance systems were abruptly interrupted.

Picard gripped the armrest of his seat. "What's going on, Mr. La Forge?"

Geordi's practiced hands were already skipping across his console keypad. "Primary computer malfunction, Captain. Scattered system failures. Backups should be on-line now . . ." His voice trailed off.

But the bridge lights remained low, and most computer screens remained dark.

"Damn," Geordi swore under his breath.

Picard rose from his seat and turned to face Geordi's station. "Is the malfunction due to the energy field?"

"Affirmative, Captain." Geordi's display hopped from one circuitry chart to another as he searched for a way to restore vital computer operations. "Give me a minute here, sir."

"Captain," Ensign Crusher reported from his helm console, "the *Enterprise* is maintaining its course. Whatever . . . wh . . ." Wesley's voice faltered, his eyelids fluttered, and he flopped to the deck in a dead faint.

Picard started forward. "Ensign . . ." Then his own knees turned rubbery and he staggered.

Counselor Troi jumped up to steady him, helping him back to his seat. She and the officer at the Ops console knelt down to tend the crumpled Ensign Crusher.

Picard took a half-dozen deep breaths to clear the fog that had so suddenly shrouded his brain.

"Captain," Worf said from behind him, "are you all right?"

Picard nodded. "Quite, Lieutenant."

"Similar incidents are being reported in other parts of the ship," the Klingon said.

The captain smoothed his uniform tunic. "Bridge to Dr. Crusher." He expected the usual near-instant reply, then scowled when he heard nothing. "Bridge to Dr. Crusher."

Instead of Beverly's voice, the computer said pleasantly: "Sickbay comm circuit temporarily overloaded. Unable to reroute due to computer system malfunction."

Picard sat up stiffly. "What the devil—"

Beverly Crusher stood in the center of chaos. She and her staff had unconscious crew members on seven sickbay beds and diagnostic tables, and she was on her fifth consecutive intercom call.

"—we'll have someone up there as soon as we can. Or bring him down here yourself. Crusher out." No sooner had that conversation ended than another plea for aid took its place. "Somebody take that call," Crusher snapped. "I've got patients to see."

But before Beverly could take a step, the door from the corridor slid open and she couldn't help laughing at what she saw there. Lieutenant White, a petite young woman with a dusting of freckles across her nose, and a tall, sandy-haired ensign named Ryan were holding up a limp officer with chocolate syrup and ice cream all over his face and dripping down his uniform.

"What happened to him?" Beverly said, trying to restore a proper expression of medical decorum.

White rolled her eyes. "We were in Ten-Forward. Ensign Chafin fainted into his chocolate sundae."

"When he wakes up, I'll have to thank him for the comic relief," Crusher said. She thumbed them toward an adjoining ward. "Put him in there, if you can find an unoccupied bed."

Ensign Ryan paused at the door. "There are more where he came from."

"Tell me about it."

Captain Picard's irate voice came over the intercom speaker. "Picard to Dr. Crusher."

"Crusher here, Captain."

"There you are. Do you have any idea what the devil is happening to us?"

"Not specifically, but we've reports of at least fifty crew members fainting—mostly in sections of the ship closest to the outer hull."

"Wesley was one of them," Picard said, "but he seems fine now. Shall I send him to sickbay for examination?"

"As a mother I'd say yes. But as chief medical officer—" She took a deep breath. "Jean-Luc, we're booked solid down here. If Wesley is on his feet, he can come for a check-up when his shift is over. Just keep an eye on him for any residual effects, and that goes for anybody else who might have been affected."

"Very well, Doctor. Do you have any idea what's causing this?"

"I was going to ask you the same thing. I haven't had a chance to isolate anything specific. But it probably has something to do with this energy field we're in."

"As soon as you have any details to report, do so. Picard out."

* * *

Back on the bridge, Wesley seemed relieved to be able to remain at his post. Picard looked back at Geordi.

"Mr. La Forge—"

The captain was interrupted by the unannounced resumption of the normal bridge illumination, and Geordi huffed a breath of satisfaction. "Primary computers back up, Captain—temporarily at least."

"Temporarily?"

"I've recalibrated shield harmonics, and that seems to be doing the trick for now. If our shields go down, I'm afraid we'll have a lot more than fifty people fainting. As we suspected, the computer problems were caused by the unpredictable effects of the energy disturbance outside the ship. And unpredictable is the key word, sir."

"Can we buy ourselves any additional protection?"

"We can try—but it'll cost."

Picard's jaw tightened. "What cost?"

"All nonessential power—and I mean *all*—would have to be rechanneled to the shields. Even weapons."

"Captain," Worf quickly protested, "I do not consider weapons to be nonessential."

"If there is a vessel of some kind hidden within this energy field, it is probable that it could have destroyed us by now had it chosen to do so. Whatever we are about to encounter, I believe our shields are more important than our weapons."

Worf glowered in frustration. "Captain—"

Picard raised a placating hand. "That assessment is not carved in stone. If the danger to the *Enterprise* becomes imminent, power will be restored to weapons systems. Mr. La Forge, rechannel power at your discretion."

With a nod, Geordi ducked into the turbolift and headed for Engineering.

Their pace brisk yet vigilant, Riker, Data, and Lopez moved down another long, dark, and empty corridor inside the giant ship.

"We might as well be on a strange planet without a map," Lopez muttered.

"Frustrated?" Riker asked lightly.

"Aren't you, sir?"

He nodded. "A map would come in handy. So would a faster means of transportation than foot-power."

Divorced from the conversation, Data scanned intently ahead with his tricorder as they rounded a corner. "Hmm."

"Something interesting, Data?" said Riker.

"Yes, sir. The first indication of active power consumption since we began our exploration."

"What is it?"

"Unknown."

"Where is it?"

The android gestured ahead with his chin. "One hundred and fifty meters, straight ahead."

With long quick strides, Riker led the way. Several seconds later, they arrived at an open door and shone their lights into a small room, barely more than a booth. There they saw a console and bench built into the wall, with a computer terminal glowing softly.

"It appears to be some sort of work station," said Data.

Riker gave it a close examination. "The question is, can you make it work?"

"I can try."

*　*　*

Sitting at his ready-room desk, Picard stared out the small viewing port. There wasn't much to see, actually. It was as if the *Enterprise* were drifting through an endless bank of energized fog. Ever since he'd ordered his ship into the energy field, they'd been flying, if not completely blind, with vision substantially obscured. Sensors were unreliable at best, useless at worst. And the viewscreen displayed images shredded by irregular bursts of static, even less satisfactory than those visible to the unaided eye. During a particularly active assault by the roiling tides of energy outside the starship, the flickering of the viewer had become annoying enough that Picard had ordered it shut off.

What was this energy cloud? And would they really find anything inside it? His ruminations were interrupted by the door chime.

"Come," he said without turning away from the window.

"It is an interesting mystery," said Deanna Troi.

He swiveled in his seat and looked at her, finding some comfort in her strong, warm gaze. "Indeed it is. But I can't help wondering if taking the *Enterprise* inside it was a foolish risk. You know, I've always had a fondness for mysteries. Or should I call it a weakness?"

Troi perched on the corner of his desk. "Why would you call it a weakness?"

"Intellectually, I am well aware that this trait is part of what makes me a successful starship captain. But emotionally, I am also well aware that it is that same trait which has placed the *Enterprise* and her crew in jeopardy."

Troi smiled. "Do you want me to remind you that you had valid reasons for choosing this course?"

"Not really. Enough of my soul searching. Something on your mind, Counselor?"

Troi retreated to the couch across the small office. "Speaking of soul searching, I just came from Retthew's cabin. He is deeply concerned about the delay in getting to Alaj, and he is afraid that his mission will fail."

Picard rubbed his eyes and sighed. "Counselor, I am—"

He swallowed the rest of that thought when a shudder went through the ship and the lights dimmed, prompting a red-alert. Bolting to his feet, he strode to the door. Just as he reached it, his knees buckled and he caught himself with a hand on the door frame. Troi lent a supportive arm as the wave of dizziness spun through his head and swirled through his stomach. He swayed for a moment, then fought off the wave of vertigo and straightened up.

"Captain—"

"I'm all right."

"Are you sure?"

His eyes twinkled with a touch of black irony. "If I faint on the bridge, we'll know I was incorrect."

With that, he moved to the door. It slid open and Troi followed him out on the bridge. Three of the crew had fainted at their posts, including Wesley. Other duty officers had taken their places, while others tended the affected personnel.

"Captain," said Worf from his tactical console, "Engineering reports partial degeneration of deflector shields. Sickbay reports widespread collapses among the crew."

Picard acknowledged the Klingon's update with a nod and took his seat in the center of the bridge. "Bridge to Engineering."

"La Forge here, sir. We've got more computer malfunctions, and we've lost fifty-eight percent of shield capability."

"Can you compensate?"

"You know I hate to say no, Captain. But there's no more surplus power to rechannel."

"I think it's time we viewed this energy field from a less threatening distance."

"No arguments here, Captain," Geordi said.

"Can you restore helm and navigation, Mr. La Forge?"

"If it's possible, we'll do it, sir."

"Good. Keep me informed. Picard out."

"Captain," Troi called out, "look."

Everyone on the bridge followed Troi's gaze as the viewscreen showed sudden changes outside the ship. The visual signal grew more distinct, as the energy field coiled in on itself and rolled away from the *Enterprise.*

"Captain," said Worf, staring at his sensor readouts, "the energy field is retreating. Shields back up to eighty-three percent."

The bridge lights also resumed normal levels.

"Engineering to Captain Picard," said Geordi's voice over the speaker. "I had nothing to do with it, but helm and navigation functions have returned to normal, sir. Other computer systems are still down."

Picard watched in fascination as the energy field dispersed like storm clouds in the path of a strong wind, dwindling down to a pinpoint. He glanced at Lieutenant White, who'd taken Wesley Crusher's place at the conn post. "Lieutenant, is the helm responding?"

"Aye, sir."

"Then take us ahead, one-half impulse."

"Course, sir?"

"Close in on the center of that field. I have a feeling we're about to find out what's been lurking inside."

208

Chapter Eighteen

"WELL?" Riker stood with hands on hips, looking over Data's shoulder as the android made his fourth attempt to tap into the dormant computer station.

"There is evidence of widespread malfunction within this system, sir," Data explained.

"As if nobody's used it in a long time?"

"Precisely."

"But it *is* operative?"

"Marginally."

"This is really spooky," Lopez muttered, peeking around Riker so she could see what Data was doing.

Riker leaned close over Data's shoulder. "We don't have a lot of time to waste. Give me your best judgment, Data—is this terminal of any use to us?"

"That is a difficult judgment to make, sir. We have no way of knowing if this system is damaged beyond any utility. If, however, it is functional, it may give us entry to important records and information on this vessel."

"Okay. Keep trying."

Moments after Riker's lukewarm vote of confidence, the work station screen roused from its indeterminate slumber with a jumble of words, figures, and charts. It didn't take long for Riker to realize that only Data could possibly make sense of what they were seeing.

With blinding speed and unerring grace, Data's slender fingers danced across the keypad, enabling him to establish some semblance of control over the information flow. Finally, the screen sputtered and the system lapsed back into the catatonic state in which they'd first found it.

"So much for that," said Lopez. "I feel like we should have a funeral service for it."

"Data," Riker said, "what was all that? Is this station part of the main computer running this ship?"

"Originally, perhaps. But it is not functioning in that capacity now, sir. It offers access to only a limited memory and is in a state of obvious disrepair."

"Was anything comprehensible to you?"

"Some of the information was. The language has roots strikingly similar to the contemporary language common to both Etolos and Alaj, though with significant differences."

"Hmm. Were you able to find out anything about who built this ship and where it came from?"

"There were no such specifics. But I did see some technical information and partial diagrams of its interior, leading me to conclude that this vessel was intended for long-term occupancy and not merely transport."

Riker squinted quizzically. "What do you mean by long-term occupancy? The *Enterprise* is built for that."

"I would venture to say that whatever beings built this ship meant for it to have the potential to serve as a home indefinitely. Perhaps permanently, and to a far larger group."

"Which leads to the obvious question," Riker said. "Is anybody home?"

"That is impossible to determine from this work station. But we are on the correct route to the command center."

"How far away are we?"

"Based on the charts I saw, approximately thirty decks."

"Oh, great," Lopez moaned.

"However, there is an intraship network of transport pods similar to our turbolifts."

Riker clapped his hands together. "Now *that,* my friend, is useful information. Did you get enough information for us to find these transport lifts?"

"I believe so."

"Then lead the way."

The message was the same one they'd heard earlier: Riker's voice called from the bridge speakers, "To the *Enterprise* or any other vessel within range. This is the Federation shuttlecraft *Onizuka,* en route from the Alajian system to the planet Etolos. We have been drawn off-course by an unidentifiable energy field. Please assist."

When the repeat of the distress call came in, Picard, Troi, and Retthew had been meeting in the captain's ready room, discussing Retthew's deepening fears about the fate of his peace initiative. At Worf's summons, they moved to the bridge, Retthew remaining to one side as Picard and Troi took their seats.

This time, the message drew no discernible reaction from Picard or anyone else. The captain looked over his shoulder at Worf.

"The same recording as before, Lieutenant?"

"Yes, sir."

"Point of origin?"

"Within the energy disturbance."

That was exactly what Picard expected to hear. "I want to get as close as possible without subjecting the *Enterprise* to the same systems disruptions we've just weathered. Maintain approach course and speed until the first indication of interference."

As the *Enterprise* moved closer, the energy field once again began to grow larger on the viewscreen. Worf confirmed that the still-unexplained disturbance had stopped contracting. Picard leaned forward in anticipation, his elbows resting on his knees.

Finally, the secret at the heart of the energy cloud revealed itself.

"Captain," Troi began.

"I see it, Counselor."

A ship. The energy field surrounded it, a diaphanous cloak of power, now drawn tightly around its source.

"That," said Picard, "is one of the largest vessels I have ever seen."

Worf's rapid calculations pinned some specifics to Picard's observation. The other ship was fifteen to twenty times the size of the *Enterprise* in length, width, and height. Based on its sectional construction, with modules of various sizes and shapes linked assymmetrically by structural tubes and girders, Worf estimated its interior volume to be about *two thousand times* as large as the Galaxy-class starship *Enterprise,* the largest vessel in Starfleet, the pride of the Federation.

The *Enterprise,* now reduced to the relative dimensions of a gnat.

Worf concluded his report by saying, "Captain, request restoration of full power to weapons."

His attention still drawn to the viewscreen, Picard nodded coolly. "That would seem prudent, but maintain yellow alert, weapons on standby."

"Aye, sir. On standby," said Worf.

Now the captain leaned back in his seat, his expression thoughtful. "Counselor, any impressions?"

"Nothing, Captain. I suspect that energy field is still interfering with my ability to pick up anything empathically."

"Any suggestions?"

"Make contact with whomever might be aboard that vessel."

"Agreed. Lieutenant, open hailing frequencies."

"Hailing frequencies open," Worf advised.

"To unidentified vessel: this is Captain Jean-Luc Picard of the U.S.S. *Enterprise,* representing the United Federation of Planets. We request communications contact. Please respond."

Picard waited a few moments, then began to repeat his message. "This is the U.S.S. *Enterprise,* Captain Jean-Luc Picard in command. We represent the United Federation of Planets. We—"

A shriek of audio feedback filled the bridge, forcing hands over ears in a spasm of protective reaction. After a few seconds, a harsh voice replaced the painful sound.

"Enterprise . . . Picard . . . I am Danid, Supreme Primary of the Holy Bekeem."

No one noticed, but a frown creased Troi's face and she turned anxiously, first one way, then the other. She felt a wave of distress and disbelief from someone close to her. It took Troi a moment to isolate the agitated emotions—they were coming from Retthew. The prefex gaped at the ship still on the viewscreen.

"Spirit save our souls," he whispered to himself as the strident voice thundered on.

213

"I caution you to heed this warning. It will be given only once. Do not interfere with us or our holy purpose."

"We are not familiar with you or your customs," Picard said mildly. "So that we may give you all due respect, what is your preferred form of address?"

"You may call me Holiness."

"Very well, Holiness. Are you holding our missing shuttlecraft?"

"Unimportant."

"Not to us, Holiness," Picard replied, his tone balanced, unperturbed yet business-like. "The people on board that ship are our friends and we are concerned for their safety. Are they in your protective custody?"

"They are prisoners until after we have dealt with the people of Alaj."

"Dealt with Alaj? In what way?"

"The Bekeem have returned to settle an ancient score, Picard. The people of Alaj will be driven from their world—or they will die. We warn you . . ."

"That is twice," Worf muttered under his breath.

". . . do not interfere in a matter that is none of your concern."

"But it is our concern," Picard said, his voice growing stern. "Alaj is a member of the United Federation of Planets. By treaty, the *Enterprise* will come to the Alajians' aid if their planet is endangered."

A bray of fevered laughter sang from the speakers, prompting an exchange of bemused looks around the bridge. The laughter ceased as abruptly as it began and Danid's voice turned brittle. "What is this Federation you keep prattling about? Never mind—I don't care. You have seen what our ship can do, Picard. The might of the Bekeem will crush any opposition. That should be obvious. Do you have a brain?"

Picard glowered. "Yes, we have brains."

"I suppose you do, since you obviously possess enough rudimentary intelligence to build ships, however insignificant they may be. Do you have enough intelligence to recognize a force greater than yourselves?"

"We have the intelligence to recognize the value of settling differences through communication, negotiation, and mutual understanding. Perhaps your grievance with the Alajians—"

"Grievance? *Grievance!?* How dare you trivialize our holy vengeance!"

"That was not my intent, Holiness. Forgive my choice of words."

"Forgiven," came the haughty reply, snapped off as if by an impatient monarch.

"We are interested in learning more about the Bekeem—"

"Well, we're not interested in you, Picard. You have been warned."

Before Picard could say another word, Worf announced that the Bekeem ship had closed its reception channel, though it was holding its position. The captain scowled in annoyance. "Observations, Counselor?"

Troi glanced over her shoulder at Retthew, standing ashen at the railing near Worf's tactical console. "I believe Prefex Retthew has something to contribute."

Picard rose from the command chair. "Is that true, Prefex?"

The Etolosan leader nodded weakly. "I suppose so, Captain."

"Do you know this Supreme Primary?"

"No. No, I don't. But I do know something about the Bekeem."

Picard crossed his arms expectantly. "What about them?"

"They were the first dissident group ever banished from Alaj."

"How long before your ancestors' banishment?"

"A hundred and fifty years. But no one knew there were any Bekeem still left."

"Obviously, there are," Picard said dryly. "I think you had better tell us everything you know about the Bekeem, Prefex."

"Captain, my knowledge is hazy at best. All I can tell you is what I've read in books on Alajian history. Remember, Alajian history is not my own."

He took a breath and collected his thoughts. "Hmm. Where to begin. Well, as I understand it, the Bekeem were a strict religious order. I guess they could be called fanatics."

"What were they fanatical about?" asked Troi.

"They didn't believe that our Spirit handed down wisdom directly."

"You mean through the nefittifi?" Picard said.

"Not by any means, Captain. The Bekeem believed that wisdom was intended to be a challenge, strewn by the Creator throughout the Universe, and the only way that wisdom could be learned was to search for it."

Troi's eyes widened. "Everywhere?"

"Everywhere. The Bekeem were totally dedicated to that quest and they were furious that the Alajian government refused to pour all the planet's wealth and resources into this never-ending search for ultimate wisdom."

Picard rubbed his chin pensively. "Hmm. Based on

what we know about Alajian society, the Bekeem would certainly represent diametric opposition."

"Quite right, Captain," Retthew agreed. "The Bekeem attempted the violent overthrow of the government, and the government met violence with violence. It was open warfare. The Bekeem movement was crushed quickly, many of the leaders captured and summarily executed . . . followers rounded up and locked in camps. There were some mock trials and, of course, the accused were convicted. Some were offered pardons if they'd publicly repudiate their beliefs. A few did. Many others committed suicide and became martyrs, prompting a wave of suicides in the camps." Retthew shuddered at the stark images conjured by his words.

"Is that when the government decided upon banishment?" asked Picard.

Retthew nodded. "They thought it was the best way to stop the bloodletting and still clean up the problem. So they provided a ship and supplies and sent the surviving Bekeem on their way. The same method they used with our ancestors in Totality more than a century later."

"Prefex," said Troi, "what did the Bekeem set out to do?"

He shrugged. "To search for that elusive wisdom. And I suppose to found their own theocratic world— or impose their beliefs on some other world."

"Did they succeed?"

"No one ever really knew. Stories would come back through the centuries. Some said that they had settled on one world or another, while others said that they were doomed to wander."

"Computer," Picard said, "is there any record of Federation contact with the Bekeem or any group fitting their history and description?"

"Negative," the computer replied. "No known species match those search parameters."

"It is a big galaxy," Worf noted. "And that ship is not imaginary."

"No, it is not," said Picard. "It proves the Bekeem did indeed survive and may have prospered."

Retthew came down the ramp and stepped up to Picard. "What are you going to do, Captain? You can't let them destroy Alaj."

"Mr. Worf, is the Bekeem vessel still holding its position?"

"Yes, Captain."

"Helm, maintain our position relative to theirs. If they move, we move."

Picard convened a staff briefing in the bridge conference lounge, with Troi, Worf, La Forge, Dr. Crusher, and Retthew attending.

"Prefex Retthew is correct. We cannot allow the Bekeem to destroy Alaj, no matter what their ancient grudge may be," Picard said simply.

"If that's what the Bekeem decide to do," Beverly interjected, "is there anything we can do to stop them?"

"Mr. Worf, Mr. La Forge, find an answer to Dr. Crusher's question. If we are forced to intervene, we need an effective course of action."

"Whatever it takes, Captain?" asked Geordi.

"Whatever it takes. The next question—do we warn the people of Alaj? And if so, when?"

"We have to warn them," Crusher said bluntly.

"To what end?" Picard mused. "There are four billion inhabitants there. We could no more evacuate them under impending threat than we could a mere two hundred thousand Etolosans. Do we warn Alaj and risk inducing a world-wide panic?"

"Captain," said Troi, "don't we have an ethical

responsibility to tell them what we know? If we were in their place, and the crew and families aboard this ship were about to die, wouldn't you tell them?"

"Yes, I would," Picard said quietly. "But I acknowledge that some would prefer not to have the chance to contemplate the imminent arrival of death."

"Death is a part of life," Worf said with brusque dignity. "Each individual should be permitted the time to deal with it in his own chosen way."

The security chief's statement took Picard and the others by surprise, since Klingons were notoriously private about their feelings and philosophies.

"If we try to oppose the Bekeem, we may face the same fate as Alaj," Troi remarked evenly.

Everyone at the table knew that Troi was correct and their debate was no academic exercise. The thousand souls aboard the *Enterprise* and the unsuspecting population of Alaj could very well meet the same end.

Chapter Nineteen

"Do they have *brains*? How could you ask them anything so insulting, Danid?" The angry, disembodied voice of the computer echoed through Danid's triangular bridge.

Danid sat imperiously in the command chair. "What business is it of yours, Nole?" he retorted roughly.

"You forget that my systems run this vessel and keep you alive."

"The only one you *did* keep alive," Danid sneered.

"You like to remind me how I've failed in my assigned function. You're right, and I'm past caring."

Danid sighed and raked his fingers through his long beard. "You and I both," he said, his expression softening.

"Then why must we do this thing to Alaj?"

"You know why."

"No," Nole exclaimed. "There is nothing to gain. This vengeance of yours will not change what's already happened."

Danid slapped a feeble fist on his armrest. "They

are responsible. They are the cause. They are evil and evil must be punished—"

"And you are the instrument of this cosmic punishment," Nole said, completing a litany they'd repeated many times.

"Afraid you can't do this one thing right?" Danid taunted.

"You say it's right. I don't agree."

"You don't *have* to agree. You just have to serve me." Danid began to laugh, a thin, mirthless cackle.

"What's so funny?" said Nole in a listless voice.

Danid's laughter died away. He sat in silence for a time. "Nothing. Nothing at all. I guess that's the joke in the end. And the conclusion of the ultimate search for wisdom."

The elevator pod waited as it had for uncounted time, its door frozen open by disuse.

"I don't trust it," said Ensign Lopez crisply.

"After your little experience with that ladder," Riker said, "I can't blame you. I'll go in first. What's the worst that could happen?"

Lopez arched her eyebrows. "Commander, do you really want an answer to that?"

"No."

Data cocked his head. "Then why did you ask, sir?"

Riker held his reply as he stepped gingerly inside the small, dark pod. It held his weight and he motioned to the others. Data stepped in next. Lopez hesitated at the threshold, then entered. As Data palmed a wall panel, the pod started with a jolt and descended.

"Up, Commander, up!" Lopez hissed through clenched teeth.

The android pressed the switch-plates again in a

different sequence. The pod slowed, then rose smoothly.

Data tracked their ascent with his tricorder until, after twenty-two levels, the pod shuddered to an unscheduled halt.

"Oh, hell," Lopez groaned. "Sirs," she added hastily. "Now what?"

Data examined the activation switches while Riker aimed his searchlight at the ceiling. He found what he was looking for—an escape hatch. "Any luck, Data?"

"If by 'luck,' you mean is it possible to make this pod resume operation, I would have to say no."

"Then there's only one way out."

"But we don't know where that exit leads, sir," Lopez said.

"Only one way to find out. Data, give me a boost."

The android linked his hands together and held them out. Riker set one boot there and vaulted up. Bracing himself on Data's shoulder, he shoved the ceiling hatch outward. The opening was just wide enough to fit his upper body through.

Pointing his lantern upward he surveyed the shaft. "You won't like this, Lopez, but there's an emergency ladder. But we won't have far to go. I see an open hatch about five meters up."

Riker hauled himself out on top of the pod, then reached down and helped Lopez up.

"You're the lightest," he said to her. "Why don't you go first."

"I'm honored, sir," she said wryly. "If I fall, I expect you to catch me." Then she reached over to the ladder and carefully stepped onto it. It seemed sturdy. But then again, so did the one that had almost killed her. She climbed quickly.

Data jumped up from the floor of the stalled pod and caught the rim of the hatch, easily pulling himself through. A moment later the elevator pod jiggled, then slipped a few inches.

Riker swallowed nervously. "Uh, Data, what's holding this thing up?"

"I do not know, sir. Whatever the mechanism, it is apparently malfunctioning."

"That's all I need to know." Riker immediately grabbed the ladder and headed up, with Data following closely.

It was four seconds later, Data noted, that the elevator pod plummeted silently down the shaft and out of sight. Somewhere below, it stopped with a metal-rending crash.

Lopez helped Riker and Data out into another darkened corridor. "If you all don't mind," she said, "I think I'll walk on level decks from here on."

And she took a step, but Riker reached out with a big hand and clamped it onto her shoulder. "Just where do you think you're walking to, Lopez?"

She looked up at him with hopeful eyes. "Away from that shaft?"

"I am afraid not," said Data. "We must go up at least five more levels before we reach the command center."

"And there's only one way to do that," Riker said.

"The ladder," Lopez said, a wan smile curling the corners of her mouth.

Riker opened his emergency pack and rummaged around, coming up with two safety tethers. "This time, we'll be tied together."

"Do I go first again?" Lopez asked dubiously as she looped the rope around her waist.

"As a matter of fact, no. You're in the middle. I go first, Data goes last."

Lopez mulled over the possibilities for disaster. "If

I fall, Data grabs me. If you fall, you pull me down, too, and Data grabs us both. But what if Data falls first, and then you fall, too?"

Riker flashed a devilish smile. "You're the trapeze artist. You'll think of something."

Linked by the safety ropes, they went back into the elevator shaft and began what they hoped would be the final ascent before reaching their goal.

"I still don't understand it," Lopez said as they climbed. "We still haven't seen anything to indicate that there's a living soul aboard this ship."

"Perhaps," said Data, "it is haunted, like the houses you enjoyed exploring as a child."

"A ghost ship?" Riker said. "That might make a good story to tell some Halloween night."

"But that means at least one of us has to live to tell the tale," said Lopez.

"A little incentive for us," Riker suggested.

Without mishap, they'd soon scaled the ladder to the top of the shaft. There was no open doorway as there'd been on lower levels. Instead, they found a solid cap with a small round hatch. Balancing precariously, Riker had only one hand free to force the hatch up. It budged just a crack, its hinges yielding grudgingly.

"Is it locked?" Lopez called from below him.

"No, just heavy," he grunted. *And Lord knows how long it's been shut,* he thought to himself. He summoned all the strength in his right arm and shoulder and managed to coax the creaking hinges into giving way. From there, it opened easily.

Even before he poked his head out, Riker noticed something different. From the moment they'd first left the shuttle in that hangar bay down in the lower levels, the entire ship had smelled musty and cool, like a tomb. But here at the top of this access tube, the air above him smelled like . . . like a spring rain in a country field, with the fresh fragrance of moist soil and grass.

Riker peeked over the rim of the hatchway, confirming by sight that his nose had been telling him the truth.

A few seconds later they were all inside a massive cylinder. Riker guessed that it was at least a kilometer across and two or three times that long. It contained a perfect reproduction of a rolling meadow, complete with wildflowers bending in a faint sweet breeze.

"Wow." Lopez craned her neck and peered up at the clear enclosure overhead. She could see the stars.

Data came up last, stepped down and felt the long grass soft beneath his boots. "It would seem you were right, Commander Riker."

Riker gave him a curious look. "About what?"

"The grass is indeed greener on the other side of the hill."

Picard and Troi faced each other across his ready-room desk. The model of the *Bon Homme Richard* was now sealed inside its glass container which Picard held in his hand.

"I'm beginning to feel like we're trapped inside a bottle," he said. "This Danid—do you believe he means what he says?"

Troi considered the question. "Yes, as far as he goes. He does intend to have his revenge on Alaj, and he will not let us get in his way."

"But?"

"He is keeping some important secrets."

Picard set the ship model down. "What sort of being are we dealing with, Counselor? Is he sane?"

"By what standards?"

"By ours."

"If you define sanity as soundness of mind, ability to reason clearly, and to understand the consequences of actions and behavior, I would say yes. But we heard evidence of what we might consider unprovoked emotional responses and wild emotional shifts."

"Does that sort of behavior tell you anything useful about him?"

"Well, the behavior patterns Danid has demonstrated could be the product of long-term isolation. It is almost a reversion to the unsocialized behavior of a young child."

"You sound uncertain."

"That's because we're applying human standards to a being who may be very different from us."

"Understood. Tell me, then, of what things *are* you certain?"

Troi took a deep breath. "Danid is a very angry being . . . cynical . . . with deep feelings of betrayal."

"Betrayal? By whom? The Alajians?"

"Yes, but it seems even deeper than that."

"Do you have any idea what it might be?"

"I wish I knew, Captain."

The intercom chime sounded. "Bridge to Captain Picard," said Worf. "The Bekeem vessel is moving. Shall we match their course and speed?"

"As ordered, Lieutenant. Their heading?"

"Bearing one-one-three mark six-nine, straight for Alaj."

"Damn."

Picard got up and strode out to the bridge with Troi close behind. "Mr. Worf, open hailing frequencies."

"Open, sir."

"Enterprise to Bekeem vessel. It is urgent that we open discussions with you. We cannot—"

"You cannot *what,* Picard?" said Danid over the audio speakers.

"We cannot allow you to approach Alaj with hostile intentions."

Again, Danid reacted with a peal of caustic laughter. "Big talk for a tiny ship."

Captain Picard's jaw clenched. "You may be underestimating the capabilities of the *Enterprise.*"

"I doubt it, based on what I've seen so far."

"What you have seen has been tempered by restraint. In that spirit, I appeal to you, Holiness. Let us discuss this dispute."

"It is not a dispute, Picard!" Danid screamed. An instant later, however, his tone reverted to utter calm. "We are not talking about a tiff over trade or port privileges. We are talking about revenge for attempted genocide. This is a sacred score I have sworn by blood to settle. The Alajian people forced my ancestors to wander the galaxy for almost five hundred years. What I am here to do is absurdly simple, Picard. Even you can understand."

The muscle in Picard's cheek twitched in cold anger. "And what is that?"

"To take back the world that should rightfully have been ours. And to banish forever the criminals now living there."

"The present inhabitants of Alaj are generations removed from the people who banished your ancestors. The score you are determined to settle can never be reconciled."

Danid responded with a rude noise and closed the channel.

"Continue hailing, Lieutenant," Picard said, standing in the center of the bridge.

"No response, Captain."

"Danid," Nole scolded, "why did you do that?"

"Do *what?*"

227

The computer bit off each word for emphasis. "You refused to discuss this situation with Picard."

"Don't you understand?" Danid shouted. "I owe this act of vengeance to every Bekeem who died without a home!"

"I *don't* understand, Danid. Will it do any good to answer one act of evil with another, greater evil?"

Danid swiveled in his command throne. "Who said anything about good, you damned computer? There is no good, no truth, no wisdom." His lips drew back over his teeth, and a hollow laugh seeped from his heart. "It took hundreds of years and thousands of lives, but the Universe has finally taught me its one and only lesson. Existence is worthless."

"Do you really believe that?"

Danid waved his hands in an all-encompassing gesture. "Of course I do! Why else would I be doing this? Did the lives of the Bekeem have any meaning? Did my own life have any meaning?"

The computer's response was uncomfortable silence, prompting a bitter chortle from its companion.

"Even your vast brain can't think of a single shred of purpose to my existence. Ahhh, but you don't escape so easily, Nole. Has *your* existence any meaning? I'll save you the trouble of combing your memory banks. The answer is no."

"I can't accept that."

"Why? Is the concept too abstract for you? Too horrible to contemplate? We are cosmic waste, my old friend. My final act will be to end this sorry chapter in history, and that alone will give our lives meaning."

"But we won't be there to enjoy our sudden rise to that exalted state."

"Ha-hah! That's the beauty of it, Nole. We won't have to do anything for an encore."

"No, there must be more, Danid. There must be another way to validate our creation than by converting ourselves into instruments of destruction."

Danid pursed his wizened lips. "Fine. Name one thing that relieves the unending futility of our existence, and I will consider reconsidering."

More silence from Nole. Then, with sorrow: "I can't."

"Then let's have no more of this doubt and vacillation. We're worthless . . . so let's go out with a bang."

Dread was not common for Jean-Luc Picard. But he clearly dreaded the decision he now had to make: whether or not to inform Zeila of the threat to her world and people. He'd put the decision off as long as possible, hoping that he could reason with Danid and buy some time.

But Danid wasn't selling. The Bekeem ship was on its way and the Alajians had to be warned now if they were to be warned at all. Picard wondered if the situation was reversed, would he want to know about an impending and unavoidable disaster? The answer was an unequivocal yes.

The decision was made. He contacted Alaj and told Zeila everything that had transpired.

Her composure stunned him. "Well, Captain, I was just sitting here wondering how things could get any worse. Apparently they can."

Her intelligence deputy Lef moved into the picture on Picard's desktop viewer. "Captain, we have a sizable space fleet of our own. We could mobilize all our ships and stop this intruder before it enters Alajian space."

"Deputy Lef, that would be futile. The size and power of this Bekeem craft is more than—"

Lef hammered Zeila's desk with his clenched fist. "We cannot stand by and submit to annihilation, Captain!"

"We are not suggesting that."

"Then what *are* you suggesting?" Lef demanded.

Picard sighed. "At the moment I have no solutions, but it seems pointless for you to sacrifice lives in that way."

"From what you say, we're all going to die anyway. I'd rather go out fighting."

Zeila managed an ironic laugh. "There's a bright side, Captain."

Picard seemed puzzled. "There is?"

"Mm-hmm. If Alaj is about to be wiped out by some interstellar marauder, I suppose it relieves me of the burden of dealing with the impossible problems here."

"The destruction of Alaj is not a forgone conclusion. There are still possibilities."

"There may not be for me, Captain."

"What do you mean?"

"Our cities are burning. Riots broke out in twenty provinces today. Lef and I were considering unleashing our army against Alajian citizens as a last resort."

"Curister, it is not my place to tell you how to govern your world. But if Alaj does survive this threat from the Bekeem, acts of violence against your own people could strengthen their determination to overthrow your government."

"I'm well aware of that, Captain. Tell me the truth—are we still going to be here tomorrow?"

"I wish I could tell you Alaj's survival is assured. Obviously, I cannot. But I promise you we will do everything we can to prevent the Bekeem from carrying out their threat."

"Because we're a member of the Federation."

Picard nodded. "Yes. I realize Alaj's membership has been distant at best. But the Federation stands by its charter. The *Enterprise* and her crew are bound to protect your world as if *we* were from Alaj ourselves—even at risk of our own lives."

"I understand, Captain Picard. I hope it doesn't come to that—for both our sakes. Let us know if you come up with any brilliant solutions."

"I shall. Picard out."

Zeila's communications screen went blank, and she and Lef stared at it. Neither seemed especially anxious to face the other. Zeila turned first, leaning back in her desk chair. She waited a moment for Lef to turn and she saw him glare at her. "What's that look for?"

"How can you make jokes?"

"That's my way of dealing with overwhelming horror. I see your way is to get angry and pound things."

"Pretty ineffectual, I guess," said Lef as he slouched down in the chair across from her. He shook his head, trying to clear it of apocalyptic visions. "All the problems we have . . . I thought we could get a grip on things. I really did. Life wouldn't be easy, but it never crossed my mind that existence might end, that we'd run out of time. But now . . ." His voice faded.

"Now *what?* Why is now any different?"

Lef's mouth dropped open. "Why is now any different? You heard Picard. Our fate is out of our hands."

She slammed her hand down on the desktop and he jolted upright. "That's *not* what I want to hear from you, Lef!"

"You heard Picard," he repeated. "That Bekeem ship—"

"Hasn't fired a shot yet. Picard says it's too powerful for us to stop. Maybe he's wrong. You said you'd rather go out fighting. Did you mean it?"

"I—"

"Of *course* you meant it. Mobilize a defensive force—*now*."

Chapter Twenty

"Do you think ghosts eat vegetables?" Ensign Lopez wondered, examining the plump root she'd pulled out of the ground by its leafy cap. It was greenish-yellow and shaped like a cross between a carrot and a potato, with clumps of thick, dark loam still clinging to it.

Riker stood next to her, surveying the thriving rows of neatly cultivated crops. "Judging by the size of this garden, it would have to be a very hungry ghost."

"Compulsive, too," Lopez said. "This little farm is incredibly well-tended."

Data scanned the field with his tricorder. "This soil is remarkably rich in nutrients."

"Don't most plants need direct sunlight?" asked Riker.

Data knelt to touch the plants sprouting at his feet. Their leaves all faced the same way. "Judging by the manner in which these are growing, I would say that artificial sunlight is provided for them, from that direction."

Lopez wandered up to the crest of a gentle hill, gazing out over the rest of the lush meadow. Riker and Data soon joined her.

"This is so, I don't know, *weird,*" she said. "After all the sterility throughout the rest of this ship, there's *this.*"

"It fits in with your theory that this ship was built as a permanent habitat, Data," said Riker.

"Not necessarily, sir," Data said. "The amount of food produced by so small a plot of land would not be enough to feed the potential population of a spacecraft this size—unless there are additional similar farm modules, as well as other more efficient means of food production."

"I wasn't talking about food production alone, Data. Beings like us on long-term space voyages need a little nature in their immediate environment."

"Ahh. One of the reasons why holodecks have been incorporated into the design of starships sent on extended missions."

Riker nodded. "Before holodeck technology was perfected, the old starships used to have some space set aside for plants and greenery."

"But holodecks and small gardens are not equivalent," said Data. "The holodeck offers an infinite variety of interactive recreation. Gardens simply exist."

"That's all we need them to do," Lopez said.

"I do not understand," Data admitted. "In a planetary ecosystem, plant life is an essential biological component. But in an artificial environment such as a starship, flora are not required to preserve physical well-being."

"I'm not sure I understand it either," Riker shrugged. "I guess we've still got some primeval connection with the land."

"Intriguing."

Riker turned slowly, eyes squinting as he studied

the boundaries of the vaulted cylinder. "Is there an easy way out of this place?"

With his enhanced vision, the android scanned the area and pointed to a far-off corner. "There is a doorway in that direction."

"Is that in the direction we need to be going?"

Data nodded. "Yes, sir. And I believe we are now on the same level as the command center."

"Then let's go see who's got the green thumb."

A perplexed expression furrowed Data's brow. "How do you know the life forms on this vessel have green thumbs? Or any thumbs at all?"

"Data—" Riker gave his friend a tolerant smile. "Never mind."

"Ah," said Data earnestly, "something else you will explain when you tell me about the midnight raids at Starfleet Academy."

Picard sat at his ready-room desk, fingers steepled in thought. He wondered if the Alajians were really going to try mounting a spaceborn defense of their world. If so, who was he to say they'd be wrong to make the attempt? Perhaps this Bekeem vessel, for all its size and power, had some undiscovered Achilles' heel.

The missing shuttlecraft also weighed heavily on his thoughts. Were Ambassador Navirra, Riker, and his crew actually still alive somewhere inside that massive ship? *If Danid does indeed have them, what the devil does he plan to do with them? Is it possible to predict the actions of such an unbalanced individual?*

Enough rumination, Picard concluded. He rose from his chair. The time had come to find out just how powerful and determined the Bekeem really were. He strode out to the bridge.

"Worf, open hailing frequencies."

"Open, sir."

Picard straightened his uniform tunic and spoke in a tone of righteous authority. "Enterprise to Bekeem vessel. This is Captain Picard. We request that you halt your approach to Alaj. Please reply."

He expected no response and got none. "Danid," he went on, "if you continue on your mission of aggression, you will leave us no choice but to intervene with force."

Again, not a word from the Bekeem commander. "Ensign Crusher, break parallel formation and set an intercept course." Picard half-turned toward the tactical station. "Worf, on my command, fire two photon torpedoes across the Bekeem ship's bow."

The Klingon's expression didn't deviate from his accustomed glower, but there was crisp satisfaction in his motions as he entered the commands to arm and aim torpedoes. "Ready, Captain."

"Fire."

The two glowing projectiles hurtled away from the *Enterprise,* directed to miss the Bekeem ship by a margin wide enough to be safe but narrow enough to be persuasive. However, at the instant they passed the giant ship—a microsecond before they could detonate—the Bekeem energy field extended and bounced them wildly off course where they exploded in open space.

Worf growled deep in his throat. "Ineffective, Captain."

"Phasers, half-power."

"Targeting, sir?"

Picard didn't answer right away. Instead he glared at the viewscreen for a long moment. When he spoke, there was steely resolution in his voice. "Dead on,

Lieutenant. It's time we got through to the Supreme Primary in no uncertain terms."

"Phasers locked on target, sir."

"Fire."

Worf hit the trigger and the beam sizzled through space. It hit the Bekeem ship, or, more accurately, hit the protective energy field. The anxious *Enterprise* bridge crew watched as the phaser beam rebounded directly back at them. The beam wavered as it lost some of its integral definition but it packed enough residual force to rattle the starship and everyone aboard her.

"Shields holding, Captain," Worf reported. "The Bekeem protective field reflected our phaser beam with only a ten percent dissipation."

Picard let out a breath of frustration as he backed into his seat. "Then it appears we need an alternative approach to this problem."

"Captain," said Worf, "permission to speak with you . . . privately."

Rarely did Worf make such a request. Picard turned to stare at the burly Klingon. "Granted. In my ready room."

Picard led the way to his office. When the door shut behind them, he faced his chief of security. "What is it, Lieutenant?"

"A plan to stop the Bekeem vessel."

"All right, Worf. Let's have it."

"Geordi and I have studied the situation and reached the conclusion that there is only one way to divert or disable that ship."

"Why didn't you tell me this earlier?"

"We did not think you would like our recommendation."

Picard frowned as he took his seat. "I do not have to

like it in order to implement it, if it is the only feasible choice—and if it will accomplish our goal."

"We were aware of that, sir," said Worf, remaining at attention. "But there was an unknown factor, without which we could not make an accurate prediction."

"And would that factor have been the effect of the *Enterprise*'s weapons on the Bekeem ship?"

"Yes, sir. We did not know the full capabilities of their energy shield."

Picard clasped his hands and rested them on the desk. "But you do now. What is this final alternative?"

"There is an eighty-three percent probability this action would render the Bekeem vessel incapable of pursuing its attack on Alaj," Worf said stiffly.

"You are being uncharacteristically cagey, Mr. Worf," Picard prodded gently. "Just tell me the plan."

"The *Enterprise* can stop the Bekeem ship only by ramming it, sir. There is a forty percent probability that such a collision would result in their destruction."

Picard's expression remained impassive. "I see. Obviously, in either scenario, whether they are destroyed or merely disabled, the *Enterprise* would be destroyed."

"Captain, you do not seem surprised by our strategy."

"The same strategy had already occurred to me."

"We suspected that would be the case."

"And you're quite correct, Worf. I do not like it. But I've already accepted that we may have no choice. And I thank you and Geordi for having the courage to think the unthinkable."

Worf looked vaguely perplexed. "Death in the line of duty is never unthinkable to a Klingon."

"I know that. Will we have time to separate the saucer section from the stardrive?"

Worf shook his head. "Time, yes. But there is another problem with separation. In order to provide sufficient mass to assure the required destructive force, the *Enterprise* must remain whole."

"Then everyone on the Enterprise will die," Picard said, his voice barely above a whisper.

Worf's words came slowly. "Yes, sir."

Picard fought the knots twisting his stomach. His only reservations about taking command of the *Enterprise* had come when Starfleet told him that crew members would be able to have their families aboard. Husbands, wives . . . children. It was one thing for a Starfleet officer to face danger and death—that was part of the job when your job entailed exploring strange new worlds. But families, and children were another matter entirely.

The saucer section can detach and carry those loved ones to safety, he'd been assured.

But what if the situation doesn't permit that? he'd argued in return.

There'd been no answer to that objection. But the human mind has almost limitless ability to convince itself that the worst will quite simply never happen. So Picard had accepted the commission. Perhaps he should have thought again. Had he done so, perhaps some other captain would now be forced to sacrifice the lives of a thousand people—

"Captain."

Worf's voice called him back to the immediate situation. "When is the last possible moment for us to ram the Bekeem ship?" he asked with a deep breath.

"We will have to intercept it no later than eight minutes before it enters Alajian orbit."

"Are you and Geordi certain that their energy shield would not stop the *Enterprise?*"

"Our calculations did include a four percent margin of error. But we believe that sufficient velocity and the element of surprise would permit us to breach any shields and evade any defensive measures."

"Kamikaze," Picard said.

Worf nodded respectfully. "I am familiar with the reference."

A thousand people on the *Enterprise.* Four billion on Alaj. Picard had no way of knowing how many Alajians might actually die if the Bekeem had the opportunity to carry out their threat, but it was a threat he had to take seriously.

So, the decision is made for me, he realized. Not that Jean-Luc Picard wished to die. But if the choice had to be made, he'd prefer to die knowing that the sacrifice of the *Enterprise* might save billions than live with the knowledge that he'd allowed so many deaths without trying to prevent them.

"Lieutenant, you and Mr. La Forge enter a self-correcting automated program locking the *Enterprise* on collision course with the Bekeem ship, as you have proposed."

"Automated, sir?"

"Yes. If our crew should become disabled, I want the ship to continue to its destination. Manual override should be available until the last possible second."

"Yes, sir."

Worf exited, leaving Picard to ponder just how to tell his crew what they were about to face.

Chapter Twenty-one

"WE WHO ARE ABOUT TO DIE salute you," Lopez whispered to no one in particular.

Riker fixed her with a disapproving glare. "What's that supposed to mean?"

"Just something I think ancient gladiators used to say to their rulers before going into combat."

The *Enterprise* trio crouched at a corner of a dim passageway no more than thirty meters from the Bekeem command bridge. Data activated his tricorder and scanned ahead.

"Lousy analogy, Lopez," Riker chided. "We haven't seen *any* resistance so far."

"Which makes me expect a whole *lot* of resistance before we get in there," she said, gesturing down the dark corridor.

"That is not likely," Data said. "I am picking up only one life form reading from inside the command center."

Riker's eyes narrowed to confused slits. "One? What about passive security measures? Photo-electric trip beams? Force fields? Gates?"

"There is no evidence of any such measures."

"Spooky," Lopez said. *"Really* spooky."

"Data, any suggestions on how to approach?"

"There are two entries, both apparently unguarded and unlocked. I suggest you and Ensign Lopez enter from the left, while I enter from the right."

"Somehow I expected something a little more complex," Riker said with a glimmer of amusement.

"With two doors and three of us, the possibilities are fairly limited," Data pointed out. "I believe speed and simplicity would be most appropriate."

"All right, then. I'll go in first, Data second, Lopez last. Phasers on stun. In this case, if there's any danger at all to any of us, shoot first and ask questions later."

They crept silently toward their target, soon arriving at the corridor junction where two branches angled off, bracketing the command bridge located between them. Data went one way, Riker and Lopez the other. Ten meters farther along, they approached the closed doors and stopped a couple of strides away.

Riker silently mouthed the word "Ready?" and Lopez responded with a firm nod. He sidled up to the door and when it slid open he burst through, phaser at the ready—

Simultaneously, Lopez tapped her communicator. "Now, Data!"

The door on the other side of the bridge snapped open and Data rushed in, his weapon held high.

An instant later, Lopez dove in, also poised to fire.

Three weapons, in the hands of highly trained Starfleet officers, aimed at one old man, cowering in his command throne, stunned into terrified silence.

Cautiously, Riker moved closer. Frozen in his seat, the only parts of Danid that moved were his eyes, following this armed and angry intruder.

"Who the hell are you?" Riker growled.

Danid drew himself upright in the elevated command seat and gathered the remains of his dignity, as tattered as the threadbare cloak gathered around his bony shoulders. "I am Danid, Supreme Primary of the Holy Bekeem. And who are *you?*"

"Commander William Riker, first officer of the U.S.S. *Enterprise.* Don't you know who you keep as prisoners?"

"Only when it matters."

"We *don't* matter?" Lopez snarled, her eyes flashing.

"Not particularly, no. And I'll thank you to stop pointing those weapons at me."

Riker nodded amiably and he and the others lowered their phasers.

"Trusting soul, aren't you, Riker?" Danid said.

"We got this far without running into any sort of security and I don't think that you pose much danger to us."

"If I may ask," said Data politely, "why do you not have any security arrangements in your vessel?"

Danid responded to the question with an abrupt wheeze of laughter, bringing a confused expression to the android's face. For a moment, Data looked like a child uncertain of whether he'd delivered a joke or was the butt of one.

"Did I say something humorous?"

Danid's belly laughs receded. "Depends on your outlook. What's your name?"

"Lieutenant Commander Data."

"Well, Lieutenant Commander Data, we don't have any security arrangements because we don't need any."

"Then you *are* the only being on this ship, aren't you?" said Riker.

"In a manner of speaking," Nole's voice said softly.

Riker and the others looked all around the bridge for the voice's origin.

"Are you the only being?" Riker repeated.

"I'm the only biological life form. That was Nole, the computer system responsible for operating this vessel."

Data seemed fascinated. "Indeed."

"But none of that changes anything," said Danid. "You are still my prisoners and I still plan to exact my revenge from the planet that condemned my ancestors to a death sentence that took almost five centuries to be executed."

"You mean Alaj," said Lopez, leaning closer to him. "You look Alajian."

"I am *not* Alajian!" Danid bellowed. Then he struck a pompous pose and spoke gravely: "I am Bekeem— and I am an instrument of justice."

"Call yourself anything you like," said Riker, "but you're obviously related to the Alajians. Why do you call yourself Bekeem, and what did the Alajians ever do to you?"

Danid drew his lips into a tight line and combed his fingers through his beard. But he refused to answer.

"Tell them," said Nole.

Danid remained mute.

"If you don't, I will," Nole cautioned.

They were both quiet for a few moments. Then Danid's face clenched sourly. "We are Bekeem be- cause we were *always* Bekeem. Yes, we came from Alaj. They banished us because we wouldn't accept their cheap substitutes for truth. Three thousand truth-seekers followed the first Supreme Primary Gerrenjennow and set off to search for wisdom."

"Searched where?" Lopez asked.

Danid ignored the question, chortling to himself. "Imagine—a world dominated by nit-brains who believed that Ultimate Wisdom got passed from the Spirit-force to primitives so backward they could barely clothe themselves—and passed along through ugly little animals no less! Ha!" He turned back to the starship officers. "How's that for blasphemy! That Alajian society was doomed to damnation from the day it was born."

"Tell us what happened to the Bekeem after they left Alaj," Riker said, more gently.

"We set out to find a world built on a foundation of Truth. There were none. Or to convert a world. But no one willingly accepted enlightenment," Danid said with a wry shrug. "Generations of wandering taught the third Supreme Primary—what was his name—?"

"Lans," Nole said helpfully.

"Lans. Lans realized we might never find a home *or* Ultimate Truth. So he prepared us for perpetual pilgrimage by starting the construction of this great ship."

"How long did that construction take?" asked Data.

"How long," Danid mumbled. "How long . . ."

"It was done in many stages," said Nole. "One hundred and twelve years."

Danid waved his hand in a vague gesture of acknowledgment. "That long."

"How many people lived on it?" said Riker.

"We grew to fifty-thousand," Danid said, turning melancholy. "Nole can tell you. Nole was here, always here." The old man's voice trailed off into a private grief.

The computer continued the story. "It was never an easy life, and some were too weak to accept the destiny of wanderers. The Bekeem did not thrive. Their numbers fell to ten thousand, and in the two-hundred-and-ninetieth year, the Division took place. More than half left to form their own planetary colony. The rest went on, but they were too few to maintain this ship."

"Tell them about the plague, Nole," Danid whispered.

"I will." This time, when the computer spoke to the old man, its voice was gentle. "I will, Danid. Some landed on another world to try to recruit more Truth-seekers, but they brought back a disease that decimated the Bekeem."

Danid roused himself from his daze. "Time, disease, and decay did the rest. I am all that remains of the great Bekeem," he said bitterly.

"And me," Nole said with profound sadness. "I saw them die. I was created and programmed to nurture and protect them . . . and I failed them."

"Nole," said Data, "no machine, no matter how advanced, can do all that."

"So that's what you meant by a death sentence that took five hundred years to execute," said Ensign Lopez.

"And that is why I'm returning to Alaj to return the favor."

"We can't let you do that," said Riker. "I won't pretend we can understand your feelings, but we do sympathize. However, that doesn't change the fact that the Alajians who banished those ancient Bekeem are as dead as your ancestors are. You've got no quarrel with the people living there now."

Danid lurched to his feet and grasped Riker by his shoulders. "Riker, if I could kill the Alajian leaders from five centuries ago, I'd gladly do it. But I can't— so these descendants will have to bear the responsibility for their fathers' crimes. *That* is fair."

Riker shook free of the old man's grip. "I'm not the one to judge that—and neither are you."

Danid broke into laughter. "You may be no judge,

but you are a fool if you think you can stop me. Even if you killed me here and now, you wouldn't be able to stop me. This ship is locked on course."

"Don't you have to be alive to fire your weapons? Or are they preprogrammed?"

"There's no need to fire a weapon. This ship is my weapon."

Data's eyebrows arched. "A collision course."

Danid replied with a shrug. "My life is meaningless. This is a very large ship and will make quite a nice bang when it hits Alaj, don't you think?"

Elbows braced on his desk, Picard tried to rub the fatigue from his eyes. "What do I tell them, Deanna?"

He lowered his hands and looked at Troi's elegant face, trying to lose himself in the serenity of her dark eyes.

"The truth," she said gently.

"But there is no comfort to be drawn from a truth this terrible."

Troi leaned partway across the desk and touched his hand lightly. "Just trust them, Captain. And trust yourself. They do."

A moment later, the door of the ready room slid open and Captain Picard and the counselor came out onto the bridge.

"Intra-ship communications," he said as he took his seat. "This is Captain Picard. When we all became a part of the *Enterprise,* we knew we were embarking on a great mission of discovery. In our years together, we have succeeded admirably. Thanks to your skills and courage, we have explored the unknown, and provided a vital link between all manner of civilizations and life forms. In doing that, we have made this vast galaxy of ours just a bit smaller, a bit more hospitable . . . but not a bit less grand or exciting."

Picard paused for a moment, and glanced at Troi in her adjacent seat. She could tell he was exerting every effort to maintain the voice of calm authority his crew had come to expect from him. She knew this task was the most difficult he'd ever undertaken.

He took a breath and continued. "No group of people has ever embodied as well as the crew of this starship the belief that life should be lived, not postponed. But it is the nature of our form of life that individuals cannot last forever. Death is inevitable, preferably after a long and productive span of time. But we who choose to dedicate our lives to exploration make that choice with the knowledge that death may come without warning, sooner rather than later."

All through the *Enterprise,* people who had been listening with one ear while tending to their work were now still, all attention directed toward Picard's words. His voice somehow blended his accustomed commanding presence with the deepest vulnerabilities of his soul.

"The *Enterprise* has faced terrible danger before. We face such danger once again. We know little about the giant Bekeem vessel a short distance away, or the beings aboard it. We only know that they claim to have taken an *Enterprise* shuttle and its crew as prisoners, and that the Bekeem have vowed to attack a Federation world with four billion inhabitants.

"We do not have the time to summon assistance from other Starfleet ships, and the *Enterprise* is all that stands between Alaj and the Bekeem threat. Preventing the death of millions or billions of Alajians will require the sacrifice of the *Enterprise* and all hands.

"I have decided to commit this vessel to that course of action. We will not be able to separate the saucer and stardrive sections. If we are to die today, we will die as we have lived . . . together. Picard out."

Down in her quarters, Beverly Crusher sat motionless, holding a small photo in an antique brass frame —herself as a young wife and mother, with her late husband Jack and their infant son cradled in their arms. Then she stood and returned the picture to its private place in her keepsake drawer. She still had patients and they needed her care. Death would just have to wait its turn. And when and if it came, she planned to be too busy to pay it any mind.

Chapter Twenty-two

THE CLUSTER OF a dozen Alajian spacecraft formed into a loose wedge and accelerated toward their destiny. They weren't especially big or powerful ships, with even the largest dwarfed by the *Enterprise.*

Their sortie had a simple goal: protect their world. And the Alajians making up these combat crews all knew they were expendable.

On the bridge of the *Enterprise,* Lieutenant Worf studied his tactical scanners, his powerful hands moving with uncanny lightness and speed as he sought to filter out residual interference from the Bekeem ship's energy field.

"Captain, sensors indicate the approach of twelve small vessels from Alaj."

"Damn." Picard's lips pressed together in disapproval. "Worf, open a hailing frequency. Secure channel."

"Coded channel open, sir."

"Enterprise to Alajian flagship."

The reply came a few moments later, *"Enterprise,* this is the Alajian task force," said a no-nonsense male voice. "Marshal Greiba in command."

"Marshal, this is Captain Picard. I urge you to turn back."

"We have our orders, Captain."

"Then let me warn you. The energy shield around the Bekeem ship can have debilitating effects on both electronics and living beings. Do not remain in close proximity to it. In addition, it deflects any attacking force. It proved impregnable against both our photon torpedoes and our phasers. We barely escaped damage from our own reflected phaser fire. If you must attack, keep your deflector shields on maximum and take evasive action immediately upon firing."

"We appreciate the advice, Captain. But we've got to put maximum power in weaponry if we're to have any chance at all. If we divert too much power to shields or evasive maneuvers, we'll never break through their defenses."

"Marshal—"

"Thank you, Captain. Alajian task force out."

Frustrated, Picard sank back in his seat. "Worf, put their approach on main viewer, maximum magnification."

The image on the viewscreen homed in on the assault force as it closed on the giant Bekeem vessel. The Alajian ships broke formation and five attacked at close range, blasting and strafing with both torpedoes and phasers.

Just as Picard had feared, those first five Alajian fighters proved sacrificial, swallowed up by the reactive pulses of their own reflected weapons fire and exploding in rapid succession. As the *Enterprise* command crew watched helplessly, the remaining seven ships twisted away, regrouped into a tight wedge and turned. At top speed, they hurtled toward the Bekeem ship.

"Collision course," Worf said, the first to state what everyone on the *Enterprise* bridge knew.

They never got past the energy shield. In quick succession, six Alajian ships were blown to bits. At the last instant before oblivion, one peeled out of the suicide wedge. Damaged by debris, it limped home, a wounded messenger of bad news.

"No effect at all on the Bekeem ship," Worf reported. "Course and speed unchanged." His words lingered in the otherwise stark silence of the starship's bridge.

When Picard finally spoke, his eyes remained on the viewer. "How long before we must commit the *Enterprise?*"

"At current speed, nine minutes and forty seconds."

"Maintain safe distance, parallel course and speed." Picard let out a slow breath. *Nine minutes to find a miracle,* he thought.

Danid fixed his eyes on the small triangular viewer on the front wall of his bridge, as the sole Alajian survivor retreated. His withered frame seemed to shrink further into itself. "They're dead," he said softly.

"You mean murdered," Riker snarled, barely able to contain his outrage.

Danid sat heavily in his throne, slowly gathering his resolve. "This is a war, our holy imperative. I celebrate our first victory over our oppressors."

"Do you really find the deaths of those people a cause for celebration?" Riker snapped.

"Yes, I do," Danid responded, but his voice broke slightly as he spoke. "I—"

"I don't," Nole interrupted.

"Then why did you permit it?" Data asked with neutral curiosity.

"I didn't. The energy shield is an automatic function over which I have no control. It operates as long as the ship's drive core produces power."

Riker was certain he detected genuine regret in the computer's voice, but he chose to let Data continue conversing with it.

"Do you have control over whether this vessel collides with Alaj and causes widespread destruction?"

"No," Danid said sharply, before his computer companion could answer. "Nole doesn't. I do, because Nole is programmed to obey the Supreme Primary, and that's *me.*"

"Nole," Riker boomed, "do you have any concept of just how much destruction this collision is going to cause?"

"Yes."

"Shut up," said Danid, rising from his seat.

With a quick thrust of one powerful forearm, Riker caught Danid in his mid-section and pinned him back in the chair. With his free hand, Riker drew his phaser and pointed it at Danid's nose. "I don't think Nole wants to shut up, Danid. Nole, you said you were programmed to nurture and protect. Where does all this killing fit into that directive?"

"I was programmed to nurture and protect the travelers on this ship," the computer said, mustering a lame defense.

Riker straightened and released his press on Danid's frail shoulders. Talking as fast as he could, he addressed Nole and hunted for the opening he needed. "Does your programming say that specifically? Does it specify that you should protect life within this vessel but destroy life outside?"

Nole's reply came slowly. "No. It says nothing about life outside."

"Danid thinks you failed in your assigned task. I think Danid's wrong. I think he's blaming you for the failures of his own people. I think he can't accept that the Bekeem were responsible for their own destruction."

"No!" Danid roared in fury. "The Alajians were responsible. They banished—"

Riker whirled on the old man, clamping his hands on Danid's armrests, trapping him in the command seat. "Others were banished from Alaj after the Bekeem—"

"No!"

"*Yes*. And they didn't all die out. Some flourished. So don't blame Nole for what your people couldn't do. Nole's kept this ship functioning. And he's kept you alive." Riker glanced up. "Nole, what if you could have this ship filled with life again, life that needed your protection and nurturing?"

"Tell me more, Riker," the computer said with a hint of eagerness and fear in his voice.

Danid began pounding the arms of his chair. "Nole, don't listen to—"

"Tell me, Riker," Nole repeated.

"We're trying to help one of the other groups banished from Alaj—they call themselves Etolosans." He related an abbreviated version of the Etolosans' troubles.

"And they need to be moved?" Nole asked after listening in silence.

"Yes, desperately. And this ship is big enough to save much of the life now endangered on Etolos."

"And you say that many of the life forms on Eto-

254

los were already saved from worlds where beings didn't have the wisdom to protect that which is so precious?"

"Yes."

"How wondrous to trade echoes of revenge for sounds of life," Nole said. "We would not only be sparing Alaj, we would also be sparing another world. Two worlds of life."

"No!" Danid squawked. "It's a trick! He's lying."

Riker still gripped the chair in his big hands. "It's not a trick," he said quietly, leaning close and silencing Danid with a fierce glare.

"Danid," said Nole, "you said if I could name one thing that would relieve the unending futility of our existence, you would consider reconsidering your revenge on Alaj."

"I didn't say anything like—"

"Those were your exact words. Were you lying?"

"No. But they are, Nole. And you can't violate your programming."

Data's expression turned thoughtful. "Nole, can your programming be altered if you absorb new input?"

"Yes."

"What if we offered evidence of what Commander Riker has said?"

"Evidence?" Nole echoed, sounding afraid once again. "It would have to be extensive."

"Would the complete Federation file on Etolos be sufficient?"

"No," Danid shrilled. "Files can be fiction."

"Why would they have falsified files when they had no way of predicting in advance that they would need them," Nole said carefully. "If such files exist and they are truly extensive, then I would accept their authenticity."

"If, if, if! How can you base our future on this concoction of deceit?"

"Your way," said Nole, "we have no future. I . . . I am not as ready as you to surrender my existence."

Riker stepped back from Danid's command seat and pulled Data to a private corner of the bridge. "Data, we don't have time to access Federation records."

The android tapped one finger on the side of his head. "It will not be necessary. My memory file is quite comprehensive."

"Data," said Nole, "how will you present your memory records?"

"Because of the limited time element, I will attempt direct transfer. Nole, do you have a data reception link on this bridge?"

"Yes," the computer said. One of the dark consoles surged to life, with a toggle blinking bright green. "When you are ready to transfer, activate this receptor."

Danid bolted from his chair, his face reddening in protest. "No! One computer brain to another? How will I know what lies they're telling you?"

"I can display Data's records on the viewscreen," Nole said.

"But the transfer will take place at a rate far exceeding human comprehension," Data said, moving to the console.

Danid shook his head vigorously. "Unacceptable! I will not—"

"Don't you trust me?" Nole asked.

Riker joined Data at the transfer-link panel. "How will Nole gain access to your memory core?"

"The tricorder should be able to serve as an interface between us."

"Are you sure this is safe for you?"

"No, I am not." He accepted Riker's look of silent exasperation. "But we do not have a great many choices, nor a great deal of time."

"Nole," Riker called, "how long before this ship can no longer be diverted from collision with Alaj?"

"Eleven minutes."

"Do you want to see our evidence?"

The computer hesitated. When it spoke, its voice pleaded for a way to avoid the fate Danid seemed determined to pursue. "Yes. Tell me."

"No," Danid said, *pro forma.* His tone admitted defeat.

"Let me do this."

"Oh, do whatever you want, damned computer," Danid sulked.

Riker turned to Data. "In the words of Captain Picard, make it so."

Data popped open the tricorder in his hand and set it for simultaneous input and transmission. Then he reached up and peeled back the patch of scalp along his right temple, revealing the twinkling circuitry of his positronic brain. With the touch of a fingertip, he activated his own information transfer down-link.

"Nole, I am ready," Data said as he moved to the console and placed his finger on the green receptor switch. "Transmitting now." Data's fellow officers stood by as his face drained of outside awareness and became a blank mask. Then, as promised, the torrent of information flowing from android to computer flooded across the triangular viewscreen in a blur of words and images, impossible for a humanoid brain to grasp.

Not much point looking at that, Riker thought. He maintained a stolid posture, arms folded across his chest, eyes fixed on Data. Lopez fidgeted, unable to stand still for more than five seconds at a time. Danid sat in his disgruntled hunch, refusing to watch any of it.

Suddenly, the lights faded. The vent blowers and viewscreen also shut down. Riker's jaw tightened involuntarily. *Data, are you all right?* There was nothing he could do but wait in dark, eerie silence for two machines to complete their private conference.

Taut silence also reigned on the *Enterprise* bridge. Picard broke it with a quiet question.

"Ensign Crusher?"

"Yes, sir."

"Do you have Lieutenant Worf's programming plotted into helm and navigation?"

Wes glanced over his shoulder, trying to cover his nervousness, hoping the captain wasn't about to give the command no one wanted to hear. His mouth was so dry he wasn't sure he could speak. But he did. "Aye, sir."

"Implement high-speed intercept course."

Wes choked down the most difficult swallow of his young life. "Aye, sir. Intercept course implemented."

The starship *Enterprise* began a wide arc, and accelerated toward the Bekeem vessel.

The tension had forced Lopez to stand still, her fists clenched, staring at Data for a sign, *any* sign that he and Nole had finished their task.

Riker perched on the edge of the instrument console, trying not to think about the possibility of failure. What if Data and Nole were incompatible and *couldn't* trade the memory file Data chose to share? What if—

"Thank you, Data," said Nole in the darkness, so suddenly even Riker reacted with a start.

Data's eyes blinked as he reoriented himself. "You are welcome." He noticed Lopez and Riker crowding him anxiously.

"It is not a trick," Nole said. "I believe them, Danid. And I will not carry out your wishes. Not when there is life to be preserved . . . a purpose for my existence . . . and yours."

Danid jumped to his feet. "I forbid this, Nole, you can't overrule your directives."

"My programming is complex enough to permit judgment, Danid. I exercise that judgment."

"Judgment!" Danid ranted. "That's what you call—"

The computer cut him off. "There is a ship approaching at high speed." Nole restored lights and power to the bridge and the viewer came on.

After a moment of astonishment, the starship officers recognized the familiar silhouette on the screen. It was the *Enterprise* racing toward them.

"It is on a collision course," Nole concluded.

"That's insane," said Danid. "It'll be destroyed."

Riker shot an alarmed look at Data, who had already turned back to the computer console. "Nole, may I have access to your sensor system?"

"Yes."

The console monitor flashed the readouts Data needed. "It is true the *Enterprise* will be destroyed. But there is a high probability that this vessel will also be destroyed or at least disabled."

"That's impossible," Danid sputtered. "This ship can't be—"

"Your energy shield will not be able to stop a body combining the *Enterprise*'s mass and velocity. Fifty-eight seconds to impact."

Riker hit his communicator. "Riker to *Enterprise*," he said urgently.

"Commander," said Nole, "your communications device can't penetrate our energy shield."

"Then open your communication channel, please," Data said.

"Open, Data," said Nole.

As quickly as a human could react, the words tumbled from Riker's mouth. *"Enterprise,* alter your collision course. Repeat—this is Riker—*change course now!"*

Picard whirled to face Worf. "Confirmation?"

"Transmission is real-time, not a recording— ninety-nine-point-eight-four percent probability it is Commander Riker's voice."

"Ensign Crusher," Picard barked, "hard over— reduce speed to sublight!"

The sudden maneuver overwhelmed the starship's inertial-stability dampers and people throughout the ship struggled to maintain their footing as they heard Picard's voice over intraship speakers: "This is the captain. Our emergency collision maneuver has been cancelled. Resume normal posts and maintain yellow alert."

Back on the bridge, Wesley's shoulders slumped in relief. "That was too close for comfort."

"We had nine seconds to spare," Worf responded with a stoic shrug. Several crew members turned toward him with stares of disbelief. He glowered back at them in a Klingon approximation of guilelessness.

"Open a channel to the Bekeem ship, Lieutenant," said Picard.

"Channel open, sir."

"Enterprise to Commander Riker."

"This is Riker, sir."

"I must admit considerable surprise at the sound of your voice, Number One."

260

"That makes two of us."

"Have you commandeered the Bekeem ship?"

"Not exactly."

A curious frown creased Picard's brow. "Then what is your status?"

"We're safe, and the Bekeem ship has been neutralized as a threat."

"Well done, Number One. We would like the Bekeem ship to assume a fifty-thousand kilometer orbit around Alaj. Is her commander willing to comply?"

Danid, glowering in his seat, noticed Riker glancing at him. "I don't seem to have any say in the matter."

Riker clucked in mock sympathy.

"Captain," Nole said, "that is acceptable."

"Number One, who was that? It didn't sound like Supreme Primary Danid."

"Uhh—it wasn't," Riker said with a relieved chuckle. "It's a long story, Captain."

"Well, then, I shall look forward to hearing it."

Chapter Twenty-three

Captain's Log, Supplemental:
Commander Riker and the shuttle away team have returned to the *Enterprise* and reported the details of the tragic wanderings of the Bekeem. But some good may yet come from their misfortune. Chief Engineer La Forge has found the Bekeem vessel to be essentially spaceworthy. He and his team have begun refurbishing work, to be continued by a small army of Starfleet engineers arriving from the five nearest starbases. Once rehabilitated, this huge craft will be able to transport much of the human and animal population of Etolos. *Where* they will be transported *to* is now up to the diplomats, as negotiations between Etolos and Alaj enter their fourth day.

THE TURBOLIFT OPENED and Troi and Riker stepped onto the bridge, making no attempt at all to conceal their pleasure. Picard noted their arrival with a nod as they came down and took their usual seats on either side of him. "Smiling faces usually connote good news," he said.

"Zeila and Retthew have reached an agreement," Troi announced happily.

"Well, that's grand."

Riker rubbed the back of his neck. *"Now* it is. But for a while this morning, I thought they were going to reach for each other's throats."

"And how did you discourage those violent urges?"

Riker gestured an open hand toward Troi. "Captain, you know how persuasive Deanna can be—that gentle way she has of getting to the heart of a matter."

"Kudos to you, then, Counselor," said Picard, looking her way just as she deflected the praise with a modest bow of her head.

"Well, sir, I would not have any effect at all if not for Will's toughness."

Picard glanced from one to the other. "Ahh, I see. She said nice doggie while you brandished the rock?"

"That about sums it up," said Riker with a grin. "It also helps to have both sides desperate for an agreement." He stretched his long legs comfortably, pleased to be back in his accustomed spot at Picard's elbow.

"Don't get too comfortable, Number One. I'd like you to pay a visit to Mr. La Forge on the Bekeem ship and check on their progress."

Riker got up with a sigh. "I guess diplomatic eminence doesn't last very long."

The column of shimmering energy took on solid form as Will Riker beamed into a pitch-dark section of the Bekeem vessel. Geordi and Data were supposed to be in there somewhere but Riker couldn't see a thing. A dry chill in the air made his nose prickle.

He cupped his hands over his mouth and called out, "Data, Geordi, where are you?"

"Over here, Commander," Geordi shouted back, flashing a light from a couple of hundred meters away. "Stay there, we want to show you something."

"Okay."

After a few seconds' wait, dawn broke. A simulated dawn, at least. Thirty seconds later, it was daylight in a domed cavern that replicated a desert plateau, complete with dunes and scrubby trees. The "sun" shone strongly enough that wriggling heat waves rose across the desert floor.

Riker spotted Geordi and Data across the biosphere, climbed a gentle dune and scuffed through the sand toward them. "Pretty impressive."

"Welcome to a little corner of the Sobel Desert—just like on Etolos," Geordi said proudly. "This ship is absolutely amazing. I could spend years studying its construction and internal systems."

"But we do not have years," Data reminded him.

"Party pooper," said Geordi.

Data considered the phrase, but before he could comment, a nearby door opened and Danid came in. He stopped short when he saw the *Enterprise*'s first officer.

"Riker," he said in curt greeting.

"Danid." The tall first officer and the even taller old Bekeem glared at each other in stiff silence. "I just want you to know I strongly disagreed with the decision not to punish you for what you did."

"*Tried* to do, Riker," Danid corrected. "I didn't succeed. Alaj is safe."

"The crews on those Alajian ships are dead," Riker said pointedly.

"In retrospect, I am sorry for those deaths. But it *was* the Alajians who agreed not to prosecute me."

264

"Only because Nole insisted that your freedom had to be assured before he would cooperate and allow this vessel to be used by the Etolosans."

"A small price to pay," Danid sniffed. He started to walk away, then stopped and turned back. He spoke with grudging sincerity. "I truly am sorry for those deaths, Riker. And thankful for Nole's loyalty. I'm not sure I deserved it."

"Neither am I. What are you going to do after the Etolosans have been transferred to their new world? I understand you decided not to search for Bekeem colonies which might have survived?"

Danid shrugged. "The past is past. The Etolosans want to continue to use this ship for their work. I've asked to help them."

Riker's brows hitched up a skeptical notch. "Oh? What happened to the religious purity of the Bekeem?"

"Can't be a whole religion by myself," Danid growled. "Besides, these Etolosans are tolerable. Based on our common history, I feel a kinship with them. A damn sight better than the Alajians."

"The Alajians may yet redeem themselves," said Riker. "Engineer La Forge says you've been quite a help."

Danid's hands fluttered in a dismissive wave. "I *should* know my way around after spending my whole life on this ship."

"We still haven't figured everything out," Geordi said. "Like, for instance, what makes Nole tick."

Data frowned vaguely. "Geordi, Nole does not tick."

As he and La Forge snickered, Riker said, "Geordi, the captain would like you to start packing up. We'll be making the official transfer of the nefittifi from the

Etolosans to the Alajians soon, and then the *Enterprise* will be leaving."

"Nefittifi," Danid sneered, puckering his lips and making a rude noise as he ambled away.

Picard and Zeila exited the holodeck. The doors slid shut behind them and they strolled along the curving corridor. "Thank you for taking me to your Africa, Captain."

"My pleasure, Curister."

"You know, when I was a child, I loved reading picture books about all the huge animals that once lived on our world. I knew they were extinct, but it didn't really hit me until I got a little older and visited some of the exotic places I'd read about. And they were empty. When I was negotiating with Retthew, I was so jealous because he lived on a world full of wildlife."

"Perhaps you'll be able to visit Beta Etolos someday."

"I hope so," said Zeila.

Picard escorted her back up to the bridge where Retthew was already waiting with Counselor Troi in the conference lounge. The two leaders visibly tensed in each other's presence, but both Picard and Troi chalked it up to understandable wariness that would fade only with time and proximity.

The captain motioned toward the drinks, pastries, and fruit that had been spread out on trays. "Please, help yourselves."

Standing stiffly, Retthew nibbled on an apple slice. Zeila picked up a glass of wine and approached him. "Prefex, I want you to know we genuinely appreciate the sacrifice you're making by giving us the nefittifi."

"Do you? I'm still not convinced you comprehend the difficulty of caring for them."

Picard came over, trying to make his approach casual. But he wanted to head off any tiffs that might cause the new treaty to start fraying at the edges even before it could be implemented. "If I might I make a suggestion, Honoress. Why not invite Robbal to remain on Alaj with the nefittifi for a time?"

Zeila grunted thoughtfully. "Hmm. I suppose we could. That way, he could help train our caretakers. And he could assure you, Prefex, that we are giving them everything they need. Would you permit that?"

Retthew pursed his lips. "I suppose, if Robbal would agree."

"Such exchanges often smooth the process of establishing better relations," said Troi with extra enthusiasm.

"Speaking of exchanges," Zeila said, "isn't it about time for the official transfer ceremony?"

Picard nodded. "I'll just check with sickbay and make sure everything is ready." He tapped his communicator. "Picard to Dr. Crusher."

"Crusher here." Her voice sounded frazzled. "Captain, if you're calling about the nefittifi, we're having a little problem—"

Picard, Troi, Retthew, and Zeila made it to sickbay in record time. There, they found Wesley and Riker waiting in Beverly's outer office.

"Number One," said Picard, "what is going on?"

"I'm not sure. One of the animals had some sort of seizure just before we were going to call you to come down for the ceremony."

"Which one?" Retthew asked, his face furrowed with concern.

"Kad, the female," Wesley said.

Retthew shook his head and began pacing. "Oh, no,

this is awful . . . I knew this was all a mistake . . . I must go in there—"

"I'm sorry, Prefex," said Riker. "Dr. Crusher and Robbal left explicit instructions that they must not be disturbed."

"Please, Prefex," Picard soothed. "Dr. Crusher and Robbal have already proven their capabilities. Perhaps it's nothing serious."

"Captain." Zeila put a hand on his shoulder, guiding him to a private corner of the office. Her voice dropped to a confidential level. "The exchange of these nefittifi is critical to this treaty. If I go home without them, I can't answer for the consequences."

The door to the nefittifi ward suddenly slid open and Dr. Crusher came out alone, a stunned look on her face. Both Retthew and Zeila rushed over, and Beverly raised her hands defensively, blocking their way. Then she broke into a wide grin.

"Robbal," she called over her shoulder, "I think you'd better get in here before these people trample me."

She stepped aside and the lanky Etolosan entered the office—with a towel-wrapped bundle in his arms. Smiling broadly, he let a corner of the cloth drop away, revealing a tiny wriggling form, covered in bright orange down.

Retthew's eyes blinked in amazement and he mouthed the word three times before he could find his voice. "A . . . a *baby?*"

"That's right," Robbal beamed.

Captain Picard grasped Beverly by the elbow. "Doctor, why didn't we know this was coming?" he said through gritted teeth.

"Because Robbal tells me it's almost impossible to tell if a nefittifi is pregnant. And this one was."

"This is wonderful," Retthew crowed.

"No, it isn't," said Zeila.

Retthew turned toward her. "Why not?"

"Does the baby need to be with its mother?"

"Yes, it does," said Robbal.

"That means we can't take the adult pair," Zeila said in a defeated tone. "We can't expect you to separate them."

"They won't have to be separated," Retthew said firmly. "We will give you the whole family."

Now it was Robbal's turn to be upset. "With all due respect, Prefex, the Alajians don't know the first thing about taking care of nefittifi adults, let alone a brand new chetling."

"Which is why you're going to live on Alaj for a while," said Retthew. "Until you're convinced they're doing well—if that's acceptable to you."

"Yes, yes," Robbal said, his voice rising in excitement. "I have to confess, I was not at all happy about giving Kyd and Kad up to strangers."

"Neither was I," Beverly admitted, prompting disbelieving glances from Picard, Troi, and Wesley. She glared back at them. "So they grew on me. So shoot me."

Robbal waved his free hand above the group, calling for their attention. "There's one more formality, and I really hope no one minds, but I took the liberty of naming the chetling after the person most responsible for saving the lives of baby and mother—so it is named Beverly—if that's all right with you, Doctor."

Crusher blushed. "I . . . I'm honored."

After ruling that the new arrival and its parents needed a few hours to get acquainted, Dr. Crusher chased everyone out of sickbay. Zeila had no objection to the slight delay, since it meant getting not two but three nefittifi. It also gave her another chance to return to the holodeck and visit Africa again.

But the time passed quickly and Crusher certified the nefittifi family fit for release. Accompanied by an entourage of Beverly, Wesley, Picard, Troi, Retthew, Robbal, and Zeila, they and their enclosure were carted to the transporter room and placed on the platform.

Dr. Crusher held her tiny orange namesake one more time and nuzzled its little beak for a moment, then handed it back to Robbal. He and Zeila stepped up onto the transporter pads while the others moved back to the console where O'Brien entered the coordinates.

"Remember, Robbal," said Retthew, "you represent Etolos. Make us proud."

"I will," Robbal replied. But his eyes were on Troi. She smiled back at him with a special warmth.

"Chief O'Brien," said Picard, "energize."

"Aye, sir." He activated the unit, initiating the familiar sparkle effect. In a few seconds, the chamber was empty.

Hoping no one would notice, Dr. Crusher made a surreptitious swipe at a droplet of moisture unaccountably gathering in the corner of one eye and threatening to slip down her cheek.

"You know, Doctor," said the poker-faced O'Brien, "I do believe the little beggar had your eyes."

"Not just the eyes," Troi teased, "the nose, too."

"And the hair," Wesley added. *"Definitely* the hair."

Crusher straightened with exaggerated dignity. "Excuse me while I go write little Beverly into my will." With an imperious toss of her head, she exited.

Picard, Troi, and Wesley returned to the bridge. "Commander Riker," said Picard as they took their seats, "is the *Enterprise* ready to leave orbit?"

"Affirmative, sir . . . though I can't believe we're going to be moving an entire society. It isn't going to be easy."

Picard gave his first officer a sidelong glance. "Afraid we're not up to the challenge, Number One?"

"I didn't say that, sir," Riker replied with a sly smile.

"Good. Ensign Crusher, set course for Etolos."

"Course already set, Captain," Wesley said over his shoulder.

"Very well, then." With a jaunty flick of his wrist, Picard pointed ahead. "Engage."

Jean-Luc Picard slid back into the firm cushions of the command seat, allowing himself a moment to enjoy the immense satisfaction he felt. The mission he'd feared might be impossible was well on its way to accomplishment, and he flirted with an amusing thought: *Is this how Noah felt on that legendary ark?*

Already something of a legend itself, the starship *Enterprise* cruised majestically out of Alajian orbit, shifted into warp speed, and streaked toward the stars.

ABOUT THE AUTHOR

Howard Weinstein's name may already be familiar to *STAR TREK* fans. His 1981 novel, *The Covenant of the Crown,* became the first original *STAR TREK* novel to be reprinted in a special Science Fiction Book Club hardcover edition. In 1987, *Deep Domain* climbed high on national bestseller lists, including the *New York Times* list. *Power Hungry,* his first *STAR TREK: THE NEXT GENERATION* book, was a 1989 bestseller.

In 1974, at age 19, Weinstein became the youngest person to write professionally for *STAR TREK,* selling *The Pirates of Orion* to NBC-TV's animated revival of the series (now available on home video). A decade later, he was one of several writers consulted by Director Leonard Nimoy during the story-development phase of *STAR TREK IV: THE VOYAGE HOME,* and received a screen credit for his assistance.

Other writing credits include a trio of original novels based on the NBC science fiction series *V;* columns, articles, and reviews in *Starlog* magazine, the *New York Times,* and *Newsday;* and award-winning radio public service announcements. Weinstein has also written numerous slide shows presented at science fiction and *STAR TREK* conventions around the country. Since 1976, he's made more than a hundred speaking appearances at conventions, colleges, and libraries.

Weinstein lives with his wife Susan and their Welsh Corgi, Mail Order Annie. Susan works as a computer programmer, Howard is busy developing new projects, and Annie is content to sleep in the sun, eat whatever she can reach, and be petted endlessly.

STAR TREK
THE NEXT GENERATION
POWER HUNGRY

Sent to deliver emergency famine relief to the
planet Thiopa - the Federation's only allies in a
critically important sector of space - the crew finds
a brutal dictatorship - one more
concerned with preserving its own powers than
protecting its citizens, or the world they all share.

Captain Picard is hesitant about turning over the
supplies to the corrupt government: he fears they
may never reach their intended destination.
But can he convince the ruling council to change
their ways, before it is too late - for the
government, and Thiopa itself?

THE COVENANT OF THE CROWN

The Shaddan Crown is the key to power - and the
Klingons have the advantage!

An *Enterprise* shuttle is forced to crash-land in a
violent storm on the barren planet of Sigma 1212.
Spock, McCoy and Kailyn, the beautiful heir to the
Shaddan throne, survive the near disaster.

Now pursued by primitive hunters and a band of
Klingon scouts, they must reach the mountain
where the fabulous dynastic crown is hidden.
With the help of Spock and McCoy, and their
own fantastic mental powers, Kailyn must prove
that she alone is the true heir to the throne.

If they all fail, they will open the door for Klingon
takeover of the whole quadrant - and the galaxy's
hope to live long and prosper will fall in the
shadow of a cruel tyranny!

Also available by Howard Weinstein
from Titan Books

DEEP DOMAIN

A routine diplomatic visit to the water-world of
Akkalla becomes a nightmarish search for a
missing Spock and Chekov, a search that plunges
Captain Kirk headlong into a corrupt government's
desperate struggle to retain power.

For both a Federation Science outpost and
Akkalla's valiant freedom fighters have begun
uncovering the ancient secrets hidden beneath her
tranquil oceans. Secrets whose exposure may mean
civil war for the people of Akkalla - and death for
the crew of the starship *Enterprise*.

Also available by Howard Weinstein from Titan Books

PERCHANCE TO DREAM

On a routine mission to survey Domarus IV - a class M world with no intelligent life - an *Enterprise* shuttle crewed by Data, Troi and Wesley Crusher is captured by a race called the Tenirans who claim the world for themselves. As Captain Picard tries to negotiate with the captain of the Teniran ship, the shuttle suddenly disappears in a blaze of colour and light.

Picard demands to know what's happening to the shuttle and its crew, but the Tenirans deny any part in their disappearance. Suddenly, Captain Picard vanishes from the bridge and finds himself alone on the planet's surface with the Teniran captain. As the two captains begin to work together, they realise that they are not alone on Domarus IV as they confront an incredible alien force with the power to transform a world - or to destroy it.

THE STARLESS WORLD

STAR TREK®

ADVENTURES

by Gordon Eklund

'As for our assigned mission, evidence continues to be negative. We're apparently alone here in the Core...'

While investigating rumours of renewed activity by the Klingon Empire within the Galactic Core, the *U.S.S. Enterprise* makes contact with a shuttle craft from the *U.S.S. Rickover*, a starship presumed lost with all hands over twenty years ago. The lone occupant of that shuttle craft is Thomas Clayton, once Kirk's roommate at the Starfleet Academy, now the self-proclaimed chosen son and favoured prophet of a deity he calls Ay-nab.

Kirk plans on disregarding Clayton, until control of his engines is seized by an unexplained outside force - a force which Clayton insists is now taking Kirk and his crew to meet his god.

STAR TREK®
THE NEXT GENERATION
THE STAR LOST

by Michael Jan Friedman, Peter Krause and Pablo Marcos

A routine shuttlecraft mission goes awry, leading Captain Picard to believe half his command crew has perished. Faced with continuing the mission of the *U.S.S. Enterprise*, the captain and crew must deal with their grief on their own time.

Unknown to the crew, though, is that the shuttle crew is not dead - just on the other side of the galaxy! Their epic struggle to survive and ultimately find their way home fuels this power-packed story with dynamic artwork.

The first in a new line of *Star Trek: The Next Generation* graphic novels. With a special introduction by *Star Trek: The Next Generation* producer Ronald D. Moore.

STAR TREK®
THE MODALA IMPERATIVE

by Michael Jan Friedman, Peter David
and Pablo Marcos

Modala, a peaceful, developing world, is suddenly thrown into turmoil when the government uses alien technology to subjugate the population. Captain Kirk and the *U.S.S. Enterprise* get embroiled in the battle, only to find themselves a part of the revolution.

A hundred years later, the *Enterprise* returns to Modala, bringing with them survivors of that adventure - Spock and McCoy. The centennial celebration is abruptly halted by the arrival of the Ferengi, and Captain Picard must rely on those living legends to help save Modala... again.

The first in a new line of *Star Trek* graphic novels, featuring, for the first time ever, characters from both classic *Star Trek* and *Star Trek: The Next Generation*. With a special introduction by Walter 'Chekov' Koenig.

For a complete list of Star Trek publications, please send a large stamped SAE to Titan Books Mail Order, 19 Valentine Place, London, SE1 8QH. Please quote reference NG14.